THE YACHT GIRL

RYAN LOCK
BOOK 13

SEAN BLACK

*To Éamonn, Jennifer, and Dylan,
with heartfelt thanks for your generosity and friendship.*

The Yacht Girl

A Ryan Lock Thriller

Copyright © 2025 Sean Black

The moral right of Sean Black to be identified as the author of this work has been asserted in accordance with the Copyright, Designs and Patents Act 1988.

All rights reserved. No part of this publication may be reproduced, stored, or transmitted in any form or by any means—electronic, mechanical, photocopying, recording, or otherwise—without the prior written permission of the copyright holder.

This is a work of fiction. Names, characters, places, and incidents are either the product of the author's imagination or used fictitiously. Any resemblance to actual persons, living or dead, events, or locales is entirely coincidental.

First edition: 2025

PRAISE FOR SEAN BLACK

Winner of the 2018 International Thriller Writers Award in New York for *Second Chance*

Nominated for the 2020 International Thriller Writers award for *The Deep Abiding*

"The Ryan Lock series is ace. There are deservedly strong Lee Child comparisons as the author is a Brit (Scottish), his novels US-based, his character appealing, and his publisher the same. "
Sarah Broadhurst, *The Bookseller*

"Black drives his hero into the tightest spots with a force and energy that jump off the page. This is a writer, and a hero, to watch."
Geoffrey Wansell, *The Daily Mail*

"Sean Black writes with the pace of Lee Child, and the heart of Harlan Coben. "
Joseph Finder, New York Times Bestselling Author of *The Oligarch's Daughter*

YACHT GIRL

yacht girl (*noun*)
A young, attractive woman who serves as entertainment for wealthy men in exclusive luxury settings, typically in exchange for money, gifts, or other compensation.

CHAPTER ONE

NO MORE BROKEN GIRLS. Not here. Not now.

That was Lock's promise. A promise he'd sworn to keep, no matter what. If he had to kill, that's exactly what he'd do. No hesitation. No mercy.

But right now, the island's security team wasn't the issue. His issue was the girl standing at the cliff edge, threatening to jump.

Twenty feet away, he watched as she backed up and her left foot slipped on the blood-slicked rock. One wrong step and she'd be gone.

"I'm not bluffing," she said. "I'll do it."

A few feet behind her was the cliff face. A sheer drop. Rocks below. Beyond the rocks, ocean. The sound of waves against stone carried up from the darkness, steady and final.

Lock took a step back, palms visible. "I believe you."

"Sure you do."

"We don't work for these people." Lock kept his voice level, non-threatening. Behind him, he sensed Ty adjusting position slightly, ready but not aggressive. Years of partnership had taught them to move as one unit.

"Liar," the girl said.

"On my daughter's life." Lock let the words hang in the salt air.

"We're security consultants hired to assess the island. I'm Ryan. This is my business partner, Ty."

Behind him the towering African-American retired Marine offered up a curt nod. Lock caught the girl's eyes flick between them, reading their body language, their positioning. She was scared but not stupid.

"I get you're scared, and you have no reason to trust us, but we came to find you and get you out of here."

Lock read hesitation in the girl's eyes. She was wavering, her weight shifting from foot to foot on the bloodied stone. Should she believe him or not?

"I'd rather die than go back there," she said, almost losing her balance for a second.

"You won't have to," Lock told her. "You have my word. We're going to get you home."

"You have a daughter?"

"Sofia. She just turned four." The words came easier than expected. Lock felt something loosen in his chest, a crack in his professional armor. "She's back home with my wife in Los Angeles. She wants me to bring her back a stuffed tiger. Big Princess Jasmine fan." He paused, watching the girl's face soften slightly.

Her breathing slowed. She was tuned in now, actually listening.

Lock held up his hands, palms open. "One of the other girls told us where we could find you."

"Who?"

That was the question Lock had been hoping for. He passed it off for Ty to answer.

As Ty started to speak he was cut off by three men emerging from the tree line behind them. Israeli security personnel in tactical gear, weapons at low ready. The three spread out, creating overlapping fields of fire. Professional, silent, lethal. Lock felt a familiar tightness in his shoulders, the automatic calculation of angles and distances.

"Mr. Lock," one of the men, presumably the team leader said. "Step away from the girl, please."

Lock didn't move. Beside him, Ty's hand drifted toward his weapon, the movement casual but deliberate. Lock caught the slight shift in Ty's stance, the almost imperceptible turn that would give him better shooting angles. They'd done this dance before.

"No can do," Lock said.

The team leader's weapon came up, not quite pointing at Lock but close enough to send a message. The barrel tracked with his movements, professional and controlled.

"This doesn't concern you," the team leader said.

"Injured young woman on resort property?" Lock smiled without humor. "I'd say that's exactly our concern."

Lock's hand moved, resting on the grip of his SIG Sauer. Beside him, Ty did the same. The message clear. Make a move and this gets ugly. Fast.

Two more Israeli security personnel emerged from the jungle, boots silent on the damp earth. Five total now, spreading into a half-circle. Lock felt Ty shift position slightly, improving his angles. The girl behind them had gone completely still, sensing the change in the air.

The team leader hesitated, weapon wavering slightly. Lock could see him running calculations, weighing odds. Five against two wasn't terrible numbers, but Lock and Ty weren't typical opposition. Their stance, their calm, their complete lack of concern about being outnumbered all spoke to experience that went beyond weekend warrior training.

"Let's all be cool. Why don't we start over?" the team leader said, first to blink.

"I'm perfectly cool," Lock said. "What about you, Ty?"

"Positively frosty," Ty said.

Back at the edge, the girl made a sound that was half sob, half laugh. "They're going to kill us."

Lock spoke to her. "Want to know something? I don't think they are." He took a beat. "I think they're going to lower their weapons, and then we're all going to walk back in like civilized people."

CHAPTER TWO

FIVE DAYS EARLIER

HARPER HOLT WAS the perfect choice.

The Matchmaker had been watching her since her arrival on the island, struck by how she stood out from the other girls. Not because she was more beautiful or sexier—she was neither. But she had other qualities that more than compensated. She was bright and intelligent, simultaneously naive and guarded.

The combination of traits excited The Matchmaker.

And her match?

He was perfect too, but in a very different way.

Ulrich Drexler was in his early sixties, a lumbering testament to the grotesque power of wealth unchecked by conscience. His bloated form sprawled across a custom lounge chair, pale flesh spilling over designer swim shorts. Everything about him was excessive—his swollen fingers adorned with rings, his neck buried in rolls of fat, his small eyes that darted constantly, always searching for the next source of gratification.

He was undeniably a creature of pure appetite. Food, drink, flesh—he consumed everything with the same mechanical intensity. The Matchmaker had watched him devour a seven-course meal the previous evening, barely pausing to breathe between courses, his fleshy lips glistening with grease and wine. The man's relationship with his senses was fundamentally corrupt. Where others might find pleasure, Ulrich found only the desperate need for more.

The German's appetites were legendary among the island's regular visitors, his methods crude. No finesse. No appreciation for the art of psychological seduction. Just brute force and the assumption that money could purchase anything.

The Matchmaker had seen Ulrich's type before. They came to the island seeking not just indulgence but transformation—the chance to shed their meticulously crafted public personas and reveal the monsters beneath. Politicians who championed family values but craved young girls. Tech billionaires who preached about making the world a better place while treating human beings as disposable objects. Media moguls who spoke of truth and justice while participating in acts that would destroy them if exposed.

They all believed they were untouchable here. That the island's promise of absolute discretion meant they could indulge their darkest impulses without consequence.

The Matchmaker had listened to Harper's conversation with her roommate the night before. The girl had been quite explicit about her feelings toward Ulrich. "Repulsive" was one word she'd used. "Gross" was another. "Like something that crawled out from under a rock."

"Like a Romanian cab driver who just won an all-expenses paid trip to Vegas," Harper's roommate, Nikki, had offered, the description sending them into a fit of giggles.

Harper's revulsion had sealed the Matchmaker's decision. The greater the resistance, the more thrilling the encounter. It was a principle the Matchmaker had seen countless times among the island's distinguished guests.

The Senator from Texas who'd arrived last month preaching moral fiber to his constituents via a video call in the morning, then spent his evenings engaged in activities that would have turned the stomach of all but the most hardened of sexual predators. Or the pharmaceutical heir who donated millions to children's charities while forcing himself upon barely pubescent girls. Or the Hungarian interior minister who got off on beating young women to a bloody pulp with whatever object she had to hand.

The Matchmaker settled down to write the invitation. Crane & Co. stationery, cream-colored with a subtle watermark. The kind of paper that whispered of old money and refined breeding. The fountain pen, a fifteen thousand dollar Montblanc Meisterstück Solitaire Royal.

Miss Holt,

Mr. Drexler cordially invites you to join him for dinner this evening at Villa Nine. A car will collect you at eight o'clock.

Cocktails will be served on the terrace, followed by a private dinner prepared by his personal chef.

The evening promises to be... memorable.

Dress: Cocktail attire

Finished, The Matchmaker summoned one of the housekeeping staff with a finger snap.

"Please deliver this to Miss Holt's quarters immediately. Thank you."

They took the invitation without a word, nodded and hurried away.

The Matchmaker settled back in the chair, happy with the selection, and mused on the others who'd come before Harper. The pre-med student from Ohio who'd arrived thinking her academic achievements made her untouchable. The marketing intern from Detroit who'd believed her street smarts would protect her. The nursing student turned OnlyFans model from London who'd thought her meticulous planning would keep her safe.

Each had possessed that same quality Harper displayed—the illusion of control. They were all used to fending off unwanted advances. They all believed they could navigate these waters on their own terms.

They had all been proven wrong.

This island they had so carefully constructed had a way of stripping away pretense, of revealing the truth that lay beneath carefully constructed facades. It wasn't just the guests who underwent transformation—the staff, the service providers, even some of the most seemingly innocent visitors could find themselves participating in acts they'd never imagined possible.

Ulrich would be the perfect instrument for Harper's education.

———

The sun was beginning its descent toward the horizon, painting the sky in shades of coral pink and gold. *Beautiful, really.*

The Matchmaker drifted to the evening ahead. The tension in Harper's shoulders when she realized she was alone with Ulrich. The moment when her practiced composure would begin to crack. The look in her eyes when she understood that all her intelligence, all her careful planning, wouldn't save her.

The Matchmaker imagined Ulrich's heavy hands reaching for her, the German's breathing growing heavy with anticipation. The man would be methodical in his approach, savoring each stage of Harper's degradation.

The girl would try to negotiate, of course. They always did. She'd attempt to use her intelligence, her charm, her polished social skills to defuse the situation. She'd offer alternatives, try to redirect Ulrich's attention.

It would all prove futile.

How had the Marquis de Sade put it? Oh, yes, that was it.

"The only way to a woman's heart is along the path of torment."

CHAPTER
THREE

"ULRICH DREXLER," Harper said, reading the fancy invitation.

Harper's roommate and bestie, Nikki Bailey, was off her bed in an instant, fire-engine red nail polish forgotten. The brush clattered onto the nightstand as she moved to read the invitation over Harper's shoulder. "Villa Nine. Eight o'clock. Cocktails and dinner."

Harper's stomach had dropped the moment she saw the name, a cold weight settling in her chest. They both knew Ulrich's reputation. The German industrialist was legendary among the girls for his excessive appetites and crude behavior. He treated the island like his personal fiefdom, demanding and taking whatever caught his attention.

"Girl, you're not actually thinking about going are you?" Nikki said, reading the tension in Harper's shoulders, the way her friend's fingers had gone white around the invitation's edges.

"What choice do I have?" Harper's voice came out smaller than she intended.

"Make an excuse. Say you're sick." Nikki moved closer, close enough that Harper could smell her vanilla body spray. "I mean, I feel sick just reading this."

Harper folded the invitation, her mind already working through the calculations. She'd been on the island for six days and had only accepted one invitation—dinner with a harmless Belgian CEO who'd spent the entire evening talking about his rescue dogs and how hard it was to be a widower at his age. The other girls whispered about what happened to those who refused too many times. Quietly asked to leave with minimal compensation, their return flights cancelled so they had to use what little money they'd earned to get home.

"I can't keep saying no," Harper said. "They'll send me packing."

"Better than what happened to Madison."

The name hung in the air between them. Madison, a pre-med student from Penn State who'd arrived two weeks before Harper. She'd spent one evening with Ulrich at Villa Nine and left the next morning—packed off the island on the first flight out, her face pale and a bruise on her throat she'd tried to cover with makeup.

Harper stared at her friend. Nikki had gotten lucky—paired with an Indian tech billionaire who was socially awkward but genuinely kind. Samir Patel treated her like she was precious, not purchased.

"I need this money, Nikki. You know I need this money."

Nikki's street-smart cynicism warred with genuine concern. She'd grown up in Atlantic City, daughter of a casino dealer who'd taught her that everyone was running some kind of angle. But Harper wasn't running an angle—she was drowning. Nikki could see it in the way Harper's hands shook slightly when she thought no one was looking, the careful way she counted every dollar.

Nikki walked to her dresser, picked up the silver letter opener lying there. "Samir gave me this," she said, running her thumb along the ornate Indian design etched into the handle. "He said he wanted me to feel safe." She paused, weighing the blade in her palm. It was heavier than it looked, sharp enough to be dangerous. "But you need it more than I do tonight."

Harper shook her head. "I don't need—"

Nikki pressed the letter opener into Harper's hands, closing her friend's fingers around the cool metal. "It's designed to look elegant, but it'll cut a bitch." Her voice was steady, but Harper caught the fear underneath. Nikki was giving up her own protection, her own peace of mind.

Harper felt the weight of it, surprisingly solid. "Villa Nine has staff," she said, grasping for reassurance. "Servers, security detail. He can't get too crazy with witnesses around."

Nikki's expression said everything she couldn't put into words.

Harper moved to the mirror, checking her makeup one final time. Nikki stood behind her, hands resting on Harper's shoulders for just a moment—a touch that said more than any words could. The young woman looking back appeared confident, composed. Someone who could handle whatever the evening might bring. A million miles from how she felt inside.

"I'll be fine," Harper said, slipping the letter opener into her small clutch. The weight of it was oddly comforting. "It's a few hours of small talk and overpriced wine. I've survived worse."

"Have you?"

Harper smoothed down her dress, avoiding Nikki's eyes in the mirror. In the reflection, she could see their shared room—two beds, clothes scattered across chairs, photos of home taped to the walls. It looked like any college dorm, except for the fear that lived in the corners.

"I'll text you when I get there," Harper said. "And when I leave. If you don't hear from me by midnight..."

CHAPTER
FOUR

RYAN LOCK PULLED into the drop-off lane at Briar Academy, the morning chaos of Manhattan Beach parents in full swing. Luxury SUVs and sports cars formed a slow-moving parade, each disgorging small children with oversized backpacks.

"I still can't believe we're paying thirty grand a year for finger painting," Lock said, watching a four-year-old climb out of a Bentley.

"It's not just finger painting," Carmen said from the passenger seat.

"They make the kids eat tofu," Lock said.

"Yeah, tofu. Yuck," Sofia announced from her car seat, clutching her Princess Jasmine lunchbox.

Lock put the Rivian in park and twisted around to face Sofia. "Hey, princess Sofia. You know Daddy has to go away for a few days, right?"

Sofia's lower lip pushed out. "I don't want you to go."

"I know, sweetie. But I'll be back before you know it. And I'll bring you a present."

Her eyes lit up slightly. "What kind of present?"

"What would you like?"

"A tiger! A stuffed tiger!"

"A tiger it is," Lock said. "Maybe even one that makes tiger noises."

"Tigers go 'raaarrrr,'" Sofia demonstrated, making Carmen laugh.

A familiar Mercedes G-Wagon pulled up behind them, and Lock

saw Ty Johnson climbing out. His partner wore a charcoal designer suit, his shoes polished to a mirror shine.

"Is that Ty in an actual suit?" Carmen asked. "What's the occasion?"

"He's trying to look professional for the client meeting in Dubai," Lock said.

"Uncle Ty!" Sofia squealed, already working at her car seat buckles.

Ty approached the Rivian, his eyes tracking a yoga-pants-clad mom pushing a jogging stroller. He tore his attention away as Lock and Carmen climbed out.

"There's my favorite girl," Ty said as Lock lifted Sofia from her car seat.

"Uncle Ty, you look funny," Sofia said.

"Funny? This is an Armani suit, young lady."

"Can Uncle Ty take me to class?" Sofia asked, reaching for his hand.

Carmen checked her watch. "Sorry, sweetheart, but Daddy and Uncle Ty need to get to the airport or they'll miss their flight." She took Sofia's hand. "Come on, let's get you inside."

Lock knelt down to Sofia's level. "Be good for Mommy, okay? I'll call you tonight."

"From the airplane?"

"From Dubai. It'll be tomorrow there already. Isn't that weird?"

Sofia wrapped her small arms around his neck. "Love you, Daddy."

"Love you too, sweetheart."

Carmen leaned in for a kiss. "Try not to get shot at this time."

"It's a security audit," Lock said. "The most dangerous thing will be the paperwork."

"Famous last words." She studied his face. "Just... be careful, okay?"

"Always am."

Carmen gave him a look that suggested otherwise but didn't argue. She took Sofia's hand and headed toward the school entrance. Lock watched them go, Sofia chattering about something that had happened in yesterday's art class.

"How'd your life get so damned domestic?" Ty said, popping the trunk of the G-Wagon.

Lock grabbed his go-bag and tactical case from the Rivian. "You're just jealous. Tough to be a *playah* when you've got arthritic knees."

"My knees not working ain't what worries me," Ty said.

"Spare me the details."

They climbed into the G-Wagon, Ty pulling smoothly into traffic on Manhattan Beach Boulevard.

"Man, I'm psyched for this gig," Ty said, "Private island. Sun, sea, and surf."

"They're paying us real money," Lock said. "That means we do real work."

"Come on, Lock. It's some rich guy's playground. How hard is it gonna be?"

They drove in silence for a moment, the morning traffic flowing smoothly for once. Lock watched planes taking off from LAX in the distance, their silver bodies catching the morning sun.

"You see Sofia with that kid when we were leaving?" Lock asked.

"The one with the Superman backpack?"

"Yeah. They were holding hands."

Ty laughed. "Better start cleaning your guns. She's four and already breaking hearts."

"She was just being sweet."

"That's how it starts, brother. Next thing you know, she's asking to borrow the car keys."

"She's four, Ty."

"I'm just saying, time flies. One day you're dropping her off at preschool, the next you're running background checks on her prom date."

Lock smiled despite himself. "I don't plan on being an overbearing father, have her so scared that she can't talk to me."

"Oh yeah?" Ty sounded unconvinced.

"She's a smart kid. She'll make good decisions."

Lock caught Ty throwing him a skeptical look.

"Plus, we already have her in jiu jitsu twice a week, and as soon as she's old enough, I'm taking her to the range, making sure she knows how to use a gun."

Ty's head tilted back as he laughed. "Hell yeah. That's more like it, brother."

CHAPTER
FIVE

ULRICH DREXLER HAD ALREADY DEVOURED half the appetizer course by the time his guest was scheduled to arrive. These girls never ate—always worried about their figures, picking at their food like nervous birds. But he would encourage them to develop other appetites.

The dining room of Villa Nine gleamed around him, all gold fixtures and marble surfaces that caught the light from an enormous crystal chandelier. Everything about the space screamed money and power, from the hand-carved dining table that could seat twelve to the floor-to-ceiling windows overlooking the infinity pool. It was a room designed to impress, to remind visitors exactly who they were dealing with.

He tore into a piece of bread, olive oil dripping down his chin as he surveyed his domain. The master bedroom lay just beyond the dining room's archway, its king-sized bed already turned down by the staff. He'd made sure of that.

A discreet knock interrupted his meal.

"Mr. Drexler?" The voice belonged to one of the villa's male staff members, a young man whose name Ulrich had never bothered to learn. "Ms. Holt has arrived."

Ulrich waved a greasy hand toward the entrance. "Show her in."

He attempted to stand with dignity as Harper entered, though his shirt was already stained with food and wine. In his mind, he cut an impressive figure—a successful man of the world welcoming a beautiful young woman into his private sanctuary.

"Ms. Holt," he said, extending his hand with what he believed was Continental sophistication. "Welcome. You look absolutely radiant this evening."

Harper accepted his handshake with a polite smile, though he noticed she kept the contact brief. Playing hard to get, perhaps. He liked that. He enjoyed a challenge.

"Thank you for the invitation, Mr. Drexler. The villa is beautiful."

"Please, call me Ulrich." He gestured dismissively toward the staff member, who took the hint and retreated toward the kitchen. "I had the entire interior redesigned by the same team that did my estate in Bavaria."

He guided her toward the dining table, his hand hovering possessively near the small of her back without quite touching. Harper noticed the positioning, the subtle claim of ownership in the gesture. She could handle this. Rich men were predictable—their egos were always their weakness.

"Wine would be lovely, thank you."

As he poured from the expensive bottle, Ulrich felt the familiar thrill of the hunt. The girl was clearly impressed by his wealth and sophistication, even if she was trying to hide it behind that composed facade.

"So," he said, settling his considerable bulk back into his chair, "I understand you're in college?"

"International relations, with a focus on—"

"Ah, politics!" Ulrich interrupted, already losing interest in her answer. "I've had dinner with more politicians than I can count. When you control as much of Germany's industrial capacity as I do, governments listen."

Harper nodded politely as he launched into a detailed account of his business empire, her wine barely touched while he refilled his own glass repeatedly. She picked delicately at her salad while he devoured course after course, and she began to recognize the pattern. He wanted an audience, not a conversation. She could work with that.

Every few minutes, she offered just enough engagement to keep him talking—a thoughtful nod, a strategic question about market dynamics. It was easier than she'd expected. He was so consumed with his own voice, his own importance, that he barely seemed to see her as a person.

―――

By the time the main course arrived, Ulrich had consumed most of the wine and was feeling particularly expansive. Harper had said perhaps a dozen words, but he found her an excellent audience—attentive, respectful, clearly hanging on his every word.

"The problem with women of your generation," he said, cutting into his steak with aggressive precision, "is that you've been told you can have everything. But deep down, you all want the same thing—a strong man who can provide for you."

His free hand dropped to her thigh, sausage fingers squeezing the fabric of her dress. Harper's body went rigid, but she forced herself to remain still. She'd anticipated this—the alcohol making him bolder, more direct. The key was not to react too strongly, not to escalate the situation before she was ready.

"You seem different from the others," he continued, his hand beginning to work its way upward. "More intelligent. More... sophisticated."

"Ulrich, your business philosophy is fascinating," Harper said quickly, shifting slightly in her chair. Her voice remained steady, controlled. "How did you manage to navigate the European Union's regulatory framework when you expanded into renewable energy?"

He moved his hand back to his wine glass, though he kept his eyes fixed on her. "Truth be told, I only moved into renewables for the carbon credits. It's like having my own bank. Elon told me about it over dinner at Bilderberg. That's how he really made his fortune. From the American government paying for all those credits."

Harper felt a small surge of satisfaction. She could redirect him, control the conversation's flow. She just had to stay smart, stay ahead of him.

"Perhaps we should continue this discussion somewhere more comfortable," he suggested, nodding toward the archway that led to the master bedroom. "I have some excellent cognac, and the view from the bedroom balcony is quite something."

Harper's smile remained perfectly in place. She'd known this moment would come. "That sounds wonderful. Perhaps in just a little while? I'm enjoying hearing about your successes so much."

"I can tell you much more about my successes in the bedroom," Ulrich said, his voice dropping to what he imagined was a seductive whisper but came off as straight up creepy.

"Of course," Harper said, standing gracefully. "Would you excuse me for just a moment? I'd like to freshen up first."

As she moved toward the corridor that led to the guest powder room, Ulrich couldn't resist reaching out to slap her backside—a playful, proprietary gesture. Harper shuddered but didn't turn around. She needed a moment to think, to plan her next move.

Harper closed the powder room door behind her, turning the lock with hands that were steadier than she'd expected. The bathroom was as opulent as the rest of the villa—gold fixtures, marble countertops, a mirror framed in what looked like actual precious metals. She took some deep breaths, using the moment to center herself.

On her way down the corridor, she'd passed one of the female staff members—a middle-aged woman with kind eyes who was arranging flowers in an alcove. When their gazes met, Harper saw something pass between them that needed no words. The woman's expression held recognition, sympathy, and something else: a subtle warning.

The woman glanced meaningfully toward the front of the villa, then back at Harper. Her lips barely moved as she whispered, "Be careful, miss."

Harper nodded almost imperceptibly. The woman knew what was happening. They all knew. But there was something else in that brief exchange—one woman looking out for another in the only way she could without risking her own position.

Harper felt the weight of Nikki's letter opener in her clutch, a solid reminder of her friend's protection. Nikki had given up her own sense of safety to arm Harper, and that gift meant everything now. She wasn't helpless. She wasn't just a victim waiting to happen.

The sound of raised voices drifted down the corridor.

"That will be all. I'm dismissing you for the evening," Ulrich was saying to the remaining staff members. "All of you."

"Sir," one of the male staff members protested, glancing toward the corridor where Harper had disappeared, "we typically remain available until—"

"Until I say."

"Sir..." the staff member protested.

"Do you know who I am?" Ulrich's voice rose. "What I could do with a single phone call?"

The young man's face showed genuine concern, his eyes darting between Ulrich and the hallway. He understood exactly what was happening, and his discomfort was obvious. But he was outranked, helpless to intervene.

"What are you waiting for?" Ulrich shouted. "Go!"

Ulrich watched with satisfaction as the staff filed out, their footsteps echoing across the marble foyer before fading into the night. The villa fell silent. He stood in the sudden quiet, savoring the moment, his breathing slightly heavier than before.

Now he could move on to the dessert.

CHAPTER SIX

THE MATCHMAKER SAVORED the moment when all the pieces fell into place. "A pair of star-cross'd lovers," they murmured to themselves, though in this case, the stars had required considerable assistance in their alignment.

Observing Ulrich's preparations, they felt the familiar satisfaction of a conductor watching their orchestra reach the crescendo exactly as composed.

The German had wasted no time once Harper disappeared into the powder room. His expensive shirt and trousers lay crumpled on the marble floor of the master bedroom, abandoned with the carelessness of a man who believed himself beyond consequences. Ulrich stood naked before the floor-to-ceiling mirror, his pale, bloated flesh gleaming with perspiration and anticipation.

The mask lay ready on the nightstand—black leather, ornate, something befitting a Venetian carnival. Beside it, a matching mask for Harper, delicate and feminine, adorned with silver filigree. Props for the evening's performance.

Ulrich was fully aroused now, his breathing heavy as he studied his reflection. In his mind, The Matchmaker knew, the German saw himself as a figure of power and sophistication. A man of refined tastes indulging in the privileges that wealth and influence afforded.

The reality was far more pathetic.

But that was precisely what made Ulrich so useful. His complete lack of self-awareness, his utter inability to see himself as others saw him—these qualities made him the perfect instrument for The Matchmaker's purposes. The man's appetites were predictable, his methods crude but effective. There would be no finesse tonight, no psychological subtlety. Just raw appetite and the belief that wealth granted a host of privileges.

Including silence.

The Matchmaker's attention shifted to Harper, still locked away in the powder room. She was gathering herself, they could see it in the set of her shoulders, the way she gripped the marble countertop. Such determination. Such faith in her own ability to navigate dangerous waters.

How deliciously naive.

She had no idea that she was now completely alone with Ulrich. No staff to overhear raised voices, no witnesses to whatever might unfold in the villa's opulent chambers. The German had been thorough in his dismissal of the help.

The girl was intelligent, resourceful, everything The Matchmaker had hoped for when they'd made their selection. But intelligence and resourcefulness could only carry her so far when faced with a man who recognized no boundaries, acknowledged no limits save his own desires.

This was the moment The Matchmaker had been anticipating. The collision between Harper's confidence and the brutal reality of her situation. The point where all her education, all her planning, all her belief in her own agency would prove utterly inadequate.

It was, in its way, quite beautiful.

"Sir?" The voice came from behind them, interrupting their observation. One of their associates, though The Matchmaker didn't bother turning around to see which one.

"What is it?"

"Some of the staff are concerned. They were told to leave Villa Nine rather abruptly. There are questions about protocol."

The Matchmaker allowed themselves a small smile. "Don't worry.

Mr. Drexler is a gentleman, The Matchmaker lied. "Ms. Holt is in perfectly capable hands."

CHAPTER
SEVEN

HARPER STEPPED out of the powder room and froze.

The villa had gone silent. Not the comfortable quiet between dinner courses. Something else. Something wrong.

Every hair on her arms stood on end.

She stood there, listening. No soft footsteps from the kitchen. No clink of crystal being cleared. No murmured conversations between staff. The absence of sound felt deliberate, orchestrated.

Just her own heartbeat, thrumming in her ears.

One step forward. Her heel clicked against marble, the sound sharp as a gunshot in the stillness. She waited for an answering sound—footsteps, a door closing, anything.

Nothing came back.

Another step. The dining room opened before her, exactly as she'd left it. Ulrich's wine glasses abandoned on the table, red stains on the rim where he'd drunk. Her barely touched salad wilting under the chandelier's light. His empty chair pushed back at an angle.

But on the side table near the archway, something new.

A mask.

Harper moved closer, her breathing shallow. Black leather, intricate silver filigree work along the edges. Expensive. Deliberate. Meant for her. The craftsmanship was beautiful and obscene—something that should have been in a museum, not waiting for her like a threat.

Her fingers hovered over it, not quite touching. The leather looked soft, supple. The kind that would mold perfectly to skin.

"Hello?" The word came out smaller than she'd intended. She cleared her throat, tried again with more force. "Is anyone there?"

The villa swallowed her voice without an echo.

Harper backed away from the mask, turned toward the main entrance. Stay calm. Think through options. There had to be a logical explanation. The heavy wooden door looked exactly as it had when she'd arrived—brass fixtures gleaming, security panel blinking green. Normal. Safe.

She reached for the handle. Her palm was already damp with sweat.

The handle turned smoothly under her grip, but the door didn't move. She pulled harder, putting her weight behind it.

Nothing.

She tried pushing instead, though she knew the door opened inward. Still nothing. The wood didn't even creak.

Ice spread through her chest. Don't panic. There are always other exits. She pressed both hands against the door, shoved with everything she had. The door might as well have been part of the wall.

"Ulrich?" Her voice cracked on his name. She swallowed hard, forced steadiness into her tone. "The door seems to be stuck."

Silence stretched for three heartbeats. Four. Five.

Then his voice drifted from somewhere deeper in the villa. From the direction of the master bedroom. But it didn't sound like the pompous businessman who'd bored her over dinner.

"If you want out, you'll have to come and ask me nicely."

The words seemed to hang in the air, poisoning it. Harper's hands were shaking now. She pressed them flat against her dress, willing them to stop. Her mother's voice echoed in her memory: *When you're scared, breathe. Count to ten. Your mind is your best weapon.*

Think. She could handle this. She'd handled worse. There were other exits. Windows. Service doors. This was a villa, not a prison.

The nearest window was six feet away, overlooking the infinity pool. Harper moved to it quickly, her fingers finding the latch. She twisted.

Nothing. The mechanism wouldn't budge.

She tried the next window. Same result. The latches were frozen in place, or locked, or broken. She worked her way around the dining room, trying every window she could reach. Each failure was another brick in the wall closing around her.

All locked.

"Just freshening up," she called out, keeping her voice light. "You know how we girls are."

No response.

The kitchen. There had to be a service entrance. Staff had been coming and going all evening. Harper hurried through the archway into the chrome and marble space. Everything gleamed under harsh fluorescent lights—industrial refrigerators, a massive gas range, prep stations that could handle a dozen or more guests.

And there, beside the walk-in freezer, a door marked "Staff Only."

Harper grabbed the handle and pulled.

Locked from the outside.

Her breathing was coming faster now, short and sharp. The kitchen felt smaller than it had a moment ago. The fluorescent lights too bright, too harsh. She could see her reflection in every chrome surface—a woman in a cocktail dress, trying doors like a trapped animal. But she wasn't an animal. She was smart. She could think her way out of this.

Back to the dining room. There had to be something she'd missed. A door to the terrace, maybe. French doors hidden behind curtains.

"You're being very quiet out there," Ulrich called. His voice was closer now. He'd moved from the bedroom. "I hope you're not having second thoughts."

"Just want to look perfect for you," Harper managed, her voice almost normal. Keep him talking. Buy time.

She found the terrace doors behind heavy silk drapes. Her hands fumbled with the curtain pulls, fabric tangling around her arms. When she finally got them open, moonlight spilled across marble floors.

The doors were glass, floor to ceiling. No visible lock, just a simple handle. Harper grabbed it, turned, pulled.

Nothing.

She threw her shoulder against the glass. Pain shot down her arm, but the door didn't even rattle in its frame.

"These new safety locks," Ulrich's voice came from right behind her. "Wonderful technology. They engage automatically after ten p.m. No one gets in. No one gets out. For security, you understand."

Harper spun around.

He stood in the archway between the dining room and the bedroom corridor. Completely naked. The mask covered the upper half of his face, but she could see his mouth, his jaw, the satisfied smile playing at his lips. His body was pale and soft in the moonlight, but his arousal was obvious, aggressive.

In his right hand, something metallic caught the light. Handcuffs.

"Villa Nine has many special features," he said, taking a step into the room. His bare feet made no sound on the marble. "Complete soundproofing, for instance. You could scream all night and no one would hear."

Harper's mind raced through options. Run—but where? Fight—but he outweighed her by at least a hundred and fifty pounds, likely more. Talk—but the look in his eyes said conversation was over. She thought of her father teaching her chess: *Always think three moves ahead. Your opponent thinks he's winning, but you're setting up the real game.*

"Actually," she said, surprised her voice came out steady, even sultry, "I brought something special to wear. Just for you. Something I think you'll really enjoy."

His head tilted. "Did you?"

"It's in my bag. Let me slip into it. I promise it'll be worth the wait."

She moved toward her evening bag on the side table, keeping her movements slow, deliberate. No sudden motions. Nothing to trigger whatever was building behind those eyes.

"I've been waiting all evening," Ulrich said. "What's a few more minutes?"

Harper's fingers closed around her bag. She could feel him watching as she opened it, items spilling onto the marble. Lipstick. Phone—useless without a signal. Wallet full of cards that couldn't help her here.

And Nikki's letter opener.

The silver blade was small, decorative, designed to look elegant rather than dangerous. But it was sharp. She'd felt that when she'd used it on the envelope. Nikki had pressed this into her hands, had given up her own protection. Her friend's voice echoed: *It'll cut a bitch.* Harper felt a surge of love for Nikki, for the bond that had put this weapon in her palm.

"You know," Ulrich said, moving closer, "I've had girls play games before. Pretend they need to freshen up. Try to find ways out. It's actually quite endearing."

Harper palmed the letter opener, keeping it hidden against her wrist. She turned to face him, forcing her lips into what she hoped looked like a seductive smile. One chance. Make it count.

"I'm not playing games," she said. "I just want tonight to be perfect."

He was three feet away now. Close enough that she could smell his cologne mixed with sweat and wine. Close enough to see the pupils dilated behind the mask's eye holes.

"It will be," he said. "I promise you that."

He reached for her.

Harper brought the letter opener up in one smooth motion, slashing at his extended hand. The blade caught his palm, opening a line of red from thumb to pinky.

Ulrich jerked back with a howl, clutching his bleeding hand to his chest. "You bitch!"

Harper didn't wait. She darted past him toward the corridor, her heels skittering on marble. If she could get to the bedroom, find the key, maybe barricade herself in the bathroom until—

A hand closed on her hair, yanking her backward.

Pain exploded across her scalp as Ulrich dragged her down. She hit the floor hard, marble cold against her back, the letter opener spinning away into shadows. But she'd drawn blood. She'd hurt him. That had to count for something.

"You cut me," he said, looming over her. Blood dripped from his hand onto her dress. "You actually cut me."

Harper tried to roll away but he dropped his weight onto her, pinning her legs. His good hand found her throat. She thought of her parents, of Sunday mornings reading the paper together, of how proud they'd been when she got into college. They were waiting for her. They believed in her. She couldn't give up.

"I was going to be gentle," he said, squeezing. "Make it nicer for you. But now..."

Stars burst across Harper's vision. She clawed at his hand, her nails finding skin, digging deep. He didn't even flinch. But she kept fighting. She would always keep fighting.

"Now I think we'll do this my way."

The pressure on her throat increased. The chandelier above started to blur, its crystal fragments multiplying into a thousand points of light. Harper's hands fell away from his, her strength fading. But her mind stayed sharp, stayed hers. He couldn't take that from her.

The pressure released suddenly. Harper gasped, air burning into her lungs. Through tears, she saw Ulrich reaching for something.

The handcuffs.

"No more games," he said. "No more running."

He grabbed her wrist, the metal cold against her skin. The first cuff clicked shut.

Harper twisted, using the last of her strength to drive her knee up between his legs. It wasn't a solid hit—the angle was wrong, her leverage gone—but it was enough. She was still here. Still fighting.

Ulrich grunted, his grip loosening for just a second.

Harper rolled hard to the right, the loose cuff clanging against marble. She made it to her knees, then her feet, stumbling toward the bedroom.

Behind her, Ulrich's breathing had gone ragged. "You can't get out. Biometric lock. My thumbprint only."

She reached the bedroom, slammed the door behind her. No lock on this side. Of course not. Why would there be?

The room was massive, dominated by a king-sized bed with silk sheets. Floor-to-ceiling windows showed the moon hanging over dark water. A door on the far wall—the bathroom. Another door beside it— a closet.

And on the nightstand, a black safe the size of a shoebox. Red light glowing where the biometric scanner waited.

Footsteps in the corridor. Slow, measured. He wasn't running. He knew she had nowhere to go. But Harper's mind was cataloging everything—exits, weapons, anything that could be used. She wasn't done yet.

Harper grabbed the nearest chair, wedged it under the door handle. It wouldn't hold for long, but maybe—

The door exploded inward. The chair went flying, wood splintering against the wall. Ulrich filled the doorway, his pale body heaving with each breath.

"Enough," he said.

He crossed the room in three strides. Harper tried to dodge around the bed but he caught her arm, spun her into the mattress. She bounced once, tried to roll away, but he was already on her.

His weight pressed her into the silk sheets. She couldn't breathe, couldn't move. The handcuff on her wrist clinked against the headboard as she struggled. But in her mind, she was somewhere else—with Nikki, with her parents, with everyone who loved her and believed in her strength.

"Look at me," he said.

When she didn't, his hand found her jaw, forced her head around. Behind the mask, his eyes were bright with something that made her stomach turn.

"I said look at me."

She spat in his face.

For a moment, neither of them moved. Then Ulrich smiled, wiping the spit away with the back of his hand.

"Perfect," he said. "I was hoping you'd have some fight in you."

He shifted his weight, reaching for something beside the bed. Harper used the movement to drive her elbow into his ribs. He wheezed but didn't let go, his hand coming back with a length of silk rope. She kept fighting because that's who she was. That's who she would always be.

"Villa Nine has so many amenities," he said, catching her free wrist. He placed a small key on the nightstand within easy reach. "The previous occupant was quite the enthusiast."

Harper fought as he wound the rope around her wrist, her movements growing more desperate as she realized what was happening. But he was too heavy, too strong, and in seconds both her wrists were bound to the headboard.

She pulled against the restraints. The rope was soft but unyielding, the knots professional. But her mind was still working, still calculating angles and possibilities. He could control her body, but he couldn't control her thoughts.

"There," Ulrich said, sitting back to admire his work. "Much better."

He stood, moving to the foot of the bed. Harper could see herself reflected in the mirror on the far wall—arms stretched above her head, dress riding up her thighs, makeup smeared with tears she didn't remember crying. But when she looked at her own eyes in the reflection, she saw something he couldn't touch. Something that remained entirely hers.

"You know what I love about this island?" Ulrich asked, running his hand along her calf. "The complete privacy. No phones. No cameras. No witnesses."

His hand moved higher.

"Just us."

Harper turned her face into the pillow, not to hide but to center herself. She thought of Nikki's laugh, of her parents' voices on Sunday phone calls, of everything worth fighting for. Her body might be trapped, but her spirit was elsewhere—with the people who loved her, who were waiting for her to come home.

"Don't disassociate now, Ms. Holt. Don't hide from me," Ulrich said.

She felt the bed shift as he climbed back on. Felt his hands on her dress, heard fabric beginning to tear. But inside her mind, she was building walls he could never breach, keeping safe the parts of herself that mattered most.

"Please," she whispered, hating herself for the word.

"Please?" Ulrich laughed, the sound muffled by the mask. "Oh, I do like it when they beg. But it's far too early for that."

The silk of her dress gave way with a soft ripping sound. Cool air hit her skin. Harper held onto the image of Nikki pressing the letter opener into her hands, of her parents hugging her goodbye when they'd dropped her at college. Memories he couldn't storm.

"We have all night," he said, his breathing getting heavier. "And I have so many things planned for us to explore."

Harper stared at the ceiling, at the crystal chandelier that threw rainbow patterns across white plaster. She tried to go somewhere else in her mind, tried to float away from what was happening to her body. And she found she could—not completely, but enough. She was Harper Holt. She was loved. She was more than this moment.

But Ulrich's voice kept pulling her back.

"Stay with me now, Harper," he said, his hand on her face again. "I want you present for this. I want you to be able to remember every moment."

Even then, even as her world narrowed to this terrible room, Harper held onto one thought: *I will survive this. I will find a way. I am not his to break.*

CHAPTER
EIGHT

A BEAD of Ulrich's sweat dropped onto Harper's cheek, and slid toward the edge of her mouth. She twisted her face away, but his weight pressed down, trapping her against silk sheets that smelled of expensive fabric softener and something else. Something wrong.

His breathing filled her ears—wet, labored, excited. The mask made it worse, turning him into something inhuman hovering above her. She could see his eyes through the leather, small and bright with anticipation.

"Don't look away," he said, his voice muffled. "I want to see your face when—"

Harper's knee drove up between his legs with everything she had.

Ulrich's words cut off in a strangled gasp. His body folded forward, his full weight collapsing onto her chest. She couldn't breathe, couldn't move, pinned under his bulk as he wheezed and groaned.

But his grip on her had loosened.

Harper twisted her right wrist, feeling the silk rope give slightly. The blood from his cut hand had made everything slippery—the sheets, the restraints, her skin. She worked her wrist back and forth, ignoring the burn of rope against raw flesh. Something had shifted inside her, some primal survival instinct taking control. This was her moment. Her only chance.

"Du... Schlampe..." Ulrich managed, trying to push himself upright.

The loose handcuff dangled from Harper's left wrist, its metal warm from her body heat. As Ulrich raised his head, she whipped her arm sideways, the steel striking his temple.

The shock of the blow sent him off balance. A trickle of blood began to run from beneath the mask's edge. His hands clutched at his groin, then his head, unable to decide which pain demanded more attention.

Harper's right hand slipped free of the silk rope. She immediately reached across to her left wrist, her fingers working frantically at the knots. The blood had made them slippery too, and within seconds she'd loosened the rope enough to pull her left hand free.

She rolled toward the edge of the bed, the handcuff still dangling from her wrist, but she could move now. She could fight. The realization flooded through her like electricity—she was no longer helpless. No longer at his mercy. The power had shifted, and it belonged to her now.

Ulrich was making sounds—not words, just animal noises of pain and rage. He tried to grab her ankle as she swung her legs off the mattress.

Harper kicked backward, her heel connecting with something soft. His nose, maybe, or his mouth. The impact sent fresh pain through her foot, but Ulrich's grip fell away.

She stood on shaking legs, her dress torn and hanging in strips. The handcuff swayed from her left wrist as she reached for the nightstand. Her movements felt different now—controlled, purposeful. She thought of Nikki's fierce loyalty, of her parents' strength, of every person who had ever believed in her. They were with her in this moment.

Her fingers closed around the small metal handcuff key just as Ulrich struggled to his knees on the bed. Blood covered the lower half of the mask, and his breathing had gone wrong—too fast, too shallow. The predator had become prey, and they both knew it.

"Help..." he gasped, one hand pressed to his chest. "Help me..."

Harper stared at him for a long moment. This pathetic, wheezing thing that had tried to destroy her. That had locked her in this room like a toy for his amusement. But more than that—she saw Madison's haunted face, the bruises poorly hidden by makeup. She saw all the girls who would come after if someone didn't stop him.

The letter opener lay on the floor where it had fallen during their struggle. Harper picked it up, the silver blade catching the moonlight. Nikki's gift. Her friend's protection made manifest.

"Help..." Ulrich whispered again, his eyes wide behind the mask.

"You said we had all night," Harper said, fitting the key into the handcuff's lock. The metal clicked open, freeing her completely. The sound of liberation. "You said you wanted me to remember every moment."

The handcuff fell to the marble floor with a sharp ring.

Harper moved closer to the bed, the letter opener steady in her hand. Her mind was crystal clear now, her purpose absolute. Ulrich tried to crawl backward but his body wasn't responding properly.

"Don't hide from me," Harper said, echoing his earlier words. "We're just getting started."

She pressed the blade's point against his inner thigh, just above the knee. Ulrich's whole body went rigid. Harper felt a cold satisfaction at his terror—not cruelty, but justice.

"Please," he gasped. "Please, I—"

"I like it when you beg," Harper said. The words tasted different in her mouth than they had in his. Like power reclaimed.

She traced the edge of the blade down the inside of his thigh. Ulrich's whole body trembled. Harper found herself thinking with perfect clarity: this man would never hurt another woman. Not after tonight. That certainty filled her with something that wasn't quite peace, but was close to it.

"Please," he gasped. "I can give you money. Whatever you want."

"So you can do this to the next girl?"

"No, no, I swear."

Harper placed her free hand on his face, her fingers gentle against the leather mask. The gesture was almost tender, but her eyes were steel. "Stay with me," she said softly. "I want you here for this. I want you to remember all of it."

She drew the blade back. Ulrich's eyes never left the silver edge.

"Every moment."

CHAPTER
NINE

THE MATCHMAKER WATCHED Harper Holt's pale legs disappearing through the bathroom window of Villa Nine. One moment she was there—a flash of torn fabric and desperation—and then nothing but darkness beyond the frame.

"No," they said. Then louder: "No!"

Their fist slammed into the console. Pain shot through their knuckles but they barely noticed. On the center screen, Ulrich Drexler writhed on the bedroom floor, his grotesque body convulsing, blood pooling beneath his head.

This wasn't supposed to happen. This wasn't the plan.

The Matchmaker grabbed their radio, their hands shaking. "Security, all teams. Code Black at Villa Nine. I repeat Code Black!"

Static crackled back at them. Where were they? Where was everyone?

"I need containment teams at Villa Nine immediately," they said, forcing control into their voice that they didn't feel. "Medical team to the master bedroom. And I want every available unit searching the grounds. The girl is running."

"Copy that," a voice finally responded. "Teams en route. What's the nature of the medical—"

"Just get there!"

The Matchmaker switched camera feeds, searching for Harper. The villa's exterior cameras showed nothing—just manicured gardens and empty pathways lit by soft landscape lighting. She'd already vanished into the darkness beyond their reach.

Their perfect composition, ruined. Their carefully orchestrated evening, destroyed by one stupid girl who didn't understand her role.

"Base, this is Team Three. We're at the main resort. Should we—?"

"Keep all guests in their villas," The Matchmaker interrupted. "No one moves. Tell them it's a security drill. Anyone asks questions, you know nothing."

"What about the staff?"

"Lock down the staff quarters. No one in or out until I say otherwise."

On the monitor, Ulrich had stopped moving. His chest still rose and fell, but barely. The mask had come partially off, revealing his bloodied face. If he died...

The Matchmaker's throat constricted. A dead billionaire meant investigations, questions, scrutiny they couldn't afford.

"Medical team approaching Villa Nine," a voice reported.

"Send them straight to the master bedroom. And get me eyes on that girl!"

They cycled through every camera feed on the property. The pools, the restaurants, the beach club—all empty at this hour. Where would she go? A barefoot girl in a torn dress, traumatized and desperate. She'd run for help, but where?

The jungle. She'd gone into the jungle.

"Teams Five and Six, sweep the tree line behind Villa Nine. She's on foot, barefoot, injured. She can't have gotten far."

"Copy. Moving to intercept."

The Matchmaker's leg bounced under the desk, a nervous tic they hadn't displayed since childhood. This was wrong. All wrong. Harper should have broken gradually, artfully, her resistance crumbling under Ulrich's assault until she accepted her role in their design. Instead, she'd turned the tables, transformed from victim to...

To what? Survivor? Avenger?

"Medical team is with the client," someone reported. "He's

conscious but unresponsive. Possible cardiac event. They're requesting permission to—"

"Do whatever it takes to keep him alive," The Matchmaker said. "I don't care if we have to fly in specialists from the mainland. He doesn't die. Understood?"

"Understood."

Another monitor showed security teams spreading across the resort grounds, their flashlights cutting through darkness. They moved in coordinated patterns, professional and efficient. But Harper had a head start, and the jungle was vast.

"Sir?" A new voice on the radio. "We've found something."

The Matchmaker leaned forward. "What?"

"Blood trail leading from Villa Nine toward the eastern jungle. Fresh. She's definitely heading inland."

"Understood."

The Matchmaker stood, pacing behind their desk. Their perfect system, their flawless operation, undone by one girl who refused to play her part. The other guests would start asking questions soon. The staff would whisper. Word would spread like infection through their carefully cultivated paradise.

Unless they contained it. Unless they fixed this.

"All teams, listen carefully," they said into the radio. "The girl is confused, possibly drugged. She attacked one of our valued guests and fled. We're conducting a wellness check for her own safety. That's the only story. Anyone deviates from that narrative, they're gone. Clear?"

A chorus of confirmations came back.

On the monitors, Ulrich was being loaded onto a medical gurney. The man's face had gone gray, his breathing labored despite the oxygen mask. If he died, if he actually died...

Harper Holt would pay for this. When they found her—and they would find her—they'd make sure every girl on this island understood what happened when you forgot your place.

CHAPTER
TEN

HARPER CRASHED THROUGH THE UNDERGROWTH, branches tearing at what remained of her dress. Her bare feet seemed to find every sharp edge—broken shells, volcanic rock, thorns that embedded deep. Each step sent pain surging through her soles but she couldn't stop. Wouldn't stop.

The jungle pressed in from all sides, a living wall of vegetation that grabbed at her with thorny fingers. What had been a manicured paradise in daylight quickly transformed into a maze of shadows. Her torn dress caught on a branch, ripping the fabric further until it hung like rags from her shoulders.

Behind her, flashlight beams cut through the canopy. Radio chatter echoed off the trees, too close. Way too close.

A vine caught her ankle and she went down hard, palms skidding across rough bark. The impact knocked the air from her lungs. For a moment she lay there, chest heaving, tasting dirt and blood where she'd bitten her tongue. The adrenaline that had carried her from Villa Nine was fading, leaving behind a catalog of hurts—scraped palms, bleeding feet, bruises blooming across her ribs where Ulrich had pinned her.

But she wasn't helpless anymore. She'd proven that. Whatever happened next, she would never be trapped again, never let someone else hold absolute power over her body, her choices, her life. The memory of taking control, of turning the tables, burned bright inside her chest.

Get up. Get up now.

She pushed to her feet, ignoring the warm wetness running down her shins. The dress hung in strips now, one strap completely torn away. Sweat stung the scratches covering her arms and shoulders. Every breath was a struggle, but she forced her legs to move, one step, then another, deeper into the darkness.

"You can't go out there," the security guard said, blocking Nikki's path. He was young, local, trying to look authoritative despite the uncertainty in his eyes. "All staff return to quarters immediately."

"My friend is at Villa Nine," Nikki said, her voice rising with each word. Heat built behind her eyes—fear and guilt and helpless rage all mixing together. She should have done more. Should have found a way to stop Harper from going. "I need to check on her."

"Quarters. Now." His hand moved to the radio on his belt. "Don't make me call for backup."

Two more guards appeared behind him, hands resting near their equipment. Not quite touching weapons, but the threat was clear. These weren't the usual security guys who smiled and flirted with the girls. These were the Israelis, the inner circle, faces grim, movements coordinated.

Nikki backed away slowly, mind racing. Harper had taken the letter opener. Harper had gone to Villa Nine. And now security was locking down the entire resort like something terrible had happened. The weight of understanding settled on her shoulders—her friend was in real danger, and there was nothing she could do to help.

She turned and ran for the staff building, her heels clicking against the pathway. Other girls clustered in doorways, whispering behind their hands. They'd all heard something—a commotion, raised voices, orders barked over radios.

"Get inside," one of the guards called after her. "No one leaves until morning."

The threat in his voice made her run faster.

Harper heard them before she saw them—voices calling coordinates, boots crushing undergrowth, the mechanical squawk of radios. They were organized, methodical. This wasn't a random search. They were hunting her.

She veered right, deeper into the jungle's embrace. The canopy here was so thick that even the moon was blocked out, leaving her to navigate by instinct and desperation. Her ankle rolled on uneven ground, shooting jagged pain up her leg. She bit down on her lip to keep from screaming, tasted fresh blood.

Not broken, but wrong. Each step sent lightning through the joint.

The sounds of pursuit multiplied. They were spreading out, trying to flank her. Drive her toward something. Or someone.

For a second—just a second—doubt crept in. What if she'd just let it happen? Survived it? Collected her money and gone home with another horror story to bury deep?

The memory of Ulrich's hands on her throat answered that question. The look in his eyes behind that mask. That wasn't about sex or power or any of the usual rich man's games. That was about destroying her, piece by piece, because he could. Because it entertained him. Because he saw her as nothing more than an object for his amusement.

She'd felt what it was like to be completely powerless, completely at someone else's mercy. The terror of realizing that her life, her dignity, her very self could be taken away on another person's whim. She would rather die than feel that helpless again.

No. Fuck that. Fuck him.

She'd fought back. She'd won. And now she had to survive the consequences.

Harper pushed through a curtain of vines, her twisted ankle screaming with each impact. Behind her, a dog barked. Then another.

She froze.

The door to their shared room stood open. Three other girls huddled on Nikki's bed, faces pale in the fluorescent light. The youngest one—she couldn't be more than nineteen—had tears streaming down her face.

"Where's Harper?" she asked.

"Villa Nine. With Drexler." Nikki moved to the window, peering through the blinds. Security teams swept across the grounds, flashlights creating crazy patterns in the darkness. The sick feeling in her stomach grew worse. She'd pressed the letter opener into Harper's hands, but it felt so inadequate now. A tiny blade against whatever forces had been unleashed tonight. "Something's happened. Something bad."

"You need to calm down," an older blonde girl called Natasha said, examining her nails with practiced indifference. She was one of the veterans, months on the island, designer everything. "Making a fuss isn't going to help anyone."

"Are you serious right now?" Nikki spun on her. "Harper could be—"

"Could be what? In trouble?" Natasha's laugh was bitter. "We're all in trouble, honey. That's why we're here."

"Shut the fuck up," Nikki said. The rage felt good, cleaner than the guilt and fear. She'd failed Harper when it mattered most, but she wouldn't fail her now by staying silent.

Natasha shrugged off the outburst.

Through the window, more teams appeared. Moving with purpose now, spreading out in a search pattern that looked military in its precision. And in the distance, carried on the wind—

Dogs barking.

"Oh god," the young girl whispered. "They brought out those dogs."

Harper burst through a wall of ferns and suddenly the jungle ended. She skidded to a stop, stones scattering over an edge she couldn't see in the darkness.

The cliff.

Here, finally free of the canopy's embrace, moonlight turned the scene silver. During daylight, this was where the girls came to show off. Forty feet down to crystal-clear water, deep enough if you jumped right. She'd done it twice herself, running full speed to clear the rocks below, screaming all the way down before the cool ocean swallowed her.

But that was in sunlight. When you could see the edge, judge the distance, spot the safe zone between the coral heads.

Now, despite the moon's glow, the ocean was just a black void below. She couldn't even make out where water met rock.

Behind her, the dogs were getting louder. Excited now. They had her scent and knew they were close. She could hear their handlers shouting encouragement, promising rewards.

She limped to the cliff's edge, trying to peer down. Moonlight caught the wave caps far below, but the landing zone was invisible. Jump too close and she'd hit the rocks. Too far and she'd miss the deep channel, land in the shallows where razor-sharp coral waited.

The smart play was to surrender. Take whatever came next. Let them drag her back to face the consequences of what she'd done to Ulrich.

But she'd left smart back in Villa Nine, with her shoes and her dignity and her belief that money could fix anything. And more than that—surrender meant going back to being powerless. It meant letting them decide what happened to her body, her future, her life. She'd tasted what it felt like to take control, and she couldn't give that up. Not now. Not ever.

"Search line, spread out!" The voice was maybe fifty yards back. Professional. Calm. "She's running out of room!"

So they knew where she was. They'd been herding her here all along.

Harper backed away from the edge. Ten steps. Fifteen. Her twisted ankle screamed with each movement, but the pain felt distant now, overwhelmed by something larger. This wasn't just about escaping—this was about refusing to be hunted like an animal. About claiming the right to choose her own fate, even if that fate was falling through darkness toward unknown water.

In daylight, the run-up was twenty-five steps. She'd counted once, laughing with the other girls. Twenty-five steps to build enough speed to clear the rocks. She thought of Nikki's letter opener, still back in Villa Nine, stained with Ulrich's blood. Her friend's protection had served its purpose. Now Harper had to protect herself.

She couldn't see to count now. Had to guess.

Twenty steps back. The dogs sounded like they were right behind her, crashing through the undergrowth.

Twenty-five. Her feet found a relatively flat stretch of packed earth.

Flashlight beams broke through the trees. She saw them clearly now— men in tactical gear, dogs straining on leashes, converging on her.

"Miss Holt!" one called out. "There's nowhere to go. Let's talk about this."

Another voice. The head of security, Ethan Efron. "You're not in trouble. I assure you that no one is going to hurt you."

Harper almost laughed. They still thought they could control her with their false promises.

Her mind was made. She couldn't let them take her. She needed to escape. Or die in the attempt. She had made this jump before. But never like this—never as an act of pure defiance, never as a declaration that her life belonged to her and no one else.

She bit down on her lip. Her mind set.

The flashlights were getting closer. The dogs' barking filled the air. Somewhere back in the compound, Nikki was probably watching from a window, worried sick, maybe even blaming herself. Harper hoped her friend would understand. This wasn't about giving up—this was about refusing to give in.

Taking a final deep breath, Harper Holt pushed off, running as fast as she could for the cliff edge. Then she was over, falling, caught in the darkness, tumbling down, legs pedaling for traction.

CHAPTER
ELEVEN

TY JOHNSON SLID BACK into his business class seat with the satisfied look of a man who'd just secured a phone number he'd never use.

"Her name's Amelia," he said, glancing back at the supermodel-esque blonde flight attendant he'd just been talking to. "From Brisbane. Says she flies this route twice a month."

Lock didn't look up from his laptop screen. "Fascinating."

"I think so." Ty settled into the leather seat, reaching for the stack of documents in the pocket beside him. The cabin was quiet around them, other passengers either sleeping or lost in their own screens. Outside the small window, endless ocean stretched in all directions. "Man, if you have to do long haul, this is the way to do it."

Lock glanced over. "We still talking about Amelia?"

"The whole deal, brother. I remember those C-130s I used to deploy in? Cargo netting for seats, pissing in a tube, eating MREs that tasted like cardboard soaked in motor oil." Ty accepted a warm towel from a passing attendant. "This beats the hell out of that."

As Ty took a trip down Marine Corps memory lane, Lock's attention was already back on his screen. The technical specifications filled the display—camera positions, sensor arrays, communication protocols. It was the kind of detailed work that required complete focus.

"The Japanese IFF integration is going to be the problem," Lock said, fingers moving across the keyboard.

Ty picked up his orange juice. "Come again?"

"The island's anti-drone defenses." Lock turned the laptop so Ty could see the schematic. Blue and red lines connected various points across what looked like a detailed map. "They're running Japanese radar integrated with Israeli countermeasures."

"This is why God invented subcontractors."

"Already on it. I've got a technical team coming in after us. They'll handle the electronic assessment while we focus on physical security."

"We're gonna use a Red Team?" Ty asked, settling deeper into the plush seat.

Red Team exercises involved hired experts, almost always former special forces or high-grade ex-military, who would attempt to breach the security systems and test defenses from an attacker's perspective. Penetration testing was the official jargon.

"Arriving a few days after we get there. Covertly," Lock said.

"Sneaky, I like it."

Ty lifted the NDA from his document stack, cream-colored paper that felt expensive between his fingers. The thing was thick as a small book, dense with legal language that made his eyes water. "Should I sign this thing? It's been burning a hole in my briefcase since LA."

"Not yet. Carmen flagged some issues."

"Such as?"

"Perpetual confidentiality, unlimited liability." Lock closed the laptop with a soft click. "Plus clause seventeen basically says if we breach, they own our children."

"Joke?"

"Barely. We'll negotiate when we get there. Face to face." Lock accepted a water bottle from a passing flight attendant, the condensation cool against his palm. "Harder to be unreasonable when you're looking someone in the eye."

"These guys sound wound pretty tight."

"The more you have to protect, the more protective you become." Lock twisted the cap off his water. "Plus, they're trusting us with their entire security profile. Every camera position, every weak point, every protocol. In the wrong hands, that information is worth more than whatever they're paying us."

"Which is?" Ty asked, though he suspected he already knew why Lock had been cagey about the numbers.

Lock had held off telling Ty the specifics of the fee, just that it was more than generous. Ty had a habit of spending money before it had landed in his account, and clients like this had a corresponding habit of slow-rolling payments.

"Two-fifty upfront. Another two-fifty when we're done."

Ty whistled low. "Half a million for two weeks' work."

"It's not about us. It's about what we represent to their guests. These people don't just want security—they want reassurance." Lock shifted in his seat, the leather creaking softly. "Big Dave Carter's word didn't hurt either. His recommendation carries weight in these circles."

"Big Dave from England? That Big Dave?" Ty said. "Guy looks like he should be fixing your sink, not running security ops."

"Appearances are deceptive. Guy's a stud. Twenty-two SAS, squadron sergeant major before he went private." Lock's tone carried the respect of one professional for another. "I met him during my stint with the Royal Military Police. We saved a principal's life twice in one week. I wouldn't have walked away from the first one without Carter."

"And now he's vouching for us to protect rich people's privacy while they play golf. Sweet."

"He's second in command. Head is Ethan Efron." Lock pulled the organizational chart from his own folder, spreading it on the small table between their seats. "Didn't you read this?"

"Oh yeah, the Israeli. Former Mossad," Ty said, glancing at the neat boxes and connecting lines.

"The kind of former where you're never really former, if you know what I mean," Lock said. His analytical mind was already working through the implications, the way it always did when he encountered new variables.

Ty nodded slowly, reaching for a handful of nuts from the dish beside his seat. "Those guys run tight ships. Makes our job easier. They'll have their protocols locked down, their people trained right."

"Maybe." Lock stared out the window at the endless ocean below, but his mind was on the briefing materials, the gaps in information that always bothered him. "The Barzanis have brought in three different security consultants in two years."

"So they're thorough."

"You don't redesign a system that's working. You don't bring in outside eyes unless inside eyes are missing something." Lock turned from the window, his expression thoughtful rather than concerned. It was the look Ty recognized—Lock's brain working through a puzzle, not anticipating danger.

"Could be they're just rotating firms. Keep it fresh, different perspectives."

They sat in comfortable silence, the hum of engines filling the space between them. The cabin lights had dimmed for the overnight portion of the flight, and most passengers were settling in for sleep. Lock could feel his mind working through the details, the way it always did when he encountered an interesting professional challenge.

"You're doing that thing," Ty said, his voice amused rather than worried.

"What thing?"

"That thing where you turn every job into a puzzle. It's a security review, Lock. We look at their cameras, test their response times, write a report." Ty's tone was relaxed, confident. "We're consultants now, remember? This is what consulting looks like."

Lock reached for his laptop again, but kept it closed. "You're right."

"But?"

"But three teams in two years, Ty. That's not standard operating procedure." He tapped the laptop's surface with one finger, an unconscious habit when he was thinking. "And who hires ex-Mossad to run security for a beach resort."

"Rich people do. It's a flex."

"Efron wasn't just Mossad. He was Kidon." Lock's voice carried professional interest rather than alarm—one security professional noting another's credentials.

Kidon was the elite covert assassination unit within Mossad. The literal translation from Hebrew to English was bayonet. They weren't spies. They were killers.

CHAPTER
TWELVE

THE SMELL of blood still hung in Villa Nine's master bedroom despite the industrial fans churning humid air through open windows.

Amira Barzani stood in the doorway, her Hermès sandals carefully positioned to avoid any lingering traces of blood. She watched the cleaning crew work with the detached interest of someone calculating depreciation on a damaged asset. The workers moved with practiced efficiency, yellow hazmat suits rustling as they bagged evidence for disposal and scrubbed surfaces.

"The mattress goes," she said, her voice cutting through the whir of ventilation fans. "The carpets, obviously. The headboard too—see those scratches? Replace it all."

Patrick appeared behind her, his linen shirt already showing sweat stains despite the early hour. The humidity seemed to cling to everything.

"Do you have any idea what Harper Holt could have been worth to us?" Amira's voice could have frosted glass.

The cleaning crew continued their work, pretending not to understand English. They'd been flown in specifically for their discretion and poor language skills. What they could understand was the thousand-dollar cash bonus for finishing before noon, and the unspoken consequences of talking about what they'd seen.

"Sure, but she was difficult," Patrick said, but his tone suggested he knew the argument was already lost. "Ethan warned us when her profile came back—"

"Ethan warned us she was intelligent. Educated. Exactly the kind of girl we needed for the Azerbaijani defense minister." Amira stepped into the room, her heels clicking against the marble where plastic sheeting didn't cover it. Behind her, Patrick and Ethan exchanged a look.

Ethan was directing two workers who were removing the bed frame, his movements economical and precise. The former Mossad operative had overseen enough crime scene cleanups to know exactly what needed to be done, in what order, and how long each step should take.

"I believe Drexler requested her specifically," Ethan said without looking up, his attention focused on a worker spraying luminol on the walls. "He was very insistent."

"And since when do we let guests dictate operations?" Amira's accent sharpened, her Swiss finishing school polish cracking. She moved to examine the damaged walls more closely, noting each gouge and stain with professional assessment. "Harper was tagged for development. International Relations student, spoke several languages, which is rare for an American. Six months of coaching and she could have been bringing in more girls for us. High-end girls, maybe some from the Ivy schools. The kind we need."

Patrick shifted uncomfortably, recognizing the signs of Amira's controlled fury. "Maybe that was the problem. Too much potential. Some guests prefer them broken."

Amira turned. "Then why didn't you give him her roommate? The black one?"

"She's been getting close to Samir Patel. We didn't want to complicate that relationship."

"So instead you complicated ours." Amira watched a worker hold up a piece of torn fabric, questioning. She nodded and he placed it in a burn bag with other evidence. "All the time I spent. All my investment. Gone."

"Not gone," Ethan said, straightening from his examination of the floor. "Missing. There's a difference."

"You haven't found the body."

"We have three boats out. The current patterns suggest she'll wash up on the eastern rocks by tomorrow." He paused, peeling off his latex gloves with clinical precision. "If marine life hasn't interfered."

Patrick moved to the window, looking out at the perfect blue water that concealed so many secrets. The view was pristine, deceptive—all surface beauty hiding the currents and creatures beneath. "What if someone else finds her first?"

"Then they find a young woman who tragically drowned after drinking too much." Ethan's smile held no warmth. "My contacts in Dubai are already prepared. The medical examiner there is very understanding about tourist accidents."

"Speaking of Dubai," Patrick said, "Our consultants arrive this afternoon."

The temperature in the room seemed to drop several degrees. Amira's expression, already cold, turned arctic.

"Perfect. An incident like this and we have outsiders coming to examine our security."

"It's routine," Ethan assured her, moving to stand beside the window where Patrick waited. The three of them formed a natural triangle. "Ryan Lock and Ty Johnson have excellent reputations. They'll review our visible systems, make some recommendations, collect their fee."

"And they won't see anything else?"

"They'll see what we show them." Ethan gestured vaguely at the room around them, where workers continued their methodical erasure of the night's events. "The same systems the previous two teams reviewed. They won't have access to the operational infrastructure."

A worker approached with a fragment of silk, blood-stained and torn. Amira examined it briefly before nodding toward the burn bag. Every piece of evidence had to disappear, every trace of what had really happened in this room.

"Lock isn't stupid," Patrick said. "Carter vouched for him. Said he's got instincts."

"Everyone has instincts," Ethan replied, his tone suggesting vast experience with people who thought they were cleverer than they were. "What matters is whether they're motivated to follow them."

"And if they are?"

Ethan shot them a professional smile. "Then we'll handle it. We've handled worse."

Amira walked to the bathroom, noting the open window where Harper had made her desperate escape. The frame showed scratches where she'd forced her way through, small signs of her desperation still visible despite the cleaning. "She went through there?"

"After incapacitating Drexler. He's lucky she didn't kill him."

"Lucky," Amira repeated, her tone suggesting she disagreed with that assessment. "A dead billionaire would have been cleaner. Now we have a witness."

"Sedated and managed. His people think it was a heart attack brought on by overexertion." Ethan checked his watch, the gesture automatic. "They're more concerned about his recovery than asking questions."

"Questions will come later."

"And we'll have answers by then." Ethan moved toward the door, already shifting into his next role—head of security preparing for important guests. "I need to prepare for Lock and Johnson's arrival."

Patrick nodded, understanding his part in the performance they were about to stage. "Warm welcome, island paradise, routine security review."

Amira turned from the window, her reflection ghostlike in the glass. The room was almost clean now, the workers packing their equipment with the same efficiency they'd shown in using it. Soon there would be no trace of what had happened here—except for the people who remembered.

"What about the roommate?"

The question hung in the air like smoke. The workers continued their methodical packing, but the three principals had gone perfectly still. Years of partnership had taught them when a conversation had reached its crucial point.

"They were close. She'll be asking questions."

"Let her ask," Ethan said. "Girls disappear from places like this all the time. They meet someone rich, they run off to Monaco or Miami."

"Does Nikki strike you as someone who'll accept that story?"

Patrick glanced at Ethan, reading the micro-expression that passed between them. Some communications didn't require words.

"Then perhaps," Amira said, her tone suggesting the matter was settled, "someone should have a word with her."

CHAPTER
THIRTEEN

THE POOL at Villa Seven was smaller than the main resort's infinity edge, but Samir Patel preferred it that way. Less chance of unexpected social interaction.

"Hold still," Nikki said, squeezing more SPF 50 onto her palm. "Your shoulders are already burnt."

"The UV index is particularly high today," Samir said, sitting rigid on the lounger. "Eleven point three according to my weather app. That's extreme on the scale."

"That's why we're doing this." She worked the sunscreen into his shoulders, feeling the tension in his muscles. He never fully relaxed when being touched, even by her. "Can you lean forward a little?"

He complied, his tablet balanced on his knees. The screen showed a business report, something about optimizing server farms that would probably earn him another fifty million this quarter.

"Samir," she started, keeping her voice light. "I need to ask you something."

"The answer is yes, we can stay another week if you want. I'll have Priya rearrange my meetings."

"It's not about staying." Her hands paused on his back. "It's about Harper."

"Your roommate? The one who went to dinner last night?"

"She never came back."

Samir twisted to look at her, nearly dropping his tablet. "What do you mean?"

"I mean she's gone. Her bed wasn't slept in. Her stuff is still in our room." Nikki resumed applying sunscreen, needing something to do with her hands. "I'm worried."

"Did you report it to security?"

"They said she probably met someone and went to their yacht. But Harper wouldn't do that. Not without telling me."

"People do impulsive things on vacation," Samir said, turning back to his screen. "Psychological studies on vacation behavior show a thirty-seven percent increase in risk-taking activities."

"Believe me, this date wasn't a vacation. It was work."

"Oh." He considered this. "Then it's probably a misunderstanding. I can ask Patrick about it. He knows everything that happens here."

Nikki moved around to face him, kneeling on the deck. "Would you? I know it's asking a lot, but—"

"It's not asking a lot." Samir looked genuinely puzzled. "Why would it be? If your friend is missing and you're anxious, we should find her. That's simple logic."

"You're sweet." She kissed his cheek, tasting sunscreen and sweat.

"I'm not sweet. I'm practical. Missing people should be found." He set down his tablet with the decisive air of someone about to solve a problem. "The Barzanis run an excellent operation here. Very secure, very organized. I'm sure they have protocols for this."

"I'm sure they do," Nikki murmured.

"Don't worry." Samir stood, already reaching for his phone. "I have resources. Whatever the problem is, we can solve it."

Nikki watched him stride toward the villa, phone pressed to his ear, already asking to speak to Patrick personally. His confidence was that of someone who'd never encountered a problem his bank account couldn't fix.

THE YACHT GIRL 57

Twenty minutes later, she was crossing the main pool area when she saw them. Amira and Patrick Barzani, holding court near the bar with a cluster of guests. Amira wore white linen that made her look like a goddess. Patrick's smile was wide enough to see from across the deck.

Nikki's temper, already frayed from a sleepless night, snapped.

"Mrs. Barzani," she called out, not caring that heads turned. "A word?"

Amira's smile didn't waver, but something shifted in her eyes. "Of course, dear. Patrick, would you—"

"You set her up with that German pig," Nikki said, her voice carrying. "Harper didn't want to go. She was scared of him. And now she's—"

"Perhaps we should continue this conversation somewhere more private." Amira's hand was on Nikki's elbow, grip firm, already steering her toward the beach club's office. "You seem upset."

They were through the door before Nikki could protest. The office was all white leather and chrome, cold despite the tropical heat outside.

"Sit," Amira said. It wasn't a request.

Nikki remained standing. "Where's Harper?"

"I assume she's wherever she chose to go." Amira moved behind the desk but didn't sit. "Girls like Harper are free spirits. They come, they go. Surely you of all people understand that."

"She wouldn't leave without telling me."

"Wouldn't she?" Amira's smile was sharp. "You've known her, what, two weeks? That hardly makes you an expert on her character."

"I know she was terrified of Drexler."

"Then perhaps she made a choice to remove herself from a situation she found uncomfortable. That shows initiative. I admire that in a girl."

"You're not even going to look for her?"

Amira came around the desk, moving closer. "Nikki, you have such a wonderful opportunity here. Samir is quite taken with you. Do you know how rare it is to find a connection like that in a place like this?"

"What does that have to do with—"

"You're a smart girl. You understand how delicate these situations can be. One misunderstanding, one unfortunate scene, and suddenly

Samir might see you differently. As someone dramatic. Difficult. Troublesome."

"Is that a threat?"

"It's reality." Amira reached out, touched Nikki's cheek with one manicured finger. "You have maybe five more years of looking like this. That tight skin, that body. Five years to secure your future. Don't waste them asking questions about girls who make different choices."

Nikki jerked away from her touch. "Harper didn't choose anything."

"We all choose, darling. Every day. Right now, you can choose to return to that sweet, generous man by the pool. Or you can choose to make problems." Amira's smile was maternal, poisonous. "Which one do you think will work out better for you?"

The door opened. Patrick stood in the frame, no longer smiling.

"Everything alright?" he asked.

"Perfect," Amira said. "Nikki was just leaving. Weren't you, darling?"

CHAPTER
FOURTEEN

THE TENDER CUT through clear blue water so clear that Lock could see the coral formations forty feet below. The tender operator handled the vessel with the confidence of someone who made this run multiple times daily.

"First time here?" the tender operator asked over the engine noise.

"Yup," Lock said, studying the approaching shoreline.

The island revealed itself in layers. First the beaches—white sand that looked like it had been sifted through a fine filter. Then the vegetation, manicured to seem wild but with every palm tree positioned for maximum aesthetic impact. Finally the structures, emerging from the greenery. Nothing gaudy or ostentatious. Clean lines and natural materials such as limestone, teak, glass, and brushed steel.

"Jesus," Ty said. "Even the birds look like they've been detailed."

He wasn't wrong. A formation of pelicans glided past in V-formation, their flight path taking them over a dock that belonged in a super yacht magazine. The pier stretched into deep water, constructed from some kind of tropical hardwood that had aged to silver. Every plank looked individually selected and placed.

"That's the main dock," the tender operator said, following their gaze. "But Mr. Efron asked me to bring you to the security pier. More private."

Lock nodded, noting the separation. Smart. Keep the operational aspects away from guest areas. The security dock was smaller but no less pristine, tucked into a natural cove that provided cover from multiple angles.

As they approached, Lock counted cameras without appearing to. Six visible, which meant probably twelve total. Overlapping angles, no blind spots on the approach.

"Gentlemen."

The man waiting on the dock looked like a tourist who'd gotten lost. Board shorts, flip-flops, a Tommy Bahama shirt with parrots on it. But Lock caught the tell immediately—how he stood with his hands free and his back to the water. Tourist clothes, operator instincts.

"Ethan Efron," he said as they climbed onto the dock. His handshake was firm, dry despite the humidity. "Welcome to paradise."

"Ryan Lock. This is Ty Johnson."

"I know who you are." Efron's smile was warm, reaching his eyes. "Dave speaks very highly of you both. Sorry he couldn't be here for your arrival."

"No problem," Lock said. "He mentioned he might be traveling."

"The Barzanis have him looking at a property in Turks and Caicos. Another island, but more of a fixer-upper. Nothing like this." He gestured at the pristine landscape. "Dave said to tell you that the tea here is muck, but the views make up for it."

Lock laughed. "Sounds like the big guy."

"He also said you'd want to get straight to business. No pool drinks and orientation videos." Efron turned to the tender operator. "Their gear?"

"I'll deal with it, sir."

"Outstanding." Efron started up the dock, moving with an easy stride that covered ground faster than it looked. "I've set you up in our business center. Full access to our security infrastructure, blueprints, procedures, everything you need for your assessment. The previous teams found it useful to have a dedicated space away from guest areas."

Lock fell into step beside him. "How many previous assessments?"

"You're the third in twenty-four months. The insurance companies love seeing the paperwork, and our guests and their security teams like knowing we submit to regular independent review. Trust but verify, as your President Reagan said."

They followed a path that wound through tropical landscaping so perfect it looked artificial. Every flower faced the right direction. Every shrub trimmed to mathematical precision. Even the mulch appeared to be sorted by size and color.

They passed a maintenance crew touching up paint on a fence. The workers nodded respectfully but didn't stare. Well-trained.

"Your background is Israeli intelligence, correct?" Lock asked.

"Yes. Though these days I'm more about making sure the towels are folded properly than folding interrogation subjects." Efron's self-deprecation was practiced but effective. "The Barzanis wanted someone who understood both security and hospitality. Turns out the skills translate better than you'd think."

"How so?"

"Intelligence work is about making people comfortable enough to tell you things they shouldn't. Hospitality is about making people comfortable enough to pay you money they shouldn't. Same principle, different application."

That made sense to Lock.

They came over a small rise and the business center came into view. It was built like a boutique hotel, all glass and natural wood, but Lock noticed the reinforced window frames, the subtle camera positions, the way the landscaping created natural barriers while maintaining sight lines.

"Home sweet home for the next two weeks," Efron said. "Your office is on the second floor. Staff suites on the third if you prefer to stay here rather than the guest villas. Though I should warn you, the villas are significantly nicer."

"We'll stay here," Lock said. "Easier to work late."

"Dave said you'd say that." Efron used a key card to open the main entrance.

The interior was corporate sterile but comfortable. Cool air conditioning after the tropical heat, the smell of cleaning products and electronics. Lock felt himself relaxing slightly. This was familiar territory.

"One question," Ty said as they waited for the elevator. "An island this exclusive, this private—what exactly are your main security concerns?"

Efron pressed the button for the second floor. "The usual. Paparazzi with telephoto lenses or drones. Disgruntled former employees. Privacy issues mostly. Nothing dramatic."

"Nothing dramatic," Lock repeated.

"We're boring by design, Mr. Lock. Rich people come here to relax without worrying about their private moments ending up on social media. Our job is to be invisible while making sure their privacy remains absolute."

The elevator opened onto a hallway lined with offices. Efron led them to a corner conference room with windows overlooking the ocean.

"This is you. Full network access, all our procedures and protocols loaded onto the system. I'll give you the full briefing whenever you're ready."

"We're ready now," Lock said.

"Of course you are." Efron's smile was knowing. "I have a few things to deal with and I'll be right back with you."

"You mind if we look around in the meantime?"

"Of course not. Be my guest."

Efron paused at the door, suddenly serious.

"The truth, Mr. Lock, is that we run the tightest operation you could imagine. But you're not paid to take my word for it. You're paid to prove me wrong." He gave a small salute. "Good luck."

After he left, Ty moved to the window. "Friendly guy."

"Very," Lock said opening his laptop bag. "You catch the maintenance crew when we walked in?"

"You mean the ones painting a perfect fence?" Ty asked.

"Yup, those ones," Lock said.

CHAPTER
FIFTEEN

THE NEXT MORNING

Ethan Efron held the door as Patrick and Amira Barzani entered the conference room. Lock clocked the order of entry: Patrick breezing in with charm dialed up to eleven, Amira trailing behind like she was holding a knife behind her back. He noted the optics—deliberate, rehearsed. The body language said something different. She let him lead, but not because she deferred.

"Ryan, Ty," Patrick said, his handshake enthusiastic. "Welcome, welcome. I trust Ethan's been taking good care of you?"

Lock stood as Ty looked up from the stack of security protocols he'd been reviewing, his expression all business now. The vacation mood from the plane had evaporated. This was work mode Ty—focused, serious, catching details others missed.

"Gentlemen," Amira said. No handshake offered. She took a seat at the far end of the conference table, posture perfect, expression neutral. "I understand you haven't signed the NDAs yet."

"The review period is over." Amira's fingers drummed once on the table. "Are you signing or not?"

Lock reached for the documents. "Of course. We'll sign now."

Ty's head snapped up. He caught Lock's eye, the question clear on his face. Lock gave a tiny shake of his head.

"Excuse us one second," Ty said, standing. "Ryan?"

They moved to the corner of the room. Ty kept his voice low. "What happened to all those objections? The liability issues? The part about them owning our children?"

"Don't worry about it," Lock said.

"Don't worry about it? Yesterday you were—"

"Trust me. Just sign."

Ty studied his partner's face for a moment. Lock's expression hadn't changed, but something in his posture had—more guarded, like he'd already calculated the cost of saying no. Ty didn't like it. He nodded anyway. They returned to the table, both men signing the documents without further comment. Amira collected the papers, checking each signature before sliding them into a leather portfolio.

"Excellent," Patrick said. "Now we can speak freely. Tell us how you plan to proceed."

Lock opened his laptop, pulling up the assessment framework. "We'll be working in phases. My technical team arrives shortly. They'll evaluate your electronic systems—cameras, access control, cyber security. I understand you have a separate consultant for maritime security?"

Efron nodded.

"Good. Maritime is specialized. We'll review procedures but it's not going to be our primary focus." Lock turned the laptop so the Barzanis could see the screen. "Our main concerns are physical security, controlling access and egress, ensuring guest and staff safety during all conditions including severe weather events."

"We're particularly interested in the privacy protocols," Ty added. "That's what your guests are paying for."

"Yes, absolutely," Amira said. "Privacy is paramount."

"Which is why we'll need to conduct a thorough counter-surveillance sweep," Lock said. "Not just of guest areas but the entire property. Our tech team specialize in detecting devices that standard sweeps miss."

Patrick raised his brows. "Devices? You think someone might be—"

Lock had already anticipated the question. He kept his tone flat.

"Precautionary. Part of our standard assessment. We also may do a small amount of penetration testing."

Amira's expression tightened. "Explain."

"We may attempt to breach your security using various methods. Social engineering, physical infiltration, technical exploits."

"Absolutely not," Amira said. "We can't have people skulking around trying to break in. It would terrify the guests."

"They won't even know it's happening," Lock said. "That's the point. If your guests notice them, then your security works."

"When?" Ethan asked.

"Sometime during our stay. I can't say when or what form it will take because otherwise it wouldn't be a surprise now, would it?"

Ethan's smiled at that one. "It is standard practice," he said to Amira.

"The point of them," Ty said, "is to identify vulnerabilities before someone with bad intentions does."

"Fine," Amira said. "But if a single guest complains—"

"We know how to operate in this type of environment," Lock said.

Patrick clapped his hands together. "Wonderful. What else do you need from us?"

"Unrestricted access," Lock said. "We'll need to move freely around the property. Speak with staff. Observe operations."

"Of course," Patrick said.

"And guests," Lock added. "We may need to interview some guests about their security concerns, their experience with privacy protection."

Amira's jaw tightened. "Certainly not."

"Mrs. Barzani—"

"Our guests come here to escape scrutiny, not to be interrogated by security consultants."

"It was mentioned in our terms. And," Lock said firmly. "It's non-negotiable."

Amira considered this. "Okay, but only if absolutely necessary. And only with my prior approval."

"And staff? We'll need unrestricted access to interview staff members."

"Staff can be a weak point," Ty added.

Amira's gaze shifted to Ethan, her stare flattening. "I'm well aware."

The look held for a moment too long. Something in Ethan's eyes flickered—a recalculation, maybe. Body language experts called it a micro-expression. A flash of tension that Lock caught but couldn't interpret.

"Interview whoever you need," Patrick said, breaking the moment.

"Perfect," Lock said. "We'll start with perimeter assessments today. Physical walk-through."

"I'll accompany you," Ethan said.

"That won't be necessary," Lock said.

"It's no trouble."

"It is, actually. We need to see how your security functions without management present. How staff respond to anomalies when they can't check with superiors."

Ethan's smile didn't waver. "Of course. Though I should mention, my people are quite capable of independent action."

It came off more as a threat than a boast.

"Good to know," Ty said.

Lock closed his laptop, signaling the meeting's end.

"One last thing," Lock said. "We'll need all incident reports from the past year. Break-ins, staff terminations, guest complaints, medical emergencies. Everything."

"That's confidential," Amira said.

"So are our findings. NDA, remember?"

Patrick stood, extending his hand again. "You'll have everything you need. Ethan will coordinate. We want this to be thorough. Our guests deserve nothing less."

"They'll get it," Lock said.

As the Barzanis moved toward the door, Amira turned back. "Mr. Lock, I hope we understand each other. This is a place of absolute discretion. Whatever you see, whatever you think you see, remember that context matters."

"I always consider context," Lock said.

"Glad to hear it."

She left without waiting for a response. Patrick followed, still smiling. Ethan lingered in the doorway.

"Incident reports will be on your secure server within the hour," he said.

After he left, Ty moved to the window, watching the three figures walk back toward the main resort.

"You get the feeling the lady with the stick up her ass doesn't like us?" Ty asked.

Lock joined him at the window, watching Amira's retreating form. Her posture was rigid, her movements too tight for the easy sunlit setting. Ty was right, something about Amira Barzani was off. Or maybe she was just having a bad day. Either way, they'd figure it out.

CHAPTER SIXTEEN

LOCK COUNTED three couples before they'd even reached the main pool area. A silver-haired executive type with a girl who couldn't be older than twenty-two. A heavyset Russian with someone who might have been celebrating her twenty-first birthday. An elderly Japanese man whose much taller blonde companion looked like she should be writing her college admission letter.

Contrary to their agreement, Ethan Efron had decided to tag along, as had Patrick Barzani.

"Popular spot," Ty said.

"We cater to a specific clientele. Successful individuals who value their privacy," Ethan noted.

"And appreciate beauty," Patrick added, appearing beside them in a pink polo shirt and madras shorts. "I love these tours. Always fascinating to see how the magic works."

They passed another couple at the pool bar—this time two men, one gray-haired in Versace swim trunks, his companion decades younger in a Speedo that left nothing to imagination.

"We don't discriminate," Patrick said, following Lock's gaze. "Love is love, as they say."

"More like money is money," Ty muttered.

If Patrick heard, he didn't react. "Come, let me show you the beach club. The security arrangements there are particularly clever."

They followed a path through manicured gardens where young women in designer resort wear clustered at small tables, sipping drinks that matched their nail polish. Their older companions sat separately, conducting business calls or scrolling through tablets. The separation was subtle but consistent—together but not together.

"The beach club operates on multiple security tiers," Ethan explained as they walked. "Perimeter defense against maritime approach, obviously. But also privacy shields—those cabanas have special glass that defeats telephoto lenses."

"Paparazzi must love this place," Lock said.

"They try. Last month we caught a photographer trying to swim ashore at night with waterproof equipment. The response time was quite satisfactory."

"What happened to him?"

"He was discouraged from returning," Efron said, his tone flat.

They reached an overlook above the beach. Below, more of the same demographic pattern played out on pristine sand. Lock noticed the strategic positioning of security cameras, their fields of view overlapping perfectly.

"Impressive coverage," Lock said.

"We've learned from experience. Three years ago, an Italian tabloid published photos taken from a yacht two miles offshore. The lawsuit was... educational."

Patrick laughed. "Twenty million euros educational. But we learned. Show them the radar array, Ethan."

Ethan led them to a discreet installation near the tennis courts. Three radar domes sat atop a concrete structure designed to look like a utility building.

"Military-grade drone detection," Ethan said. "We can spot anything larger than a hummingbird at two kilometers. The system automatically deploys countermeasures—signal jamming, GPS spoofing. We've even tested directed energy weapons, though those remain backup options."

"Seems like overkill for celebrity photographers," Ty said.

"Our guests' privacy is worth any price," Patrick said. "Some of these men—people—their entire careers could be destroyed by a single photograph taken out of context."

Lock and Ty exchanged glances. Context again.

"Speaking of privacy," Ethan said, "let me show you something else."

He led them toward the villas, each a masterpiece of tropical architecture. They stopped at Villa Seven, where Ethan produced a key card.

"May I?"

The door didn't open. Ethan frowned, tried again.

"That's odd." He examined the card reader, then pressed his thumb to a scanner beside the door. It beeped green and clicked open. "There we go. Biometric backup. Each villa is programmed specifically for its current occupant and their guests."

"What about staff?" Ty asked. "Housekeeping, maintenance?"

"Same. Key card with biometric backup."

They continued the tour, passing Villa Nine. Construction hazard tape crossed the entrance, and Lock could see workers moving inside through gauze curtains.

"Refurbishment?" Ty asked.

"Always something," Patrick said quickly. "When your guests live in six star homes we have to provide seven star accommodation."

"Must be nice," Lock said. "Surprised you don't wait for the off-season."

Ethan stepped smoothly into the conversation. "What off-season? We're booked solid year-round. If we waited for vacancies, nothing would ever get done."

Lock made a mental note. The construction crew looked more like a cleaning service than renovators. Too many mops, not enough paint.

"Would you like to see the control room?" Patrick asked. "I never get tired of it."

"Lead the way," Lock said.

The security complex sat at the island's highest point, offering panoramic views. Inside, the control room did indeed look like a film set. Banks of monitors showed feeds from across the property. Operators in crisp uniforms tracked movement patterns, logged entries, monitored maritime approaches.

"How many cameras total?" Lock asked.

Ethan reeled off the numbers for each area. "Each villa has exterior coverage, but naturally, we respect our guests' privacy indoors."

"Naturally," Ty said.

Lock studied the monitor array. Professional setup, but something felt off about the configuration. Too many blank screens in active rotation.

"Impressive," Lock said.

"Would you like to meet some of our guests?" Patrick offered. "I'd be happy to make introductions."

"Maybe later," Lock said. "We prefer to observe operations without management present first. Get a feel for normal patterns."

"Of course," Patrick said, though he looked disappointed. "Ethan, why don't we leave them to their work? Dinner is at eight if you'd like to join us. The chef is doing something incredible with local grouper."

"We appreciate the offer," Lock said.

After they left, Lock and Ty stood in the control room, watching the monitors cycle through their feeds. Young women by the pools. Older men in the restaurants. Security guards who moved like soldiers.

"Thoughts?" Lock asked.

"I've seen this movie before," Ty said. "Usually doesn't end well."

"Yeah, but for who?" Lock said, watching a girl who couldn't have been older than twenty-one help a man old enough to be her grandfather who was struggling to get out of his beach chair.

CHAPTER
SEVENTEEN

"NIGHT NIGHT, Daddy. Love you to the moon."

"Love you to the stars, princess," Lock said to the laptop screen.

Sofia's face pixelated briefly before the connection stabilized. Behind her, Carmen leaned into frame.

"Ty, don't let him work too late," Carmen said. "He gets cranky."

Ty laughed.

"Okay, be safe you two," Carmen said.

"Always am," Lock said.

"No promises," said Ty.

The screen went dark. Lock stared at his reflection in the black glass for a moment before closing the laptop.

"Miss them already?" Ty said from across the room.

"Always do."

Lock leaned back in his chair. "Can you imagine Sofia ending up like that girl we saw today? The one helping that old man with the walker?"

Ty was quiet for a moment. "Not a chance. She's got two parents who give a damn. These girls? Different story."

"That's what bothers me."

"Look, this is the oldest transaction in the world. Girls who need cash, men who have it. Everyone knows the deal."

"Except I'd bet these girls aren't trading so much as surviving."

"You can't know that."

"You see any of them smiling when they think no one's looking?"

Ty was quiet for a moment. "We're not here to save anyone, Lock. We're here to review security protocols."

"Right." Lock turned from the window. "So let's review. What'd we see today?"

"Professional operation. Good camera coverage, overlapping fields of fire. The biometric systems are current generation, maybe six months old. Radar array seems like overkill for paparazzi."

"What else?"

"Staff moves like military. That maintenance crew at Villa Nine wasn't doing any maintenance."

"You caught that too."

"Hard to miss. Same four dudes from the fence holding mops and buckets to refurbish a color scheme? Bullshit." Ty pulled up a chair. "Whatever happened there, they're cleaning it, not remodeling it."

Lock nodded. "The control room setup bothers me. Too many blank monitors for a system with hundreds of cameras."

"Could be privacy zones. Ethan said they don't monitor inside villas."

Lock opened his notebook, started sketching the monitor layout from memory. "Tomorrow we do our own walk-through. Starting with Villa Nine."

CHAPTER
EIGHTEEN

THE GUARD WAS CHECKING his phone. Perfect.

Nikki slipped behind the maintenance shed, her bare feet silent on the stone path. She'd left her heels hidden in the hibiscus bushes—too noisy for what she had in mind. The second guard stood near Villa Nine's side entrance, but his attention was fixed on something in the distance. A boat, maybe. Or just daydreaming about being anywhere else.

She'd watched them for twenty minutes from the beach bar, timing their patterns. Every seven minutes, the one with the phone did a lazy circuit of the villa's perimeter. The other never moved from his post but spent most of his time staring at nothing.

The tape across the front entrance had been her first clue. No construction crews despite the story Patrick was telling everyone about renovations. Just guards protecting an empty villa where Harper had spent her last night.

Nikki waited for Phone Guard to round the corner, then moved. Quick steps across open ground, ducking low beneath windows. The side entrance had a service door—the kind housekeeping used. She'd borrowed a keycard from a maid's cart that morning. Fifty-fifty chance it would work.

The lock clicked green.

Inside, the villa smelled wrong. Beneath fresh paint and industrial cleaner, something chemical lingered. Bleach. Ammonia. The kinds of smells that meant serious cleaning.

She moved through the kitchen into the main living area. New furniture sat wrapped in plastic. The walls were bare, showing pale rectangles where artwork had hung. In the corner, rolls of wallpaper leaned against—

"Looking for something?"

Nikki jumped. She spun around.

Amira Barzani stood in the bedroom doorway, holding fabric swatches. She wore white again—white pants, white silk blouse, white leather slides.

"I was just—"

"Breaking and entering?" Amira moved into the room with casual grace.

"The door was open."

"Was it?" Amira set the swatches on a plastic-covered table.

They stood facing each other across the empty room. Nikki felt sweat gathering between her shoulder blades despite the air conditioning.

"Harper mentioned you were clever," Amira said.

"When did she mention that?"

"Oh, we spoke many times. I had high hopes for her. Such potential." Amira ran her fingers along a roll of wallpaper, examining the pattern. "Do you like this? It's Italian. Hand-painted."

"Where is she?"

"Who?"

"Don't play games with me."

Amira's eyebrows rose. "Games? My dear, you're the one sneaking around like some bargain-basement spy. I'm simply trying to redecorate after an unfortunate incident."

"What incident?"

"A guest was taken ill. Very sudden. These things happen with older men who overexert themselves." Amira moved to another wallpaper sample. "This one's too busy, don't you think?"

"Harper was here. With Drexler. Now she's gone and you're redecorating like nothing happened."

"Things always happen, dear. The question is how we choose to respond." Amira turned to face her fully. "Take you, for instance. You could choose to accept that your friend moved on to better opportunities. Or you could choose to make trouble."

"I choose truth."

"Truth?" Amira laughed, sharp and cold. "How refreshingly naive. You're what—twenty-five? Twenty-six? Old enough to know better."

"Twenty-three."

"Ah. That explains it." Amira sat on the plastic-covered sofa, crossing her legs. "Let me share some truth with you, since you're so eager for it. Your friend Harper made choices. Some wise, some less so. Now she's no longer here, and you have choices to make."

"Is she dead?"

The question hung between them. Amira's expression didn't change.

"What a dramatic imagination you have. Harper simply decided this life wasn't for her. It happens. Girls arrive with one set of expectations, reality intervenes, they leave."

"Without her passport? Without her clothes?"

Amira studied her manicure. "I hear Samir is quite taken with you. How exciting."

Nikki's jaw tightened. "Don't."

"Don't what? Express interest in your fairy tale romance? But it's so sweet. The tech billionaire and the yacht girl. Like a modern Cinderella."

"I'm not a yacht girl."

"Of course not. You're special. Different. Not like the others. Not an escort." Amira smiled without warmth.

"Samir wouldn't date an escort."

"Not knowingly perhaps."

"Fuck you."

"Such language." Amira stood, smoothing her pants. "This is what Harper never understood either. That anger, that pride—it's a liability, not an asset. Men like Samir don't want complicated. They want grateful."

"Samir loves me."

"I'm sure he believes that. This week." Amira picked up a different wallpaper sample. "But what happens when you're in California? When you meet his friends? His family? When he introduces you as... what? The girl he met on vacation?"

Nikki's hands had curled into fists. "We're leaving soon."

"Are you? How wonderful. And I'm sure when you're living in his Palo Alto mansion, going to charity galas, pretending you belong in his world, you'll never wonder what happened to Harper. Never feel guilty that you got your happy ending while she got—"

"While she got what?"

Amira set down the wallpaper. "Forgotten."

She moved toward the door, then paused. "You know what the difference is between a Disney princess and a yacht girl?"

Nikki didn't answer.

"A princess knows when to shut up and smile," Amira said with finality.

CHAPTER
NINETEEN

THE GUARD at Villa Nine didn't even pretend to check his list.

"No access," he said, not looking up from his phone.

Lock held up his assessment credentials. "We have authorization to inspect all facilities."

"Not this one."

"Since when?"

The guard shrugged, thumb scrolling through what looked like Instagram. His partner stood by the side entrance, slightly more alert but equally unmoved by Lock's credentials.

"I'll need to hear that from management," Lock said.

"So call them."

Ty stepped forward. "How about we save everyone's time and you just—"

"Gentlemen." Ethan Efron appeared around the corner. "Is there a problem?"

"Your security won't allow access," Lock said.

"My apologies. There was a miscommunication." Ethan spoke rapid Hebrew to the guards, who immediately stepped aside. "Please, go ahead. Take all the time you need."

The first guard pocketed his phone, suddenly professional. Lock filed away the instant transformation—these weren't rental cops. They were soldiers playing dress-up.

"Miscommunication," Ty repeated.

"Staff scheduling error," Ethan said. "It won't happen again."

Lock nodded, making a mental note. First denial. First crack in the helpful facade.

"We'll be inside for a while," Lock said.

"Of course. The renovation crew is on break, so you'll have privacy." Ethan gave them a practiced smile. "I'll ensure you're not disturbed."

He walked away without waiting for a response. The guards returned to their posts, pretending Lock and Ty had already ceased to exist.

Inside, the smell hit immediately. Not paint fumes or construction dust—something sharper. Chemical cleaners, the industrial kind.

"Renovation," Ty said, but his tone suggested skepticism.

They moved through the living area. Furniture sat wrapped in plastic, walls freshly painted. Lock ran his finger along a baseboard.

In the kitchen, he checked under the sink. Bottles lined up in neat rows—all heavy-duty cleaners. No paint supplies, no renovation materials. Just cleaning products that belonged in a hospital or a veterinary clinic.

"Thorough maids," Ty said.

They moved to the bedroom. More wrapped furniture, more fresh paint. But small things felt off. The outlet covers were brand new while the switches showed their age. The carpet had been deep cleaned, furniture indentations visible in the pile. But the furniture sitting here now didn't match those impressions.

"Look at this," Lock said, checking the paint cans in the corner. "It's all primer."

In the bathroom, the chemical smell was strongest. Every surface gleamed. New caulking around the tub stood out white against older fixtures. The mirror had been replaced recently—Lock could see fresh adhesive at the edges.

"UV light equipment," Ty said, pointing to gear in the corner.

Lock knew UV had multiple uses, but in a renovation context? "Interesting choice for interior design."

They worked their way back through the villa, each observation adding to a pattern. Missing items—curtains gone but rods remaining. Intense cleaning in specific areas while others showed normal wear. Multiple coats of primer on certain walls.

"So what are we looking at?" Ty asked when they were back in the living room.

"Not a renovation," Lock said. "This is... something else. You don't deep-clean before you redecorate. You don't replace outlet covers for a color change. You don't need industrial chemicals to prep for new wallpaper."

"Could be they had a maintenance issue. Plumbing leak, maybe. Those can require serious cleaning."

"Could be." Lock looked around the too-clean space. "But why the guards? Why deny us access? Why does Ethan have to personally authorize entry to a villa being redecorated?"

They stood in the sanitized space, both feeling the weight of something they couldn't quite pinpoint. Something had happened here. Something that required more than a mop and bucket.

CHAPTER
TWENTY

NIKKI BAILEY DIDN'T SCARE easy. There was no way Amira was going to stop her from finding out what had really happened to Harper.

She'd slipped back into Villa Nine through a service door at the rear just as the clean up crew had left for the day, timing her entry perfectly.

Now she'd have all the time she needed to look around. There had to be clues left here. There had to be.

She slipped into the kitchen. Her bare feet were silent on the marble floor—she'd ditched her sandals in the bushes outside. Every surface gleamed under recessed lighting.

Voices.

Nikki's body moved before her brain caught up, ducking behind the kitchen island as footsteps approached from the main hallway. Two men. She recognized Ethan Efron's measured cadence before he spoke.

"—told you the renovation story would hold," Efron said.

"Cameras are off, right?" Patrick asked.

"Of course. They're only ever on when we need them to be."

"I don't know if they believed us. They spent forty minutes in here," Patrick said. His voice carried the whine of a man used to problems disappearing with a phone call. "What if they found something?"

"Found what? We stripped everything. New paint, new fixtures, new furniture. Even replaced the outlet covers."

They were in the living room now, maybe twenty feet away. Nikki pressed herself lower, cheek against the cold marble. Her heart was racing so hard she was certain they'd hear it.

"All the blood?"

"Is gone," Efron said. "We used luminol ourselves. Nothing. They saw exactly what we wanted them to see. A villa being updated for a demanding guest."

"Still, bringing them here so soon after—"

"Would you prefer we denied them access? Nothing raises suspicion like a locked door. This way they've seen it, filed their report, moved on."

Footsteps again. Coming closer. Nikki held her breath.

"Patel's new girl has been asking questions," Patrick said.

"Let her ask. She'll be gone soon."

The footsteps paused. Resumed. Moving away now, toward the main entrance.

"Make sure the guards are back in position," Efron said. "And Patrick? Relax. It's under control. It's always under control."

The front door opened and closed. Nikki stayed frozen for a full minute, then two. The villa fell silent.

She stood on shaking legs and moved to the door. The grounds crew's mower had stopped. No guards visible yet, but they'd return soon.

Three quick steps across the kitchen. Push the service door open. Don't run. Walking fast draws less attention than running. Her sandals were right where she'd left them but she didn't stop. Bare feet on hot concrete, then grass, then the sandy path between villas.

Only when she reached the hibiscus hedge did the tears come.

He watched her stumble past, face wet with tears she didn't bother to hide. She was practically running now, bare feet slapping against the path. Her breathing came in short gasps that might have been sobs.

She'd been inside Villa Nine for twelve minutes. Whatever she'd heard or seen seemed to have sent her into a panic.

He memorized her face—young, pretty despite the tears, with the kind of street-smart look that meant she didn't scare easily. But she was scared now. Terrified.

She disappeared around a bend in the path, probably heading back to her quarters or to find that boyfriend he'd seen her with earlier.

He waited before easing out from his observation position and slipping away.

CHAPTER
TWENTY-ONE

"THE BLACK GIRL who's staying here—the one with the tech billionaire. Just watched her in tears. Crying hard," Ty said.

Lock kept his eyes on the boats moored in neat rows. A maintenance crew worked on a sixty-footer three slips down, close enough to look busy, far enough to avoid conversation.

"And?" Lock said.

"She was sneaking out of Villa Nine."

"Nine?"

"Yup, that one," Ty said.

Lock's pace didn't change. "Anyone see her? Or you?"

"Negative. I kept to those blind spots we mapped from the camera schematics. Northwest approach, behind the utility sheds."

"How long was she inside?"

"Ten or twelve minutes, give or take. Here's the kicker—Efron and Patrick showed up while she was in there. They went inside, stayed maybe eight minutes, then left."

"She hide?"

"Must have. They didn't drag her out, and she left on her own after they were gone."

They reached the end of the dock. Open water stretched ahead, choppy with the incoming weather. Lock turned, leaning against a piling like a man enjoying the view.

"Could be anything," Lock said. "She wants to surprise her boyfriend with villa access. Gets caught somewhere she shouldn't be, gets a talking-to."

"While crying?"

"Guys like that make young women cry all the time."

Ty studied his partner's face. "I don't think they saw her and I don't think she'd cry for being told off. She had to be sneaking inside there for another reason."

"Which is?" Lock asked.

"No idea, but that's one hell of a deep clean they got going on for a villa they're about to paint over."

"Right," Lock said.

They started back down the dock. A speedboat roared past, sending waves slapping against the pilings. Two men in their fifties with three girls who looked like they should be studying for midterms.

"Thing is," Lock said, watching the boat disappear around the point, "even if something happened, it's not technically our business. We're here to assess security, not investigate... whatever this might be."

"I feel you, Ryan," Ty said, his tone suggesting he was unconvinced.

"We keep our eyes open. We do our job."

"Absolutely."

They walked in silence for a moment. Watched as a Pelican dove into the water and surfaced with a tiny fish thrashing helplessly in its beak.

"These girls," Lock said.

Ty waited.

"Like throwing goldfish in a shark tank and calling it an aquarium." Lock watched another boat cruise past—older man, younger woman, same story. "They think they're players but they're just prey."

"Not our business either."

"No. It's not." Lock's jaw tightened. "Sofia's four years old."

"These girls aren't children."

"Maybe not, but they're not equipped for this either. Whatever made that girl cry—you think she saw it coming?"

"Probably not."

"Kids that age, they stumble into situations thinking they can handle it. By the time they realize they're in over their heads it's too late." Lock shook his head. "The cleaning in that villa wasn't routine, Ty. We both know it."

"Yeah."

"But like you just said, we're not investigators," Ty told him.

They'd reached the shore end of the dock. The path split—left toward the business center, right toward the guest areas.

"Still," Lock said, "might be worth knowing more about our tech billionaire's girlfriend. Just for context. Security assessment context."

"Like Amira said, context is important, right?" Ty said.

"She did say that, didn't she?" said Lock.

They turned left, toward the business center, two professionals discussing nothing more dangerous than security protocols and camera placement. But Lock's eyes tracked to Villa Nine, visible through the palms.

Something had happened there. Something that required industrial cleaning and made young women cry.

Not their business. Not what they were being paid for. But then again, Lock thought, every one of these girls was someone's daughter.

CHAPTER
TWENTY-TWO

AT DAWN the pool was empty. Steam rose from the water into cool morning air. Ty dropped his towel on a lounger and dove in, the shock of warm water after cool air waking every nerve. A few laps to clear his head.

A woman was already swimming in the far lane, smooth freestyle strokes that barely disturbed the surface. Ty recognized her immediately—the crying woman from Villa Nine—but she was different now. Tense. Her head kept turning toward the resort buildings between strokes, like she expected someone to appear.

He started his own laps, keeping to the opposite side of the pool. She noticed him but didn't acknowledge his presence, just continued her methodical swimming while checking the approaches every few strokes.

When he paused at the shallow end after his tenth lap, she was treading water near the ladder, clearly preparing to leave. Up close, he could see the stress etched around her eyes, and in the way she held herself. He'd noticed that most of the women on the island carried themselves the same way. Like they were on guard, waiting for something bad to happen.

"Early swimmer too," Ty said, keeping his tone casual and unthreatening.

She studied him. "Pool's quieter this time of day."

"Before the circus starts, right?" He gestured toward the resort. "We're doing a security assessment of the island. Amazing how different a place looks without people around."

The words had their intended effect. Her posture shifted slightly—still wary, but now with interest. "Security assessment?"

"Independent contractors. My partner and I." Ty kept his voice matter-of-fact. "We don't work for the resort. Just evaluating their systems, mostly for compliance and insurance purposes. Guests want to know they're getting what they've been promised kind of a deal."

Something flickered in her expression. "How long have you been here?" she asked.

"Not long. You?"

"Not long." The words came out flat, tired. "But it feels like forever."

Before Ty could respond, footsteps echoed across the pool deck. Samir Patel appeared at the gate, designer swim trunks and anxious energy radiating from him. His eyes immediately locked onto the woman in the pool, then shifted to Ty with obvious suspicion.

"Nikki?" Samir's voice carried an edge. "I woke up and you were gone."

"Just swimming, baby." Nikki's demeanor changed instantly, shoulders drawing inward. The confident woman from moments ago disappeared, replaced by someone trying to manage a volatile situation. "You know I like the early morning laps."

"Who's this?" Samir's attention fixed on Ty with the intensity of someone who'd already decided he didn't like what he was seeing.

"Nobody," Nikki said quickly. "Just another early swimmer."

Ty pulled himself out of the pool in one smooth motion, reading the dynamics clearly. Samir was marking territory, but Ty guessed there was real anxiety beneath the posturing. Fear that she might leave him, might choose someone else.

"Pool's all yours," Ty said easily, reaching for his towel.

Samir moved closer to the pool's edge, standing over Nikki while she remained in the water. "I don't like waking up alone, Nikki. I thought you understood that."

"I know. I'm sorry. I just needed to clear my head." Her voice had taken on the careful tone of someone managing an unpredictable situation.

Ty headed toward the gate, but the conversation followed him across the quiet morning air. "Why didn't you wake me? We could have swum together." Samir's questions carried the weight of ownership rather than partnership.

"You hate getting up early," Nikki replied, but even from a distance Ty could hear the strain in her voice.

As he reached the path leading back to the business center, Ty glanced back once. Samir had crouched beside the pool, one hand trailing in the water near Nikki, the gesture more possessive than romantic.

CHAPTER
TWENTY-THREE

THE CONFERENCE ROOM smelled like freshly ground coffee and lies.

Lock counted six department heads around the polished table, all wearing variations of the same corporate mask. Ethan Efron sat at the head, relaxed in an aloha shirt that didn't match his military bearing.

"Let's start with personnel screening," Lock said, pulling up his checklist. "Walk me through your hiring process."

The HR manager—a compact woman with cropped gray hair—slid a binder across the table. "Complete background checks on all staff. Criminal records, employment verification, reference checks. The works."

"What about security personnel specifically?"

Efron leaned forward. "Our security team undergoes additional screening. Psychological evaluations, polygraph testing, extensive background investigation including military service verification."

"I noticed most of your security staff are Israeli," Ty said.

"The best training in the world." Efron's hands remained flat on the table. "IDF special operations, Mossad, Shin Bet. When it comes to protecting high-value individuals, nobody does it better."

Lock made a note. "No diversity concerns? Different perspectives, skill sets?"

"Our clients value effectiveness over diversity," Efron said.

They moved on.

"When it comes to operations, guest privacy is our absolute priority," the operations manager offered up. "Every staff member signs extensive NDAs. We conduct regular training on confidentiality protocols."

"How regular?" Lock asked.

"Monthly sessions," another manager said. "We emphasize that what happens here stays here."

"No exceptions," someone else chimed in. "We've terminated staff for even minor breaches."

Lock and Ty exchanged glances. Every answer came too fast, too rehearsed. Like a legal deposition where they'd practiced the exact conversation more than once.

"Tell me about incident reporting," Lock said.

"All incidents are logged in our secure system," Efron said. "I personally review each report within twenty-four hours."

"What constitutes an incident?"

"Any breach of protocol, any complaint, any security concern—no matter how minor." Efron's smile never wavered.

"While maintaining absolute discretion for our clients," the operations manager added.

"Discretion is paramount," someone repeated.

"The foundation of our business model," another voice confirmed.

Lock kept his expression neutral while he made his notes. In his experience, people who talked this much about discretion were usually hiding something.

"What about medical incidents?" Ty asked.

A beat of silence.

"We maintain a full medical facility," Efron said smoothly. "Rotating physicians on-site twenty-four seven, helicopter for emergency evacuations. Complete medical records, naturally."

"With privacy and discretion being paramount, right?" Lock said.

"Exactly," three people said simultaneously.

An hour later, Lock and Ty followed the housekeeping director through the service corridors. She moved with the efficiency of someone who'd spent thirty years in hospitality—short, graying hair, Manila accent softened by decades in service.

"Each villa requires specialized attention," she said, leading them past supply rooms stocked like small warehouses. "Our clients have particular preferences."

"Must be challenging when a villa goes offline," Lock said casually. "Like Nine. Renovations can disrupt the whole rotation."

Her step hitched slightly. "We adapt. The Barzanis requested deep cleaning before the renovation. Very thorough."

"How thorough?" Ty asked.

"Industrial-grade sanitization. Mr. Efron personally supervised." She opened a supply closet, revealing shelves of cleaning products. "We use hospital-standard protocols when requested."

Lock studied the inventory. Heavy-duty stuff. The kind used for biohazard cleanup.

"Often requested?"

"Sometimes our clients have... accidents. Too much champagne, rough seas." She paused. "Incontinence can be an issue with some of the very elderly gentlemen. We're prepared for anything."

"You say incontinence or impotence?" Ty asked, pretending to make a note on his phone.

She didn't smile, ignored his question.

"I noticed UV equipment in Villa Nine," Lock said.

"Blood detection." She caught herself. "I mean, for ensuring complete cleanliness. Some stains only show under black light. Wine, certain foods. Or bodily fluids."

"Of course," Lock said. "And your staff reports these cleaning requests to...?"

"Mr. Efron is..." She chose her words carefully. "He's very hands-on with facility management."

They walked past a laundry facility that looked like it could handle a small hotel. Industrial washers churned behind glass doors.

"Your team must see a lot," Ty said. "Working in the villas, cleaning up after parties."

"We see nothing," she said firmly. "That's the first rule of housekeeping here. We're invisible."

"But if you noticed something concerning? Something that might be a security issue?"

She stopped walking. Turned to face them directly.

"Mr. Lock, my staff are trained to clean. That's all. A good housekeeper sees everything and remembers nothing."

"That's quite the philosophy," Lock said.

She sighed, exasperated. "It's how we keep our jobs."

CHAPTER
TWENTY-FOUR

THE LUNCH SPREAD at Villa Seven could have fed a dozen people. Lobster thermidor, seared ahi, caprese salad with tomatoes. No expense spared.

Nikki fussed with a piece of bread while Samir sat across from her, fidgeting with his water glass.

"I'm sorry about this morning," he said for the third time. "I acted like an ass."

"It's fine," Nikki said.

"It's not fine. I just—" He pushed his glasses up his nose, a nervous tic she'd noticed increased when he felt out of control. "I've never done this before."

"Done what?"

"Had a real girlfriend."

Girlfriend. Nikki kept her face neutral.

"I know how this looks," Samir continued. "Rich guy, private island, beautiful woman. Like some bad movie."

"Pretty Woman," Nikki said.

"Except I'm no Richard Gere." He attempted a smile. "More like an Indian Bill Gates with an anxiety disorder and a touch of autism."

Despite everything, Nikki almost smiled back. When he wasn't being possessive, Samir could surprise her.

"Look." He leaned forward. "I know it's weird how I met you, but this—us—it's become real for me. When I woke up and you were gone, I panicked."

"I just wanted to swim."

"With that guy."

"He was already there."

Samir set down his fork. "I asked around about him. And his friend."

Nikki kept eating, but her focus shifted. "Oh?"

"They're consultants. Security consultants." He said it like the words tasted bad. "Here to review the island's systems. Basically high-priced help."

"I know. He told me."

"Efron brought them in. Regular thing, apparently. They look at cameras, write reports, collect their check." Samir stabbed at his lobster. "The kind of guys who think they're tough because they used to be military."

Nikki filed this away.

"The guy definitely looked like he knew how to handle himself," she said, prodding at Samir's ego.

"I looked them up. Ryan Lock and Ty Johnson. They run some high-end boutique firm in LA. Glorified mall cops who somehow charge Fortune 500 prices," Samir scoffed.

Lock and Johnson. She silently repeated the names, committing them to memory.

"The one from the pool didn't come off like a mall cop," she said.

Samir's fork clattered against his plate. "Oh really?"

"I'm just saying.

"Well don't. He better keep his distance, stop sniffing around you."

The edge was back, that possessiveness that made her stomach clench. She reached across the table, touched his hand.

"Hey, what's with all this jealousy? You're the one I'm with."

He turned his hand over, gripped hers too tight. "Am I? Because sometimes I feel like you're just going through the motions. Like you're here but not really here."

Because my best friend is missing and possibly dead. "I'm here," she said.

"Prove it."

"How?"

"Promise you'll come back to California with me. For real. Not just a visit."

Nikki pulled her hand back. "Samir."

"I know it's fast. But when you know, you know." His eyes were desperate, searching. He really was like a little boy, Nikki thought.

"I can take care of you," Samir continued. "Set you up with your own place if you want space. Whatever you need."

"I don't need taking care of."

"Everyone needs taking care of." He softened his tone. "I didn't mean it like that. I just... I see something in you, Nikki. You're smart. Tough. You shouldn't be in a place like this."

"Neither should you."

"I'm here because I'm lonely." The admission hung between them. "Worth all this money, and I have to pay to fly to a private island to find someone to talk to."

"You have friends."

"I have employees. And other entrepreneurs who see me as either competition or an acquisition target." He took off his glasses, cleaned them obsessively. "Do you know what it's like to never know if someone likes you for you or just what you can do for them?"

Nikki thought about Harper, about all the girls here, about herself. "Yeah. I do."

"That's why we work. We both know the transaction, so we can get past it to something real."

She wanted to laugh. Or cry. This damaged boy-genius thought he'd found love in a place that was nothing more than an ultra high-end brothel.

"I'll think about moving to Cali," she said.

His whole face changed. "Really?"

"Really."

He jumped up, came around the table to kiss her. Awkward, too eager, but genuine.

"I need to make some calls," he said. "Lawyer stuff. Stay here, enjoy lunch. I'll be back in an hour."

He headed inside, leaving Nikki alone with enough food to feed a small country. She pushed the plates away, appetite gone. *Lock and Johnson.* Security consultants who noticed things. Who weren't part of the island's ecosystem.

Maybe—

"Miss?"

Nikki looked up. One of the housekeepers stood by the table, a young Filipino woman who looked more nervous than usual.

"Yes?"

The woman glanced toward the villa, then quickly pressed a folded napkin into Nikki's hand.

"Please," she whispered. "Destroy this after. I don't want trouble."

She hurried away before Nikki could respond. Nikki waited until she was gone, then unfolded the napkin.

The handwriting was shaky, desperate:

I'm alive. H

Nikki read the three words twice, her hands trembling. Harper. Alive. She turned it over.

A crude map of the island. More writing. At the very bottom, the words: *"Memorize and destroy."*

She looked toward the villa where Samir was making his calls, then back at the note.

The paper felt toxic in her hands. She needed fire, matches, something to destroy it.

"What's that you got?"

Samir's voice from behind her. She spun, crushing the note against her palm.

"Nothing. Just a napkin. I thought you were working."

He held up a small Tiffany gift bag, smile bright. "I almost forgot. I got you something."

"You shouldn't have," she said, crumpling the note into her fist as she took the Tiffany bag.

CHAPTER
TWENTY-FIVE

THE RHIB—RIGID inflatable boat—moved through the dark water, engine throttled down to a whisper. Four figures in tactical gear kept low profiles against the boat's rubber sides, night vision goggles turning the world green.

Ten kilometers from the island's eastern approach. The team leader checked his GPS—blue dot crawling across the display exactly where it should be. They'd jumped on these conditions. Half moon. Scattered clouds. Sturdy winds.

"Speed?"

"Four knots," the operator at the helm replied through his throat mic.

They'd drilled this approach until it became automatic. Every waypoint memorized. Every contingency planned. The eastern side offered the best infiltration point—jungle down to the waterline, radar shadows from the terrain, a forty-meter gap between camera positions if their intelligence was accurate.

The youngest operator scanned the horizon through his NVGs. Clear except for the expected patrol boat running its pattern two kilometers north. Navigation lights visible even at this distance, following the same route they'd observed for the past week.

"Engine off," the team leader said.

The water went quiet around them. Just waves against the hull and the creak of gear as bodies shifted. They'd drift the next kilometer, use paddle strokes to maintain course.

Through night vision, the island's heat signatures bloomed against the cooler background. Security lights created bright halos that they'd navigate around. Between those pools of illumination lay the darkness they needed.

"Bearing?"

"Two-six-eight. On track."

The operator in the bow had his paddle ready but hadn't deployed it yet. The current was doing most of the work, pulling them toward the planned insertion point.

The team leader consulted his tablet. Radar showed no contacts within three kilometers. Their AIS transponder had been dark since leaving the mainland. To any surveillance, they would just be another small craft among the fishing boats and pleasure craft that worked these waters.

"Movement onshore."

They tracked the figure through their optics. A guard walking a service road, maybe seventy meters inland. He paused, appeared to scan the waterline, then continued. Right on schedule according to their surveillance.

"He's clear. Resume approach."

Paddle strokes now, careful and quiet. The youngest operator had his waterproof camera ready to document security measures. Everything would go in the assessment report—camera positions, patrol timings, response protocols.

The smell of vegetation grew stronger. Diesel exhaust from generators mixed with something that might have been cooking oil. The resort's kitchen venting to the night air.

"Hold."

The bow operator pointed. Something floating thirty meters off their insertion point. Through NVGs it appeared as a dark shape against the water's surface.

"Debris?" someone asked.

"Maybe. Bring us closer."

They altered course slightly. The object wasn't moving with the current the way driftwood should. Too much mass below the surface. As they closed distance, it rolled with a passing swell.

"That ain't debris," the helm operator said.

Ten meters now. The shape had definition—longer than it was wide, substantial enough to create its own wake pattern. One end seemed heavier, causing it to list.

The team leader weighed options. They could continue to the insertion point, report the object later. But if this was connected to island operations, they needed to know.

"Alongside. Quiet."

The RHIB drifted up to the floating mass. One operator extended his paddle to nudge it. The object rolled sluggishly, resistant to the push. Waterlogged fabric became visible through the night vision. Something pale underneath.

A wave lifted the mass and more details emerged. The wrong kind of details. The kind that made the youngest operator pull back from the gunwale.

"Christ," someone whispered.

"Maintain discipline," the team leader said, though his own voice had tightened.

The object rolled again with the boat's wake. Through the green world of their NVGs, they could make out material that had once been clothing. Other shapes that shouldn't be floating in open water.

The smell hit them then—decay cut through the salt air. One operator pulled his shemagh over his nose.

The team leader processed what they were seeing. This changed things. Protocol said to document and continue, but some things took precedence over an infiltration exercise.

"Is that what I think it is?" the youngest operator asked.

"Sure as hell smells like it."

CHAPTER
TWENTY-SIX

"I CAN'T GO TONIGHT," Nikki said, pressing a hand to her stomach. "Something I ate at lunch."

Samir stood by the mirror adjusting his collar for the third time. He'd actually dressed well for once—dark jeans that fit, a linen shirt that wasn't wrinkled. The cologne was still too strong, but she'd work on that later.

If there was a later.

"The lobster?" he asked, turning from the mirror. "I knew that sauce tasted off. I'm calling Patrick right now, have him speak to the kitchen."

"No." Nikki sat on the bed, trying to look pale. "Don't make a fuss. Please."

"But if the food made you sick—"

"It happens. Maybe it was just too rich." She pulled her knees up, making herself small. "I just need to sleep it off."

Samir crossed to the bed, sat beside her. His hand found her forehead, checking for fever like she was a child.

"I'll stay," he said. "We can watch something in bed. I bookmarked a couple of romantic comedies."

"I thought you hated rom-coms."

"I hate parties more."

She almost gave up the act then. Underneath all his insecurity and possessiveness, there was something genuine about Samir. Something that made this harder than it should be.

"Go," she said. "Network. Make connections. That's why you're here, right?"

"I'm here for you."

"And I'll be here when you get back." She managed a weak smile. "Just sleeping. Very boring."

He didn't look convinced. "I don't like leaving you alone when you're sick."

"I'm not dying, Samir. Just need rest." She touched his freshly shaved cheek. "Go. Have fun. But not too much fun."

"What's too much fun?"

"You'll know because I'll kill you."

He laughed—surprised, genuine. "Any advice for surviving without you?"

"Eye contact," she said. "Remember what we practiced? Look people in the eye when they talk."

"Eye contact. Got it."

"And ask about them. People love talking about themselves."

"What do I ask?"

"Anything. Where they're from. What they do. How they made their money. Just... listen to the answers."

He leaned down, kissed her forehead. "I'd rather stay."

"Go." She gave him a gentle push. "Bring me back something good."

"Like what?"

"Just you," she said, pecking his cheek. "In one piece."

He stood reluctantly, checked his appearance one more time. "You sure?"

"Go before I throw up on your nice shirt."

That got him moving. At the door he paused, looked back. "Nikki?"

"Yeah?"

"Thank you. For... y'know, making me better at this stuff."

The Matchmaker watched the scene unfold on their monitor. Villa Seven's hidden cameras provided crystal clarity—every gesture, every word, every calculated expression on the girl's face.

Sick. Indeed.

They'd observed this performance before. These creatures thought themselves so accomplished, playing their angles, manipulating their marks. But Nikki Bailey had overreached. Declining social obligations? Behaving as though she possessed agency?

Time for education about how this world truly functioned.

They accessed another screen, scrolled through the current roster. There—sublime. Natasha Volkov. Twenty-seven, Lithuanian, statuesque and amenable to whatever circumstances required. She'd been expressing dissatisfaction with her current assignment slash beau, some Belgian pharmaceutical executive who spoke exclusively of his deceased wife and his rescue dogs.

The Matchmaker reached for their phone. Time to orchestrate a fortuitous encounter.

Nikki waited fifteen minutes after Samir left, watching from the window as he walked toward the main resort. His shoulders were squared, trying to project confidence he didn't feel.

Part of her felt guilty. Most of her didn't.

She moved quickly now. Grabbed dark clothes from the closet—black leggings, running shoes, hair tied back. In the bedroom, she stuffed towels under the comforter, shaping them into something that might pass for a sleeping body in the dark.

Harper's note burned in her memory. Whatever truth waited there, she had to know. Her friend was alive and needed help.

Nikki checked the window again. Her path was clear. She slipped out of a side door, staying in the shadows cast by landscape lighting.

CHAPTER
TWENTY-SEVEN

"IMPRESSIVE SETUP," Lock said.

And it was. The control room operated with quiet efficiency. Six operators in matching polo shirts worked their stations, monitoring multiscreen displays. No chatter. No wasted movement. Just the soft click of keyboards and occasional murmur into headsets.

Efron leaned against the supervisor's desk, arms crossed, relaxed. "We run a tight ship. Twenty-four seven coverage, overlapping sectors, full redundancy."

The main wall showed dozens of camera feeds cycling through preset patterns. Pool areas, pathways, dock approaches, service roads. All the public spaces where guests might need protection from prying eyes.

"How many feeds total?" Ty asked.

Efron told him then added: "Plus thermal overlays on perimeter zones, motion detection grids, and full radar coverage for maritime approaches."

Lock studied the layout. Professional. Clean. The kind of setup you'd find protecting an embassy, not a resort. Backup power indicators showed green. Biometric scanners at each workstation. SATCOM array status in the corner—multiple channels, all encrypted.

"Walk me through a typical night."

"Typical is boring, which is how we like it." Efron nodded to the nearest technician. "Show them sector four."

The man pulled up beachfront coverage. A couple walked barefoot along the waterline, her dress catching in the breeze. Two grounds crew members worked on landscape lighting near the tennis courts. Normal resort activity.

"Guards?" Lock asked.

"Roving patrols on randomized schedules." Efron pointed to another screen showing GPS trackers. "We know where every security team member is at all times. No gaps, no predictable patterns."

Ty moved closer to the AIS display. "Lot of boat traffic for this hour."

"Fishing boats mostly. Some pleasure craft." Efron's tone stayed casual, almost amused.

A technician adjusted his headset, spoke quietly in Hebrew. Efron's eyes flicked to him, then back to Lock.

"Shift change in thirty minutes," Lock noted, checking the duty roster on the wall.

"Staggered rotation. Never more than two stations changing at once." Efron seemed to be enjoying this, playing tour guide. "We learned from embassy protocols. Always maintain continuity."

On the thermal overlay, heat signatures appeared and disappeared. A security guard checking the marina. Kitchen staff hauling trash to the service area. Everything routine.

"Motion sensors?"

"Full grid coverage." The supervisor pulled up a schematic. Boxes of green showing clear sectors. A few amber alerts along the eastern perimeter—probably birds or small animals. "We calibrate for local wildlife. The larger animals used to drive us crazy until we dialed down the sensitivity."

Lock watched an amber box flicker to green. Then another. Natural movement patterns.

Ty had wandered to the communications station. Three men managing radio traffic, monitoring emergency frequencies, coordinating with the mainland.

"You run your own repeater network?"

"Has to be self-contained." Efron spread his hands. "Can't rely on cell towers out here."

Lock checked his watch.

On the main display, a maintenance buggy crossed between villas. Its headlights swept across manicured lawns. The driver waved at a passing guard. Both following their routes, their schedules, their training.

"Drone detection?"

"As discussed." Efron straightened slightly. "We can spot anything bigger than a sparrow at two kilometers."

One of the technicians touched his screen, zooming on movement near the staff quarters. Just someone taking out garbage. He tagged it in the log and moved on.

"No interior coverage?" Ty asked.

"Guest privacy is absolute." Efron's tone suggested this was gospel. "What happens inside villas stays inside villas."

Lock nodded, watching the screens. Watching the technicians. Watching Efron watch them.

All quiet. All normal. All exactly as it should be on a peaceful evening in paradise.

The eastern perimeter showed more amber boxes. Wildlife, probably. The man monitoring that sector didn't even look up from his coffee.

Lock kept his expression neutral. He checked his watch again. By now, his Red Team should be feet dry on the beach. Moving through those amber boxes that everyone ignored.

"Quiet night," Lock mused.

"The best kind," Efron replied.

CHAPTER
TWENTY-EIGHT

NIKKI KEPT HER PACE STEADY, unhurried. Just another guest heading for an evening walk. The path from Villa Seven to the main resort was well-lit, lined with solar lanterns every few meters.

A couple passed her going the other direction, too wrapped up in each other to notice. She recognized the man—Swiss banking executive who'd bought her a drink her first night. His companion looked new. They rotated fast here.

The party noise grew louder as she approached the beach club. Laughter, glass clinking, a DJ playing something with too much bass. The smart move would be to circle around, take the service paths. But that would look suspicious if anyone was watching. Direct was better. Confident.

She rounded the pool area and froze.

Samir stood at the bar, and he wasn't alone. The blonde draped on his arm looked like a magazine cover—long legs, longer hair, dress so tight it was basically paint.

She laughed at something Samir said, touching his chest. She moved on to playing with his collar. All moves Nikki recognized because she'd used them herself.

Nikki pressed herself behind a cluster of palms, jaw tight.

The blonde turned and Nikki saw it was Natasha. The tall Lithuanian leaned in close to Samir's ear. Whatever she whispered made him blush behind his glasses. His hand went to her waist. Tentative. Like he wasn't sure he was allowed.

Figure that out later, Nikki thought. Right now she had to find her friend.

She forced herself to move, skirting the pool's edge where the landscape lighting created shadows. If Samir looked up, looked around, he'd see her. But Natasha had him mesmerized.

She slipped past the beach bar. The jungle loomed ahead, a wall of black beyond the resort's carefully maintained boundary. The music faded as she moved away from the party, replaced by the sound of waves and wind in the palms.

A guard walked the perimeter path fifty meters ahead. Nikki slowed, timing his movement. He'd pass the maintenance shed, check the locks, continue toward the tennis courts. She'd done this walk herself during daylight, memorizing the patterns.

The guard moved on schedule. As soon as he rounded the shed, Nikki quickened her pace. The tree line was twenty meters away. Fifteen. Ten.

Her pulse kicked up. This was insane. Walking into the jungle at night with only Harper's cryptic map to guide her. But the alternative was accepting the lies, playing along, pretending everything was fine while Harper was out there alone, fending for herself.

The maintained grass ended abruptly where the jungle began. No gradual transition, just manicured lawn then wild darkness. The resort's lights didn't penetrate more than a few feet into the trees.

Nikki took a breath. Thought about Samir with his hand on Natasha's waist. Thought about Harper. Thought about all the questions nobody wanted to answer.

She stepped into the trees.

The temperature dropped almost immediately. Sounds changed too —no more party noise, just insects and things moving in the canopy above. The path was barely visible, more animal track than trail. She'd need her phone's flashlight soon, but not yet. Not until she was deeper, where the light wouldn't show.

Behind her, the resort blazed against the darkness. Ahead, the jungle waited with its secrets.

CHAPTER
TWENTY-NINE

THE MATCHMAKER ADJUSTED THEIR EARPIECE, watching Natasha work her magic on Samir via the primary feed.

"Laugh at whatever he says next," they murmured into their mic.

On screen, Natasha threw her head back, blonde hair flowing. Her hand found Samir's chest, fingers loosening his shirt buttons. Samir brightened under her attention. Men were so easy for an attractive woman to manipulate it was almost comical.

"Now whisper something about his eyes. Tell him they're soulful."

They'd orchestrated this performance countless times. The shy ones always succumbed to identical techniques—excessive attention delivered rapidly, compliments that felt intimate, touches that seemed spontaneous but weren't. Samir Patel might be worth billions, but he remained just another awkward little boy who'd never learned to decipher women and their motives.

"Your eyes," Natasha purred, leaning close. "So soulful. Like you see everything but say nothing."

Samir's hand went to his glasses, adjusting them nervously. "I, uh... thank you?"

"Don't thank me." She smiled, danger wrapped in silk. "Buy me another drink instead."

The Matchmaker checked their secondary monitor. Villa Seven

showed the fabricated scene—Nikki's supposed form tucked under covers in the darkened bedroom. Sleeping off her feigned illness while her meal ticket slipped away.

"Vodka martini. Make him order it. Then compliment his choice."

This was almost insulting in its simplicity. In an hour, perhaps two, Samir would be escorting Natasha back to his villa. Guilt would wrestle with desire, and desire would triumph. It always did. By morning, the troublesome Nikki Bailey would be yesterday's news.

"You know what I love about men like you?" Natasha said, accepting her drink.

"Men like me?"

"Brilliant men. Visionaries." She clinked her glass against his. "You change the world while others just talk about it."

The Matchmaker nodded approvingly. The script was almost foolproof—specific enough to feel authentic, vague enough to allow Samir to supply the details. Every isolated genius believed themselves misunderstood. Every wealthy boy wanted to imagine their fortune represented something much deeper about them rather than just hard work and being in the right place at the right time.

"Touch his hand when you say the next part."

"But it must be isolating," Natasha continued, her fingers grazing his. "Being so far ahead of everyone else."

Samir's eyes widened behind his glasses. "How did you—yes. It is. Isolating, I mean."

"I understand." She held his gaze. "Sometimes I feel like nobody really sees me either. Just the surface."

Perfect execution. The Matchmaker had selected Natasha specifically for this assignment. She possessed that uncommon combination of beauty and credible vulnerability. The sort of woman who could make a mark feel like a savior rather than a customer.

"Ask about his company. But make it personal. What drives him, not what it does."

"Tell me," Natasha said, shifting closer. "When you built your company, what were you really trying to create? Not the technology, the feeling."

Samir blinked, caught off-guard by the depth of the question. "I... nobody's ever asked me that before."

"I'm not nobody."

Samir was capitulating. The Matchmaker observed it in his posture, the way he angled his body toward her, forgot to check his phone. In the background, other couples danced and drank, but Samir only had eyes for Natasha.

"Connection," Samir said finally. "I wanted to create real connection in a disconnected world."

"And did you?"

"The platform did. But for me?" He looked down at his drink. "Not really."

"Maybe I can help you with that," Natasha said softly. "If you'll allow me."

The Matchmaker verified the villa feed again. Still quiet. Nikki Bailey slumbering through her own replacement. By the time she woke, her tech billionaire would have discovered a new project to rescue.

"Suggest a walk on the beach. Away from the noise. Somewhere you can really talk."

Natasha stood, extending her hand. "It's too loud here. Walk with me?"

Samir hesitated for exactly three seconds—probably thinking of Nikki—then took her hand.

The Matchmaker leaned back, satisfied. Another successful pairing. Another problem solved. In their experience, relationships were merely algorithms. Input the correct variables, execute the proper commands, achieve the desired output.

They watched the pair depart together, Natasha's hips swaying just enough, Samir falling in step alongside her like a devoted puppy.

CHAPTER
THIRTY

THE OPERATOR at station three straightened in his chair. A subtle movement, but Lock caught it.

"Thermal anomaly," the operator said, working his keyboard. "East perimeter, sector Delta-Four."

Efron didn't move from his position against the supervisor's desk. "Wildlife?"

"Checking." The operator pulled up the feed, overlaying data streams. "Ground FLIR picked up two signatures. Human-sized. Likely adult males."

On the main display, a section of the eastern grid pulsed amber. The thermal overlay showed two distinct heat blooms against the cooler background of vegetation.

"Could be staff," Efron said, but his eyes had sharpened. "Who's scheduled for that sector?"

Another technician checked his screen. "No patrols scheduled. No maintenance crews."

"Wait," the station three operator said. "I've got another contact. Single individual, moving away from resort. Sector Charlie-Two."

Multiple screens lit up. Lock watched the team work their stations, pulling feeds, running analytics.

"Guest?" Efron asked.

"Possibly. Moving through a portion of interior jungle."

Efron glanced at the screen showing the lone figure, then back to the tactical pair. "Priority?"

"The paired signatures are showing tactical movement," the operator said. "Nonlinear approach, spacing discipline."

"Focus on Delta-Four," Efron decided. "Log the single contact but maintain priority on the potential breach."

Lock kept his position by the wall, arms crossed. Beside him, Ty had gone still—the kind of stillness that preceded action. They'd both noticed the dismissal of the lone figure. Someone heading into the jungle at night warranted more than a log entry.

"Vibration sensors just triggered," the first operator reported. "Confirming footfall pattern in Delta-Four. Two individuals, moving inland."

The control room's atmosphere changed. Operators sat straighter, hands working faster. Someone switched their headset to encrypted channel.

Efron spoke rapid Hebrew into his mic. Lock caught pieces—deployment orders, sector designations, response protocols.

"What's he saying?" Ty murmured.

"Drone launch. Ground team dispatch." Lock kept his voice low. "He's not treating it as a false alarm."

On the AIS display, the maritime radar showed clear. No vessels within three nautical miles. Nothing tagged or tracked. Whatever was on that beach had come in dark.

"Give me eyes," Efron said, switching back to English.

A new feed appeared on the main screen. Drone footage, thermal imaging painting the world in whites and grays. Tree canopy, then beach, then—

Two figures in tactical gear moving through the vegetation. Disciplined spacing, weapons, evident even in thermal.

Efron's expression didn't change, but Lock caught the look that passed between them. An acknowledgment. They both knew what this was.

"Contact confirmed," an operator announced. "No badge pings. No biometric or gait analytic matches."

"Secondary validation," another technician added. "Motion analysis confirms tactical movement pattern. They're not lost guests."

Efron stepped closer to the screens. "Quick reaction force?"

"Team Two is closest. Ninety seconds to intercept."

"Deploy them. Rules of engagement?"

"Sir?"

"Observe and contain. I want to know who they are before we move."

Lock noted the restraint. Smart. Don't overreact until you understand the threat.

"The single contact is still moving," an operator reported. "Should we—"

"Log it," Efron said without looking. "Probably a guest who had too much champagne. Focus on the breach."

More Hebrew commands. The encrypted channels came alive with coordinated chatter. On screen, the drone circled higher, wider angle now. The tactical pair had stopped, possibly aware of the aerial surveillance.

"Ground team approaching intercept point," someone announced.

"Overwatch?" Efron asked.

"Tower Three has thermal scopes on target. Tower Five moving to support."

Coordinated. Layered. The kind of response that came from constant drilling. Lock was impressed.

"Lock down staff quarters for everyone who's already inside and do a count," Efron ordered. "No movement until we clear this."

"What about guest areas?" an operator asked.

"No alerts yet. Keep it contained."

Lock watched the feeds multiply. Marina cameras showing guards moving to defensive positions. Service road barriers activating. The resort's security apparatus revealing itself layer by layer.

"We've got vehicle movement," another technician called out. "Security patrol converging on Delta-Four."

On the drone feed, the two figures had gone prone in the underbrush. Solid fieldcraft if they'd heard or seen something.

"Range to target?"

"Forty meters and closing."

Efron turned to Lock and Ty. "Gentlemen, you're seeing our emergency response protocols in action. I trust you'll note the coordination and professionalism in your report."

"Impressive response time," Lock said, neutral.

"We drill constantly." Efron's smile was sharp. "Though somehow I suspect you knew we'd get the chance to demonstrate tonight."

Neither Lock nor Ty responded.

"Contact," an operator announced. "Ground team has visual."

The main screen switched to helmet camera footage. Two figures in tactical gear, faces obscured by balaclavas. Quality kit. The kind of loadout a high-end security team would use.

"Sir," the drone operator said. "I've lost the single contact in Charlie-Two. Tree canopy too dense."

"Maintain focus on the breach," Efron said.

But Lock had seen the last position. Someone had walked into the jungle alone, at night, while security descended on his Red Team. Someone who'd been dismissed as a drunk guest.

He logged that detail.

"Ground team is challenging," the operator reported.

On screen, the security team had weapons drawn but not raised. Controlled. Measured. The two tactical figures slowly raised their hands.

"This should be interesting," Efron said, glancing at Lock. "I wonder who would send a team to test our defenses without proper notification?"

Lock kept his expression neutral. The game was playing out exactly as expected.

Except for that lone figure disappearing into the jungle.

CHAPTER
THIRTY-ONE

NIKKI PULLED the hut's makeshift door closed behind her, fingers trembling as she tried to arrange the hanging vines to hide the entrance. The structure was barely visible even in daylight—at night, if you didn't know exactly where to look, you'd walk right past it.

She needed it to stay that way.

A sound froze her in place. Distant but unmistakable—dogs barking.

Then voices. Radio static. The mechanical whir of drones.

Shit. Shit, shit, shit.

They'd found her. Somehow they'd tracked her here. To this place that needed to stay hidden.

Nikki forced herself to breathe. Think. The voices were getting closer, coming from the direction of the beach. Multiple teams by the sound of it. The barking grew excited—they'd found a scent.

Move. Now.

She couldn't go back the way she'd come—that would lead them straight to the hut. Instead, she pushed deeper into the jungle, perpendicular to the approaching sounds. Every step had to count. Every broken branch could give away the path.

Light swept through the canopy. Searchlights from drones, painting the leaves in harsh white circles. Nikki dropped flat behind a fallen log as one passed overhead, the buzz of rotors loud enough to drown out everything else.

"Sector Six clear!" someone shouted. English, but accented.

Flashlights bobbed between the trees. Radio chatter crackled. They were spreading out, forming a search grid. Professional. Methodical. This wasn't some half-hearted security sweep—this was a full tactical response.

All for her. Because she'd snuck out to find the truth. It must be worse than even Harper thought it was.

The barking was louder now. Nikki could hear their handlers encouraging them in Hebrew. She had minutes, maybe less, before they picked up her trail.

She crawled along the log, staying low. Mud soaked through her clothes, insects scattered from disturbed leaf litter. Twenty meters ahead, the ground dropped into a small ravine. If she could reach it—

A drone swept directly overhead, searchlight blazing. Nikki pressed herself flat, not breathing, trying to disappear into the ground. The light passed. She waited five more seconds, then scrambled for the ravine.

"Movement, sector seven!"

"On it!"

Boots crashed through the underbrush somewhere to her left. Nikki slid down the ravine's muddy slope, catching herself on roots and vines. At the bottom, a seasonal stream had left a channel of stones. Good. Harder to track.

She followed the stream bed, moving as fast as she dared in the darkness. Behind her, the search intensified. Additional teams converging. Drones crisscrossing overhead. The barking sounded frantic now, possibly confused by multiple scent trails.

"Tighten the grid! No gaps!"

How many were out here? It sounded like an army. All because she'd—

A root caught her foot. Nikki went down hard, knees hitting stone, palms scraped raw. She bit back a cry, forced herself up. Keep moving. Don't stop.

The streambed curved left, then opened into a clearing. Bad. Too exposed. But going back meant running into the search teams.

Radio chatter erupted nearby. "Target acquired! Two subjects in tactical gear!"

Two subjects?

"Ground team moving to intercept. Maintain perimeter."

The voices shifted, moving away from her position. Orders in Hebrew, urgent but controlled. The barking grew more distant.

Nikki didn't understand. Two subjects in tactical gear? That wasn't her. She was alone, in civilian clothes.

Unless...

Unless they weren't looking for her at all.

Radio traffic continued: "Subjects contained. Repeat, we have control."

The searchlights pulled back, concentrating on another area entirely. The systematic grid pattern broke apart as teams converged on whatever they'd found.

Nikki stayed frozen in the streambed, afraid to move, afraid to hope. The jungle around her was still alive with activity but now it was flowing away from her, pulled toward some other crisis.

She waited. Five minutes. Ten. The sounds grew more distant. Whatever was happening, it was moving toward the beach, away from the hut.

Away from her.

Carefully, painfully, she climbed out of the ravine. Her clothes were ruined, cuts and bruises covering her arms and legs. But she was alive. Uncaught.

And the hut's location was still secret.

She had to get back. Get to her room. Pretend she'd never left.

If they caught her, if they found out what she knew...

CHAPTER
THIRTY-TWO

THE JUNGLE HUNG heavy with pre-dawn humidity. Lock and Ty followed the Israeli security operative down a narrow path, their shoes squelching in mud churned up by boots. The sound of surf grew louder, mixing with the buzz of insects already awake and hungry.

"Your boys made it about two hundred meters," the guard said over his shoulder. Not gloating, just stating fact.

They emerged into a small clearing near the shoreline. Three men in tactical gear stood in loose formation, hands free but clearly under guard. Two more Israeli operators flanked them, weapons slung low but ready. The Red Team's equipment lay in a neat pile—NODs, comms gear, tactical packs. Courtesy in the detention.

"Ryan."

The Red Team leader stepped forward—mid-forties, compact and weathered, with the kind of face that had seen too many ops in too many places. Ex-Delta, now running high-end security assessments for people who could afford the best.

"Heard you had some trouble," Lock said, keeping his tone neutral.

"Just so you're aware, I made the call to break cover."

Behind them, footsteps on the path. Efron appeared, still in his control room polo but with a tactical vest thrown over it. His expression radiated satisfaction, like a chess player who'd just called checkmate.

"Gentlemen." He surveyed the scene. "Impressive response time, wouldn't you say?"

"Under seven minutes," one of the Israeli guards noted.

Efron moved to stand beside Lock, close enough that Lock could smell his aftershave mixed with sweat. "Of course, using only three operators for a maritime infiltration was ambitious. Perhaps overconfident?"

"We had four. One stayed with the boat."

"Still." Efron's smile was sharp. "Against a properly trained security force, results matter. My men are all Unit 669, Shayetet 13, Sayeret Matkal. The best Israel produces."

Lock noticed how the Israeli guards straightened slightly at the mention of their units. Pride ran deep in special operations, no matter the country.

"Congratulations. But like I told Ryan, we didn't get caught. We aborted."

"Aborted?" Efron's smile flickered. "That's an interesting way to describe being surrounded and contained."

"We found something in the water. Compromised our approach window dealing with it."

Lock straightened. "What kind of something?"

The team leader looked between Lock and Efron, weighing his words. "The kind that changes mission parameters."

"Debris?" Efron asked. "Equipment malfunction?"

"No."

The single word hung in the humid air. Even the insects seemed to quiet.

"You're going to want to see this too."

He turned and walked toward the vegetation line where the RHIB had been dragged ashore and hidden. Lock and Ty followed. Behind them, Efron hesitated, then came along, his guards maintaining their positions, alert to the shift in dynamics.

The boat sat partially concealed under camo netting and palm fronds. Quality work—invisible from above, barely visible from the ground. Near it, something else lay under a rubberized tarp, half-covered with more vegetation. The shape was wrong for equipment.

The team leader crouched beside it. "Found them floating about fifty meters offshore. Right in our approach lane."

The smell hit them first—salt and decay and something sweeter. That particular wrongness that triggered primitive warnings in the brain. Ty took a half-step back. Lock stayed put, but his jaw tightened.

"My team made the call to recover it. Figured we couldn't leave it drifting into shipping lanes." He took a beat. "Or washing up next to your beach bar."

He gripped the edge of the tarp, looked up at them. "Ready?"

Lock nodded. Efron said nothing, but his cocky demeanor had vanished. His hand moved unconsciously to his radio, then stopped.

The team leader pulled back the tarp.

The body had been in the water at least two days. Skin bloated and discolored, features distorted beyond easy recognition. Female, based on the clothing remnants. Young. Likely early twenties.

"Damn," Ty said, taking a long exhale.

Lock studied the remains with tactical detachment, cataloging details. The clothing suggested staff rather than guest—practical fabric, conservative cut. White shirt, dark skirt. Housekeeping uniform? A delicate silver bracelet caught the early light, the kind of thing given as a gift.

Water pooled under the tarp where fluids had leaked. Insects already gathering at the edges.

"Where exactly?"

"Forty meters offshore, caught in the current that runs along the eastern approach. Would have drifted out to deep water by morning if we hadn't grabbed her. I assume female."

"How'd you even spot her in the dark?"

"Thermal showed a mass. Thought it was kelp or debris at first. We went to push it aside and..." He gestured at the body.

Lock looked up at Efron. The Israeli's face had gone carefully blank, but something moved behind his eyes. Recognition? Calculation? Fear?

"Your medical team should handle this. Proper documentation, identification, next of kin notification."

"Of course." Efron's voice was steady but the earlier smugness had vanished. "This is... unfortunate."

"That's one word for it," Ty said.

The team leader replaced the tarp with the same care he'd probably shown handling fallen comrades. "We marked the recovery coordinates. Everything's in my helmet cam footage if you need it for the report."

"Report?" Efron's attention snapped back. "This has nothing to do with your security assessment."

"A body in your waters doesn't concern security?" Lock kept his tone mild. "Seems relevant to me."

"An accident. A staff member or passenger from a cruise ship who had too much to drink and fell overboard." Efron was already rebuilding his composure, but the foundation was shaky. "Tragic but not unprecedented."

"Cruise ship?" said Ty.

Efron's jaw tightened. "Whoever it is, I'll handle it."

"I'm sure you will," Lock said.

The men stood in the humid darkness, the tarp-covered shape between them. Somewhere in the canopy, a bird called out—harsh and sudden in the silence. The sound of surf seemed louder now, as if the ocean was surging to reclaim the dead woman.

CHAPTER
THIRTY-THREE

NIKKI KEPT to the shadows as she approached Villa Seven, every cut and scrape throbbing. The rush from her escape was fading, leaving her shaky and exhausted. Her twisted ankle protested with each step.

The villa's exterior lights were still on. Good. Samir hadn't gone to bed yet.

She circled toward the side entrance, the one that led through the garden. Her muddy shoes squelched softly on the stone path. She'd have to hide them, along with her torn clothes. No trace of her midnight jungle run.

Movement on the terrace stopped her cold.

Two figures in the soft light spilling from the living room. Samir in his party clothes, backed against the railing. And Natasha positioned on her knees in front of him, her blonde hair catching the light as she worked.

Nikki pressed herself against a palm tree, shreds of anger and disappointment rising inside her. But not surprise. Never surprise. Men like Samir were easy marks for girls like Natasha. All it took was attention, a few compliments, sex.

Samir's hands gripped the railing, his head tilted back. Even from here, Nikki could see his glasses were fogged.

Predictable, she thought. *Couldn't even wait one night.*

Natasha was working hard, skilled and practiced. This was business, nothing more. Plant the hook deep, make him feel special, create a need only she could fill.

Nikki had seen it a hundred times. Hell, she'd done it herself when necessary.

But watching it happen to someone she'd actually started to care about...

No. This was useful. If she knew Samir like she thought she did, the guilt would eat him alive. She could use that. Turn it to her advantage.

She slipped past them, using their distraction to reach the side door. Neither noticed her—Samir lost in the moment, Natasha focused on the task in hand.

Inside, Nikki moved quickly to the bedroom. Locked the door. Only then did she allow herself to really assess the damage from her jungle escape.

Her clothes were destroyed—torn, muddy, stained with blood from various scrapes. She peeled them off carefully, wincing as fabric pulled away from dried cuts. Her knees were the worst, scraped raw from her fall in the stream. Her palms weren't much better.

She bundled everything into a plastic laundry bag, shoved it deep in the closet. Deal with it tomorrow.

The mirror showed more damage. Scratches across her shoulders and arms from branches. A bruise blooming on her ribs. Her hair was a tangled mess with leaves still caught in it.

She needed a shower. Now.

The hot water stung her cuts, but Nikki forced herself to stand under the spray. She had to wash away the traces—the mud, the blood, the smell of fear and jungle rot.

She shampooed twice, working out every tangle, every piece of debris. The water ran brown, then pink, then finally clear. Her body showed the marks of her night's adventure but nothing that wouldn't heal.

She soaped herself carefully, cataloging each injury. The bruises could be covered with makeup if needed.

Clean, she stepped out and toweled off gently. Found the sexiest nightwear she'd brought—black silk that clung in all the right places, showing enough skin to distract from any questions about where she'd been.

A touch of perfume. Lip gloss. Hair brushed out and artfully tousled.

By the time she heard the front door open, she was in bed, arranged perfectly. One strap of the nightgown sliding off her shoulder. The sheet pulled down just enough.

She knew exactly how she looked. Knew exactly what Samir would see when he walked in, reeking of another woman's perfume and his own guilt.

Nikki Bailey knew how to play the game.

CHAPTER
THIRTY-FOUR

THE CONFERENCE ROOM'S polished table created a sterile atmosphere that felt more like an interrogation than a debrief. Lock noted how Ethan Efron had arranged documents in neat stacks, everything organized. Too organized for someone dealing with an unexpected tragedy.

"Gentlemen," Efron said, his voice carrying manufactured solemnity. "First, let me apologize for the circumstances that brought your assessment team into contact with this unfortunate situation."

Lock studied Efron's face. The Israeli's expression was controlled—concerned but measured, the look of a security director handling an unpleasant but routine matter. But his eyes were calculating, measuring their reactions.

"The body your team recovered." Efron opened a thin folder. "Young female, early twenties based on preliminary examination. Cause of death remains undetermined pending full autopsy. I can confirm however that we do not have any unaccounted staff members at this time."

He spread out photographs across the table—wide shots of the recovery area, the shoreline, current patterns marked with arrows. Notably absent were any close-ups of the body itself.

"Our medical officer believes she'd been in the water for several days, possibly longer. Decomposition makes immediate identification... challenging." Efron's tone remained detached. "Water temperature, marine life, current patterns—all factors that complicate timeline estimates."

Lock found himself disturbed by Efron's matter-of-fact delivery. The man was discussing a young woman's death like he was reviewing quarterly budget reports. No emotion, no human recognition that someone's daughter had died in these waters.

Ty leaned forward. "Any missing person reports in the area?"

"We've checked with local authorities on the mainland. No missing persons matching the general description." Efron tapped the current charts. "The eastern approach where she was found is fed by currents from three different directions. She could have originated from any number of locations."

"Such as?"

"Could have fallen from a cruise ship passing through international waters. These large vessels don't always detect people going overboard immediately." Efron's explanation came smoothly, too smoothly. "By the time they realize someone's missing and begin search operations, currents can carry a body considerable distances."

Lock kept his expression neutral, but he wasn't buying it.

"Private yachts are another possibility. Alcohol, rough seas, accidents happen more often than the maritime authorities like to publicize.."

The way Efron discussed human tragedy with such casual indifference was unsettling. This wasn't detachment—this was something colder. As if the dead woman was nothing more than an inconvenient piece of debris that had interfered with his operation.

"Timeline of decomposition," Ty said. "Your medical officer mentioned several days?"

"Possibly longer. Saltwater decomposition is... unpredictable. Temperature variations, marine scavengers, current action—all factors that can accelerate or slow the process." Efron opened another section of his folder. "Without knowing the exact time of death or entry into the water, we're working with estimates."

Lock studied the photographs. The current charts were detailed, but something about them bothered him. The analysis looked like it had taken hours to prepare, not the quick assessment you'd expect from a body discovered that morning.

"Your maritime surveillance didn't detect the body approaching?"

"Our sensors are calibrated for active threats—vessels, divers, aircraft. Floating debris doesn't always register, especially in rough water." Efron's explanation was practiced. "We're reviewing our detection protocols as a result of this incident."

"Floating debris," Lock repeated. The term sat wrong in his mouth when applied to a human being.

"I apologize for my unfortunate phrasing," Efron said, his tone suggesting no real regret. "The point remains—our systems are designed to detect intentional intrusions, not... naturally occurring phenomena."

Naturally occurring. Lock felt his jaw tighten another notch.

"No guests unaccounted for?"

"Absolutely not." The response came too fast, too emphatic. "We maintain strict arrival and departure logs. Every guest is accounted for at all times."

Lock caught the micro-expression—a tightness around Efron's eyes that suggested the question had hit something sensitive. But Efron's voice remained steady as if he were reciting practiced lines.

"And definitely no staff?" Ty asked.

"Complete roster verification conducted this morning. All personnel accounted for." Efron closed the folder with finality. "This appears to be an external incident that unfortunately intersected with your training exercise."

Lock let silence stretch between them, watching Efron's face. The Israeli showed no discomfort with the pause, no urge to fill the silence with additional explanations. Either discipline, or the confidence of someone whose story was unshakeable.

"What about identification? Personal effects, jewelry, clothing?"

"Nothing conclusive. The saltwater and... other factors... have degraded most material evidence." Efron's voice carried just the right note of regret. "Without dental records or DNA comparison, identification may prove impossible."

"She'll just remain a Jane Doe forever?" Ty asked.

"Sadly, that's often the case with maritime recoveries."

Lock recognized the familiar signs of a situation being managed. Every question answered, every angle covered, every loose end neatly tied up. But something fundamental was wrong with the picture Efron was painting.

"Autopsy timeline?"

"Mainland medical examiner is conducting it now. Results within forty-eight hours, though as I mentioned, the condition of the remains may limit findings." Efron stood, signaling the debrief's end. "I've prepared a summary for your incident report. Standard documentation for training exercises that encounter external factors."

He slid a flash drive across the table. "Everything relevant to your security assessment. Photos, current analysis, our response protocols. Should cover all the details your report requires."

Lock pocketed the drive without examining it. "We'll need to coordinate with local authorities. Chain of custody, proper procedures."

"All handled through appropriate channels." Efron's smile was reassuring. "We have excellent relationships with mainland law enforcement. They trust our preliminary assessments in situations like this."

Of course they did. Lock wondered how much that trust had cost, and whether it was purchased with money or favors or something else entirely.

"The body's current location?" Ty asked.

"Secure mainland facility. The authorities prefer to handle unidentified remains with appropriate... discretion. Tourism concerns, you understand."

Lock stood, extending his hand. "Thank you for your cooperation, Ethan. We'll have our preliminary assessment ready by tomorrow."

"Excellent. I trust this unfortunate coincidence won't impact your overall evaluation of our security protocols."

The word 'coincidence' hung in the air between them. Efron had used it deliberately, Lock realized. Testing whether they'd accept that interpretation or push for something deeper.

As Lock and Ty walked down the corridor toward the elevator, neither spoke until they were out of earshot.

"That was well-rehearsed," Ty said quietly.

"Too well-rehearsed." Lock hit the elevator button harder than necessary. "And did you catch how he talked about her? Like she was a piece of equipment that malfunctioned."

"Guy's got ice water in his veins."

"Or no conscience at all." Lock watched the floor numbers descend. "Question is, what really happened to that girl? And why is Efron so eager to convince us she's nobody we need to worry about?"

The elevator doors opened, revealing their reflection in the polished steel. Behind them, Lock could see Efron standing in the conference room doorway, watching their departure.

"You know how you can tell when someone from Mossad is lying to you?" Lock said as the doors began to close.

"Their lips are moving?" said Ty.

"Correct."

CHAPTER
THIRTY-FIVE

NIKKI TOOK another bite of mango as Samir watched her from across the breakfast table.

"You're feeling better," Samir said, his relief evident. "I was worried about you last night."

"Much better." She cut another piece of fruit, noting how he fidgeted with his coffee cup. "You seem to have worked up quite an appetite with Natasha last night."

The comment landed. Samir's hand froze halfway to his mouth, toast suspended in mid-air. His face flushed behind his glasses.

"Nikki, I—"

"Relax." She kept her tone light, almost amused. "I'm not going to throw a scene."

"You're not?" His surprise was genuine.

"Should I be? We never said we were exclusive." She sipped her orange juice, watching him over the rim. "Though I have to admit, that girl works fast. Gotta give her props for that."

Samir set down his toast, going pale. "How did you—"

"I went for a walk when I couldn't sleep." Nikki let just the right note of hurt creep in beneath the casual delivery.

"It didn't mean anything," he said quickly. "I was confused, you were sick, she just—"

"Started talking to you?" Nikki finished the sentence, still not angry. That was what unsettled him most, she could see. He'd expected tears, accusations, drama. Instead, she was treating it like a mildly interesting observation.

"Yes. About my work, my vision for the company. She seemed genuinely interested."

"I'm sure she did." Nikki reached across the table, touched his wrist. "Samir, you're brilliant, I get that. It's what I love about you. But you're incredibly naive about women like her."

"Women like her?"

"Professionals. There are girls here to meet a husband, settle down, have children. Then there are the ones who y'know, work for a living."

Samir pulled back. "That's kind of harsh."

"Okay, forget about her. The question is what do you want? A girlfriend, maybe a wife and a family. Or a walking petri dish of STIs who just wants another Louis Vuitton bag before she moves on to the next mark."

He blinked at her through his glasses. "It won't happen again."

Nikki leaned back in her chair, let the silence between them stretch.

"Why don't we get away from here," she said finally, as if the idea had only just come to her. "From all these people, all these distractions. Go somewhere we can figure out what we actually have. Just the two of us."

"Get away?"

"Didn't you mention your friend has a yacht? The one who's always texting you about meeting up in Monaco or wherever?"

Samir straightened, suddenly animated. "James. Yes, he's got a two-hundred-footer anchored not too far away. But I thought you liked it here."

"I did. Before last night." She let vulnerability slip into her tone.

"I'm sorry." The words came out rushed, desperate. "I was an idiot. Nikki, you have to believe me, it didn't mean anything."

"I want to believe you, I really do. That's why I think we need some time alone."

She watched the idea take shape in his expression. Samir was the kind of man who solved problems by throwing resources at them. A yacht represented the ultimate expression of his wealth and importance.

"James would love to have us aboard," he said, warming to the concept. "He's been after me to visit for months. The yacht has everything—full crew, chef, helicopter pad."

"How many guests can it accommodate?"

"Twelve in six staterooms. But it would just be us. James is in London until next month."

Nikki filed away the details. Perfect.

"When could we leave?"

"Whenever you want. James gave me standing access." Samir was fully engaged now, planning mode activated. "I could call him this morning, have the captain prepare an itinerary."

"What about leaving here? Do we need permission or anything?"

"From who? We're guests, not prisoners." He laughed at the absurdity. "Though Patrick and Amira might be disappointed to lose the revenue."

"You're right, I guess what I meant to say was could we leave... quietly? Without making a big production?"

Samir's eyes sharpened. "Sure. Why?"

Nikki had prepared for this question. "Because I don't want Natasha knowing our business. Or any of the other girls thinking I'm running away because of what happened last night."

"Ah." He nodded, understanding male pride and female dignity in equal measure. "We could take the morning helicopter to the mainland, then head to the boat from there. Skip the whole resort departure routine."

"That sounds perfect." She leaned forward, touched his arm again. "You'd really do this? Just drop everything and sail away with me?"

"For you? Yes." The sincerity was genuine, which made what she was doing to him both easier and harder. "Nikki, I want to prove that last night was meaningless. That what we have is real."

"Then call James. Set it up."

Samir was already reaching for his phone. "I'll do it right now. We could be on the yacht by tomorrow. Maybe sooner."

"That fast?"

"When you have the resources, everything moves fast." He paused, phone in hand. "Are you sure about this? Leaving the island, I mean. What about your friend Harper?"

Nikki's pulse quickened, but she kept her expression neutral. "What about her?"

"You were worried when she didn't come back the other night. Shouldn't we check if she's okay before we leave?"

"She's a big girl. If she wanted to say goodbye, she would have." Nikki shrugged with practiced indifference. "Besides, Harper's probably halfway to Monaco by now with whatever billionaire caught her eye."

"Still, it seems..."

"Samir." She made her tone firm. "I don't want to spend our romantic getaway talking about other women. Not Harper, not Natasha, not anyone else. Can you handle that?"

He nodded quickly. "Of course. You're right. This is about us."

"Good. Now make your call." She leaned across the table and kissed him softly, letting him see down her silk top as she pulled back. Her fingers brushed through his hair, straightening it. "There. Much better."

CHAPTER
THIRTY-SIX

THE BUSINESS CENTER buzzed with surveillance equipment cycling through its routines. Lock sat at the polished table, three laptops open in front of him, while Ty worked through printed logs at the far end.

"Response protocols are well-documented. Quick reaction times, coordinated communications." Ty paused, scanning a particular page. "Interesting medical evacuation pattern though."

Lock looked up from his screen. "How so?"

"Three medical evacs in the past six months. All guests, all sudden onset conditions requiring immediate mainland treatment." Ty kept his voice neutral, consulting. "Might want to review medical facilities as part of our assessment. Make sure they're adequate for the guest demographic."

Lock pulled up the medical evacuation records on his laptop. Three incidents, all involving male guests over fifty. Heart complications, stroke symptoms, severe allergic reactions. The kind of emergencies that could strike wealthy, high-stress individuals anywhere.

But the timing bothered him. Each evacuation had occurred within days of other incidents—staff departures, minor security breaches, equipment malfunctions.

"Mr. Lock?"

Lock looked up to find one of Efron's operators standing beside the table, a young Israeli with close-cropped hair.

"Yes?"

"Mr. Efron asked me to assist with any technical questions about our surveillance systems. I'm Noam, the senior communications specialist."

"Appreciate it, Noam." Lock gestured to his screen. "Just reviewing your sensor integration protocols. Very impressive."

Noam moved closer, ostensibly to see what Lock was examining. But his eyes swept across the other laptops, the printed reports.

"The integration was challenging," Noam said. "Multiple manufacturers, different communication protocols. Took months to achieve seamless operation. We used some agentic AI but that still needs to be checked manually."

Lock nodded, opening camera coverage schematics instead. Nothing sensitive, nothing that would raise questions. Just the kind of technical review a security consultant would conduct.

"What about data retention?" Ty asked. "How long do you archive surveillance footage?"

"Ninety days for routine monitoring, one year for flagged incidents." Noam's answer came smoothly. "Storage limitations require regular archiving to offline systems."

Lock made a note. Ninety days meant anything older than three months was effectively inaccessible without special requests.

"Noam, could you pull up guest departure records for the past month? I want to cross-reference them with security camera coverage, make sure we're capturing all exit points adequately."

"Of course." Noam moved to a terminal, fingers working across the keyboard. Within seconds, a spreadsheet appeared on the main wall display. Names, dates, departure methods, destinations.

Lock studied the list, noting patterns. Most departures were scheduled helicopter flights to the mainland, followed by private jet connections. Some guests left via yacht, picked up by vessels that approached from international waters. All properly documented, all accompanied by security footage of boarding procedures.

"Can you sort by departure date?"

The list reorganized chronologically. Lock opened another laptop and began cross-referencing the departure records with actual transportation manifests—helicopter passenger lists, yacht pickup schedules, water taxi logs. Standard audit procedure to verify security coverage was capturing all departures properly.

Most entries matched perfectly. Guest departed via helicopter at 1030, helicopter manifest showed same passenger at same time. Guest picked up by private yacht, marina log confirmed the vessel arrival and departure.

Then he found the first discrepancy.

"This one here. Harper Holt," Lock said. "Listed as departed via helicopter to mainland, but she's not showing up on the helicopter passenger manifest."

Ty looked up from his reports. "System error?"

"Maybe." Lock checked the helicopter schedule again. "Noam, can you show me the security footage for the Harper Holt departure? Just want to verify your camera coverage captured it properly."

Noam's fingers hesitated over the keyboard, just for a moment. "I may need to pull it from archived storage. Give me a few minutes?"

"Sure. No rush." Lock said, casually. But something was off. The hesitation had been brief but noticeable and such a recent departure wouldn't have been archived.

A few minutes passed.

"Having trouble with that footage?" Ty asked the young Israeli.

"System's running slow today. Archive retrieval can take time." Noam's tone remained steady, but sweat had appeared on his forehead despite the air conditioning.

Lock pulled up marina records next, checking if Harper Holt might have left via boat instead. Yacht departures, water taxi pickups, private vessel transfers. Again, her name appeared nowhere in the actual transportation records.

According to the island's official departure list, Harper Holt had left the island. According to every transportation record, she'd never boarded anything that could take her away from the island.

Lock thought about the body his Red Team had found floating in the approach lanes. Young female, early twenties, condition consistent with several days in the water. He thought about Efron's carefully prepared story about cruise ship accidents and unidentifiable remains.

A paper rustled near his elbow. Ty had casually shifted position, sliding a memo pad across the table. When Lock glanced down, he saw Ty's handwritten note: "Being watched. Three observers since Noam arrived."

Lock didn't look around, didn't acknowledge the note. Instead, he continued scrolling through departure records.

"Mr. Lock?" Noam had returned, looking apologetic. "I'm sorry, but that particular footage appears to have been corrupted during archive transfer. Technical glitch. It happens sometimes with our older storage systems."

"No problem," Lock said easily. "Just wanted to verify camera coverage of the helipad area. For our security assessment recommendations."

"I can show you current coverage if that would help."

"That's fine. We'll include a note about a slight glitch in archive reliability in our report."

Noam's smile was strained. "Of course. Anything else I can help with?"

"No, thank you, I think we've gotten the answers we needed," said Lock.

CHAPTER
THIRTY-SEVEN

AMIRA BARZANI TOYED with her salad. The private dining room of Villa One commanded a view of the entire resort—pools, restaurants, guest accommodations—all of it spread below like a detailed architectural model.

""Explain to me how a dead body drifted into our security perimeter without detection?" she said without looking up from her plate.

Ethan Efron sat across from her, his tactical vest replaced by an expensive polo shirt. "Current patterns shifted due to the storm system three days ago. The eastern approach—"

"I don't want science lessons." Amira set down her chopsticks with deliberate care. "I want to know why you didn't find it first."

"It wasn't a breach. The body originated from outside our operational zone."

"You're talking to me, remember. The body originated from the island," Amira said.

Patrick Barzani sat at the far end of the table, picking at his lobster with the distracted air of someone lost in private thoughts. He'd been unusually quiet since they'd convened this emergency session, content to let Amira and Efron dissect the failure. But there was something in his manner—not concern, exactly. Almost... anticipation.

"The consultants accepted my explanation," Efron said. "Accidental drowning, external origin, routine maritime recovery. They have no reason to suspect anything."

She stood, moving to the floor-to-ceiling windows. In the distance, guests lounged by the infinity pool, young women in designer swimwear tending to older men.

"How long until they complete their assessment?"

"Original timeline was two weeks."

"Speed it up."

"On what grounds?"

Amira turned from the window, her gaze frigid. "Think of something. I don't care what it is, but I want them gone sooner rather than later."

"That might seem suspicious."

"More suspicious than a floating corpse?" Amira moved back to the table, her heels clicking against marble with mechanical precision. "They're already asking questions about departure manifests and transportation logs. How long before they start connecting names to faces?"

Patrick looked up from his lobster, sudden interest flickering in his eyes. "Which faces?"

"The Santos girl, obviously. That Romanian model who caused problems last month. The underage Brazilian girl who threatened to go to the authorities." Amira enumerated them like items on a shopping list.

"And the latest one?" Patrick said quietly. "Harper Holt."

Something passed between them—a shared understanding that made Efron straighten in his chair.

"The Holt situation is contained," Efron said. "She's been listed as departed, manifest shows helicopter transport to mainland. Clean paperwork."

"Except she never boarded any helicopter, did she?" Amira said. "If they find proof that we're lying they'll start wondering why."

Patrick leaned forward, his earlier distraction replaced by focused attention. "What about the girl with Samir?"

"Nikki Bailey," Efron supplied. "She's been asking questions about Holt's disappearance."

"What kind of questions?"

"Enough to require management."

Patrick smiled slightly, enjoying his wife's discomfort. "I thought you'd already spoken to her, Amira."

"I did."

Patrick nodded slowly, as if savoring some private amusement. "Young women can be so unpredictable."

"Never mind Nikki, I can deal with her. The consultants are who we need to worry about," Amira said, redirecting focus. "They have access to our systems, they know the questions to ask, how to build a picture."

"Agreed," Efron said. "But terminating the assessment prematurely would raise even more suspicions"

"Fine. Then we accelerate it." Amira set down her fork with finality. "Emergency situation requiring their immediate expertise elsewhere. A valued client with urgent security concerns. Something that makes early departure appear heroic rather than suspicious. Give them something else to do. Stuff their mouths with even more dollar bills if we have to."

"I'll come up with something," Efron said.

"Perfect. That gives us forty-eight hours to clean up any remaining loose ends." Amira's gaze moved between them. "This body was an embarrassment."

"Understood."

Patrick looked up again, thoughtful. "What about documentation? Their assessment report?"

"What about it?"

"Will it mention the body recovery? The discrepancies in our maritime surveillance?"

Efron and Amira exchanged glances.

"Professional consultants document everything," Patrick continued. "Every anomaly, every security gap, every incident that occurs during their assessment. It's how they justify their fees."

The implications hung in the air like smoke. A written report detailing security failures and unexplained bodies would be more than embarrassing—it would be evidence.

"The report can be managed," Efron said, though his confidence had wavered.

"Can it?" Patrick's smile had returned, subtle and knowing. "What happens when they recommend enhanced maritime surveillance specifically because of body recovery incidents?"

Amira felt something cold settle in her chest. She'd been focused on getting Lock and Johnson off the island, but Patrick was right—their departure wouldn't solve the problem if they carried evidence with them.

"Then we'll have to be more persuasive about the nature of their findings," she said finally.

"And if persuasion fails?"

CHAPTER
THIRTY-EIGHT

THE MAIN RESORT bar occupied prime real estate between the infinity pool and the beach, its bamboo frame and thatched roof designed to look casually tropical. Lock nursed a club soda with lime, positioned where he could observe the evening crowd without appearing to study them.

The blonde woman approached his table with unconscious confidence. Tall, lean, with the kind of bone structure that suggested Scandinavian genetics.

"Mind if I sit?" she asked, already claiming the chair across from him. "It's so crowded tonight."

Lock glanced around the bar. Maybe a dozen people scattered across twice as many tables. Hardly crowded.

"Please," he said.

She settled gracefully, crossing long legs.

"I'm Astrid," she said, extending a manicured hand.

"Good to meet you, Astrid." He shook briefly, noting the calculating way she assessed his clothes, his watch, his general presentation. Market research disguised as flirtation.

"You're new," she said. "I would have noticed you."

"Just arrived. Business trip."

"What kind of business?" she asked.

"Consulting," Lock said.

The bartender appeared at their table without being summoned, placing a champagne flute in front of Astrid. Clearly a regular with established preferences.

"Dom Pérignon. The resort keeps my favorites stocked." The casual mention was designed to impress, to establish her status in the island's hierarchy.

"Nice perk."

"One of many." She sipped her drink, studying him over the rim. "Though lately, the atmosphere's been a bit... tense."

Lock raised an eyebrow. "How so?"

Astrid glanced around the bar nervously, then leaned forward. "I probably shouldn't be talking about this—management made it very clear we're supposed to keep quiet—but they just found a body in the water."

"Look, even if I wanted to gossip to anyone outside about resort business, I couldn't," Lock said. "Just signed an NDA thicker than a phone book."

Something relaxed in her posture. "Some poor girl. Floating near the beach."

Lock kept his expression neutral, interested but not too interested. "Accidents happen at resorts, I imagine."

"That's what they're saying. But..." She bit her lower lip. "I think it might have been one of us."

"That's concerning. What makes you feel that way?"

"Am I crazy to think it's weird when someone just vanishes?" Astrid set down her glass. "There was this girl, Harper. Really smart, studying international relations or something. She was supposed to leave a few days ago, but I never saw her actually go."

Lock did his best not to react visibly to Harper's name. "This girl, Harper, were you close to her?"

"Not really, but usually when people leave, there's a whole production. Packing, goodbye drinks, photos. She just... disappeared. One day she was here, the next day gone."

Lock sipped his club soda. "That does sound unsettling."

"Right? "Right? And the weird thing is she had dinner plans the night before."

"Oh?"

"With this German guy, Ulrich. Really wealthy, but kind of gross. Most of the girls avoid him, even though he's insanely wealthy."

Another name that rang a bell. "But she didn't?"

"That's what's so strange—Harper was way too smart for that. She knew how places like this work, knew what men like Ulrich expect from dinner invitations." Astrid leaned closer, lowering her voice. "And then Ulrich left the island that same night. Heart problems or something. But there was a whole commotion. Everyone told to go inside until further notice. Even the men."

Lock registered the connection but kept his expression sympathetic. "Sounds like quite a coincidence."

"That's what I thought. And Harper never even said goodbye. Not even to Nikki."

"Nikki?" Lock asked, playing dumb.

"Her best friend. They were practically inseparable. Nikki's been devastated since Harper left." Astrid's concern seemed genuine. "Poor thing's been trying to act normal, but you can tell she's falling apart inside."

"That's rough. Where is she now?"

"With Samir. Sweet guy, tech billionaire from California. They've been practically living together since Harper disappeared." Astrid paused, studying his face. "Why do you ask?"

Lock realized he'd pushed too hard. Time to redirect.

"Just sounds like she's been through a lot. My consulting work involves risk assessment—when I hear about unusual incidents, my mind starts wondering about safety protocols."

"I see." Astrid's demeanor softened. "You know, you seem different from most of the men here."

"Different how?"

"Like you actually care about people as people, not just..." She gestured vaguely at herself.

Lock smiled slightly. "Most of the men here aren't here for the same reasons I am."

"Which are?"

"Business consulting. Very boring."

Astrid laughed, genuine this time rather than calculated. "I doubt anything about you is boring."

She finished her drink, signaling the bartender for another. The alcohol was loosening her tongue, making her more talkative.

"The thing is," she continued, leaning in. "Harper wasn't naive. If she agreed to have dinner with Ulrich, she must have felt confident she could handle whatever came up."

"But she couldn't?"

"I don't know, but now there's a dead girl floating in the water, and they're telling us not to discuss it with anyone." Her words carried a tremor of fear. "They're saying it was an accident, someone from the mainland who fell off a boat. But we all know that's bullshit."

Lock set down his glass, decision made. He needed to find Ty, needed to share what he'd learned. More importantly, they needed to find Nikki before anyone else realized she might have answers to questions they weren't supposed to be asking.

"Astrid, thank you for the conversation. But I should probably call it a night."

"So soon?" Disappointment flickered across her features.

"Early meeting tomorrow." Lock stood, leaving money on the table. "Be careful who you share these concerns with."

As he walked away she called after him. "You didn't tell me your name." This had to be the first time in her life a guy had walked away from her. One who wasn't gay anyway.

Lock didn't look back. He kept walking.

CHAPTER
THIRTY-NINE

THE VILLA'S front door opened before Lock finished knocking. Nikki Bailey stood in the doorway. Her dress was elegant, expensive, but her eyes held the wariness of someone who'd learned not to trust strangers.

"Can I help you?" she said, voice polite but guarded.

"Ms. Bailey? I'm Ryan Lock, this is Ty Johnson."

Her expression didn't change. "You're the security guys?"

"We're conducting a routine assessment," Lock said. "Part of that involves reviewing guest services and safety protocols."

"What does that have to do with me?"

"May we come in?" Lock said. "We'd prefer to discuss this privately."

Nikki hesitated, glancing over her shoulder toward the villa's interior. Water was running somewhere—shower, probably. She stepped aside.

"Like I said, we're reviewing guest safety protocols," Lock said once they were seated. "Part of that involves documenting any incidents or concerns that might affect future recommendations."

"Incidents?" Nikki said, voice carefully neutral.

"We understand you had a friend staying here recently. Harper Holt?"

The name struck her hard. Her composure cracked for just a moment before she rebuilt it, but Lock caught the reaction.

"Harper left a few days ago," she said.

"According to resort records, yes." Ty leaned forward slightly. "But we're finding some discrepancies in departure documentation. Transport manifests that don't match guest logs."

Nikki became very still. "What kind of discrepancies?"

"The kind that tell me people aren't actually leaving when the records say they are," Lock said. "We're trying to verify what really happened with guest departures over the past week."

"Why would you think I'd know anything about that?"

"Because you were her closest friend," Lock said.

The shower stopped running. Nikki's eyes flicked toward the bedroom, then back to them.

"Harper was... upset about something before she left," she said carefully. "She'd been invited to dinner with one of the guests. A German man. She didn't want to go."

Lock and Ty exchanged glances. Ulrich Drexler.

"Did she tell you why she was upset?" Ty said.

"She said he made her uncomfortable. But the staff... they made it clear that refusing might be an issue."

"What happened?" Lock asked.

Nikki opened her mouth to answer, then stopped. Her fingers twisted together in her lap, betraying nervousness her voice didn't show.

"I don't know. I never saw her again after that night."

"You didn't see her pack? Say goodbye?"

"No. I was... unwell. Stayed in bed most of the night."

"And you haven't heard from her since?" Ty said.

"Nope."

Lock knew she was holding something back, something important. But pushing too hard might shut her down entirely. Besides, their real purpose here was to draw a reaction from Efron and the Barzanis. If they were hiding something, news of this conversation would get back to them quickly. If they weren't, no harm done.

"Ms. Bailey, if there's anything else you can tell us about Harper's departure, anything that seemed unusual—"

"Nikki?"

They all turned. Samir stood in the bedroom doorway, hair still damp from the shower, wearing khakis and a button-down shirt. Lock recognized the type immediately—recently acquired tech money, the kind of guy who still couldn't quite believe his good fortune.

The man's eyes moved between Lock and Ty, his expression shifting from confusion to something darker.

"Who are these people?" he said, moving into the room with territorial confidence.

"Samir, these are security consultants," Nikki said quickly. "They're reviewing resort protocols."

"Security consultants." Samir's tone suggested he found the title suspicious. He looked directly at Ty. "You're the guy from the pool."

Ty nodded. "We've met."

"You were talking to my girlfriend at six in the morning. Now you're in my villa at night." Samir's voice rose slightly. "What kind of security consulting requires private conversations with female guests?"

"The kind that ensures guest safety," Lock said evenly. "We're documenting any incidents or concerns that might affect our recommendations."

"What incidents? What concerns?" Samir moved closer to Nikki, his hand finding her shoulder in a gesture that came off as more possessive than protective.

"They were asking about Harper," Nikki said.

"Harper?" Samir's confusion was genuine. "Why would they care about Harper?"

"Just checking some routine documentation," Ty said. "Guest departure procedures, transport coordination. Making sure protocols are being followed."

Samir studied them both, his earlier aggression giving way to uncertainty. Lock could see him processing the situation—two professional men with serious demeanors, asking legitimate-sounding questions about resort operations. The kind of people who might actually have authority here.

"How long will this take?" Samir said, still suspicious but less confrontational.

"We're finished for tonight," Lock said, standing. "Ms. Bailey, thank you for your time. If you think of anything else about your friend's departure, please let us know."

He handed her a business card—one of the resort's internal contact cards with his room number written on the back as well as his private cell number.

"Of course," Nikki said, accepting the card.

"We appreciate your cooperation," Ty said to Samir. "Apologies for interrupting your evening."

Samir nodded stiffly, but didn't move to show them out. Lock could feel the tension radiating from him, jealousy and suspicion mixing with wounded pride.

"Oh," Samir said as they reached the door. "I should mention—we'll be leaving the island tomorrow. Taking a friend's yacht for a few days. So if you need anything else..."

"Noted," Lock said. "Enjoy your trip."

Outside the villa, Lock and Ty walked in silence until they were well away from the building.

"She's holding back," Ty said.

"I got that too," Lock said.

"You catch what he said about the yacht?"

"Tomorrow. Convenient timing."

Nikki faced Samir's anger with practiced calm.

"I can't believe you," he said, pacing the living room like a caged animal. "First the pool, now this. What's next, inviting them to dinner?"

"They're consultants, Samir. They asked questions, I answered them. That's all."

"That's all?" He stopped pacing, turned to face her. "The same guy who was checking you out at the pool shows up at our villa asking about your missing friend, and you think that's normal?"

"Harper isn't missing. She left."

"Then why are they asking questions about her?"

Nikki moved closer to him, letting her dress catch the light in ways she knew would distract him. "Because they're thorough. Because they're good at their job. Because someone's paying them a lot of money to make sure this place is safe."

She reached up, straightened his collar with gentle fingers. "The yacht will be ready tomorrow?"

The change of subject caught him off-guard. "Yes. James confirmed it this afternoon. Captain's preparing for our arrival."

"Good." She kissed his cheek, tasting cologne and lingering anger. "I can't wait to get away from here. Just the two of us."

CHAPTER
FORTY

"GENTLEMEN."

Ethan Efron appeared beside their table, moving quietly. Lock looked up from his omelet while Ty paused mid-bite through a stack of pancakes that would have fed a small family. Around them on the breakfast terrace, other guests maintained the careful distance of people who valued their privacy above social interaction.

Efron wore pressed khakis and a polo shirt, but something about his manner suggested urgency beneath the casual clothes.

"Mind if I join you?" he said, already pulling out a chair.

"Please," Lock said, gesturing with his fork.

Efron sat, declining the server's offer of coffee with a wave. "I hope you're finding everything satisfactory with your assessment."

"Very thorough operation," Ty said. "Professional staff, quality equipment. The Barzanis should be pleased."

"About that." Efron leaned forward slightly. "I've just received word from one of our most important clients in Dubai. There's been a development that requires immediate consultation and as you can tell, with Dave elsewhere, I can't be spared."

Lock set down his fork, full attention on Efron. "What kind of development?"

"Crown Prince Khalid bin Abdul Rahman has received credible

threats against his family. His security team is requesting emergency consultation from independent experts." Efron carried practiced urgency. "The situation is... time-sensitive."

"How time-sensitive?" Lock said.

"They're requesting your presence within forty-eight hours. Preferably sooner."

Lock and Ty exchanged a look.

"Our presence?" Ty said.

"You're the experts and you're close to hand," Efron explained.

"We appreciate the referral," Lock said carefully. "But we have a contractual obligation to complete our assessment here first."

"Of course. And normally I'd insist you fulfill that obligation completely." Efron's smile was understanding, reasonable. "But in this case, the Crown Prince's situation takes precedence. Royal family security trumps resort consulting."

"Our assessment is barely half complete," Ty said. "Maritime surveillance, guest protection protocols, emergency response systems—we've only scratched the surface."

"I understand your concerns. But sometimes circumstances require flexibility." Efron applied gentle pressure. "The Barzanis are willing to consider your preliminary findings sufficient, given the urgency of the situation."

Lock sipped his coffee, buying time to think. "What exactly are we supposed to tell the Crown Prince's people? That we abandoned our current assignment halfway through?"

"That you prioritized a life-threatening emergency over routine consulting." Efron's tone sharpened almost imperceptibly. "They'll be very appreciative."

"Maybe. But our reputation depends on thorough, complete assessments. We don't do half-measures."

"Even when lives are at stake?"

Lock felt the conversation shifting, pressure building beneath Efron's diplomatic language. "Especially then. Incomplete intelligence gets people killed."

Efron sat back, studying them both. Something had changed in his manner—the helpful facade cracking to reveal calculation underneath.

"Mr. Lock, let me be direct. The Barzanis are your clients. They're satisfied with your work to date and willing to release you from further obligations. The Saudi contract represents significant future business for your firm." His words carried new authority. "Sometimes good business means knowing when to be flexible."

"And sometimes it means knowing when to be thorough," Lock replied. "We've identified several areas that require deeper analysis."

"Such as?"

"Discrepancies in departure documentation. Transport manifests that don't align with guest records. The kind of gaps that could compromise security or create liability issues."

Efron's eyes hardened. "Those are administrative matters. Clerical errors. Nothing that affects operational security."

"We won't know that until we complete our analysis."

"Mr. Lock." Efron's politeness was fraying. "I'm trying to accommodate your standards while managing urgent competing priorities. The Crown Prince is a close personal friend of the Barzanis. His situation requires immediate attention. With that in mind we are willing to compensate you fully for abbreviated services. Everyone wins."

"Except the next consultant who has to explain why our assessment was incomplete," Ty said. "Or the insurance investigators or guests who want to know why certain procedures weren't properly documented."

Efron turned his attention to Ty. "Mr. Johnson, you're former military. You understand operational priorities. Sometimes you have to choose between perfect intelligence and immediate action."

Ty straightened up. "That's combat. This is consulting. We have time to do the job right."

"Do you?" Efron leaned forward again, dropping his voice. "Because I'm not sure how much time any of us have."

The words hung between them, ambiguous but threatening. Lock felt the shift from disagreement to something more serious.

"Are you suggesting there's some urgency we're not aware of?" Lock said.

"I'm suggesting that the Crown Prince's security team doesn't like to wait. And neither do the Barzanis when it comes to accommodating valued friends." Efron stood, his movements controlled but tense. "I'll need your decision by this afternoon."

"Our decision about what?"

"Whether you're departing for Dubai tonight, or whether I need to explain to very important people why two consultants think their routine assessment is more critical than a royal family's safety."

Lock stood as well, matching Efron's height. "The decision isn't ours to make. We have a contract with the Barzanis. If they want to terminate it early that's their call."

"They're making that call now. Through me."

"I need to get it from them. In writing." Lock's manner was pleasant but unyielding. "I'll include it in our report."

Efron's smile was cold. "Of course. I understand."

He turned to leave, then paused. "One more thing. For your own safety, I'd recommend staying in the main resort areas today. We're conducting some training exercises that might involve live ammunition. Wouldn't want any accidents."

The threat was subtle but unmistakable. Lock nodded acknowledgment. "Appreciate the heads-up."

After Efron left, Lock and Ty sat in silence for several minutes.

"Well that was…" Ty paused, trailing off.

"Suspicious?" Lock offered.

"I was gonna say weird, but that too," Ty said.

"Any ideas why they want us gone?" Lock's smile was dry.

Ty looked up, like he was giving it serious consideration and didn't want to rush his answer.

"I have a couple of hunches," he said, throwing down his napkin.

Lock rose alongside him. "Guess we'd better get back to work before they throw us off this island."

CHAPTER
FORTY-ONE

LOCK WAS REVIEWING security footage on his laptop in their quarters when the soft knock came. He glanced at Ty, who shrugged and moved to answer the door.

Nikki Bailey stood in the hallway, looking like she'd barely slept. Gone was the polished woman from the night before—this version wore jeans and a simple t-shirt, her hair pulled back in a ponytail.

"Ms. Bailey," Ty said. "Everything alright?"

"I need to talk to you. Both of you." She glanced down the hallway.

Lock closed his laptop, gestured her inside. Their quarters were basic but clean—two beds, a small sitting area, a kitchenette. Most importantly, no surveillance. They'd swept the rooms themselves the first night, finding them refreshingly free of electronic monitoring.

Nikki took the offered chair but didn't relax into it. She perched on the edge like she might need to run.

"I heard you guys had been asked to leave early," she said.

"Word travels fast," Lock said.

"You said you were independent consultants," she continued. "That you don't work for the Barzanis."

"That's right," Lock said.

"And you're investigating discrepancies in guest departures."

"Among other things."

She took a breath, decision made. "Harper never left the island."

The words hung in the air.

"According to the manifests—" Ty began.

"The manifests are lies." Nikki's voice was flat, certain. "Harper is still here. Hiding."

"Hiding from what?"

"From them. From what happened." Nikki's hands twisted in her lap. "That dinner with Drexler. The German industrialist."

Lock felt the connection forming. "What happened?"

"He tried to rape her."

The words came out stark, unvarnished. Nikki's composure cracked slightly before she rebuilt it.

"She fought him off. Hurt him badly enough that they had to medical-evac him to Dubai." Nikki looked between them. "That's why he really left. Not heart problems. Harper nearly killed him defending herself."

"How do you know this?"

"Because I've seen her and she told me about it."

Lock leaned forward. "Why didn't she go to the authorities?"

Nikki's laugh was bitter. "What authorities? Efron's people? The local police who take their orders from the Barzanis? She knew they'd cover it up, make her disappear."

"So she ran."

Nikki's voice dropped to a whisper. "She's been in the jungle ever since. Wounded, scared, trying to figure out how to get off the island alive."

Ty sat heavily on the bed. "The body our guys found. We thought that might—"

"That was another girl. Who knows what happened to her." Nikki's eyes blazed. "But Harper's alive, and she's trapped, and I'm the only person who knows where she is."

Lock processed the implications. Villa Nine's "renovation." Efron's carefully prepared story about the floating body. The pressure to conclude their assessment early.

"They're covering up a rape," he said.

"Bad for business," Ty said grimly.

Nikki stood, faced them directly. "I need your help."

"What kind of help?"

"Samir arranged to borrow his friend's yacht. Two hundred feet, full crew. It's our way off this island."

"Samir doesn't know about Harper?"

"He can't know. He'd panic, try to call security, probably get me killed." Nikki's voice was steady but urgent. "I need help getting Harper from her hiding place to the yacht without anyone noticing."

Lock studied her face. "That's a big risk. For people you barely know."

"You're the only people on this island who don't work for them. The only ones who might actually give a damn about stopping this."

Lock thought it over for a New York minute.

"Where is she?" he asked.

Relief crossed Nikki's features. "There's an old research station about two miles inland. Abandoned for years, completely overgrown. She's been staying there, but it's not safe long-term."

Ty looked at Lock. "Efron's going to notice if we disappear for hours."

"So? Fuck that guy," Lock said before turning back to Nikki. "What's your timeline?"

CHAPTER
FORTY-TWO

LOCK SPREAD their equipment across the bed, methodically checking each item. GPS unit with fresh batteries and downloaded topographical maps. Compact Steiner binoculars, rubberized and waterproof. SureFire tactical flashlight with red filter for night work. Individual first aid kit—tourniquet, Israeli bandage, chest seals. Nothing overtly military, nothing that would seem out of place for security consultants conducting a site assessment.

Ty worked through his own gear at the other bed. They'd done this in worse places—Afghanistan, Iraq, Mexico City. The routine was automatic while their minds processed the real problem.

"It's maybe two miles?" Nikki said from her perch on the room's single chair. She'd been talking for ten minutes, sketching rough maps on hotel stationery, her hands trembling slightly. "I'm not good with distances. It took me more than an hour to walk there, but I was being careful. And it was dark."

"What kind of building?" Lock said, not looking up from his equipment.

"Old, concrete. Harper said it used to be for studying coral or fish or something. Marine biology?" She twisted her hands in her lap. "It's all overgrown now. Vines everywhere. If you didn't know to look for it..."

"How do we find it?" Ty said.

"There are these three dead palm trees. They're white, like skeletons. In a sort of triangle?" Nikki wavered. "God, this sounds insane. I should have paid more attention, but I was so scared someone would follow me."

"It's okay, you're doing great," Lock said. "What else?"

"From the palms, you go..." She closed her eyes, trying to remember. "Northeast? I think northeast. Harper gave me a compass bearing but I can't remember exactly. Two hundred and something meters?"

"What's between here and there?"

"Jungle. Just... jungle." Nikki's laugh had an edge of hysteria. "There's a path at first. The maintenance guys use it, I think. But then it just stops and you have to push through all these plants and vines."

Lock secured the knife inside his waistband, adjusting his shirt to cover it. "Did you see any security?"

"I don't know. Maybe? I heard things." She wrapped her arms around herself. "Every sound made me think someone was following me. There's this dried-up stream halfway there. I remember that because I almost fell climbing down into it."

"How deep?"

"I don't know. Six feet? My shoes got all muddy." She looked at them desperately. "What if I'm remembering wrong? What if you can't find it? Harper's counting on me and I—"

"We'll find it," Lock said firmly. "What does the building look like?"

"There's this big metal tank on the roof. For water, I guess? It's all rusty and falling apart on one side." She dropped her voice. "Harper made a joke about tetanus when she showed it to me. She was trying to be brave but I could tell she was terrified."

"How was she?" Ty said. "Physically."

"Her feet were all cut up from running through the jungle barefoot. And her wrists..." Nikki's eyes filled with tears. "Purple bruises, I guess from where he held her down. She kept saying she was fine but I could see her limping. I left all the medical supplies I could find but I don't know if it's enough."

"When did you last see her?"

"Yesterday afternoon. I told her about the yacht, about Samir's friend. She actually smiled." The tears spilled over now. "She said just one more day. One more day and this nightmare would be over. I promised her. I promised I'd get her out."

The door burst open with enough force to bounce off the wall. Samir stood in the doorway, his face flushed with irritation and something else—suspicion, maybe. His shirt showed sweat stains despite the air conditioning.

"There you are," he said to Nikki, carrying accusation. "I've been looking everywhere. Reception said they saw you come this way."

Nikki's face went white. "I was just—"

"Asking about sunset helicopter tours," Lock cut in smoothly, standing to face Samir. Professional consultant, helpful but not overly friendly. "For after your yacht trip. We offer security assessments for various tour operators. Ms. Bailey was inquiring about which companies the resort recommends."

Samir's gaze shifted between them, processing. Lock could see him weighing the explanation, looking for deception. The kind of jealous boyfriend who saw threats everywhere, probably with good reason given the nature of this place.

"Helicopter tours," Samir repeated flatly.

"I thought... maybe when we get back?" Nikki sounded small, uncertain. "Something fun to look forward to?"

"We won't be back for days. Maybe weeks." Samir suggested this wasn't the first time he'd reminded her. "The yacht has a helicopter. If you want aerial tours, we can arrange them from there."

"Oh. Right. I forgot." Nikki stood, unsteady on her feet. "I'm sorry. I'm just... excited about the trip."

"Clearly." Samir held out his hand, a gesture that looked romantic but carried command. "Come on. You have to pack, and I had the kitchen prepare that seared tuna you like. We should go over the sailing itinerary."

Nikki took his hand carefully. As Samir turned to lead her out, she looked back at Lock, her eyes full of fear—for Harper, for herself, for what might happen if they failed.

Lock gave her the slightest nod—message received, they'd handle it.

The door closed behind them.

"That's going to be a problem," Ty said.

"Already is." Lock resumed his equipment check, mind calculating adjustments. "She won't be able to get away again. He'll watch her like a hawk until they leave."

Lock checked his watch. "Let's go."

They made their way to the security office, footsteps echoing on the polished marble floors. The resort's public areas maintained their facade of tropical luxury—potted palms, original artwork, discrete staff who appeared and disappeared like ghosts.

The security office occupied a corner of the administrative building, its windows tinted black from outside. Lock pushed through the door to find the duty officer, feet up on the desk, reading a two-month-old copy of a boxing magazine.

"Help you?" the duty officer said without looking up. British accent, Yorkshire maybe. Ex-military by his bearing, but long enough out to have developed a paunch. For sure a Big Dave hire, so not to be judge by appearances.

"Perimeter assessment," Lock said, signing the log with practiced efficiency. "Follow-up on last night's breach points."

That got the man's attention. He swung his feet down, suddenly professional. "Oh yeah, I heard about that Red Team business. Made them look like a proper bunch of Charlies."

"Happens to everyone eventually," Ty said.

The duty officer slid over an equipment checkout form. "What do you need?"

Lock made a show of considering. "Thermal monocular for gap analysis. Maybe one of the small drones for overhead surveillance."

"Drone's good thinking," the duty officer said, fetching the equipment from a locked cabinet. "Jungle's too thick for satellite imagery. We've got some decent kit—DJI Mavic, modified for tropical conditions. Twenty-minute flight time, thermal capability."

"Perfect." Lock signed for the equipment, noting the serial numbers. Everything by the book. "Any particular areas of concern?"

"Eastern sectors showed gaps in coverage. Red Team came in from the water, but they could have just as easily penetrated from inland." The duty officer leaned back, warming to the topic. "If I were assessing, I'd start with the maintenance trails, work my way out. See how far someone could get before triggering an alert."

"Noted," Lock said.

CHAPTER
FORTY-THREE

LOCK LED them east along the maintenance trail, the drone case slung over his shoulder. The path was wide enough for a small vehicle, hard-packed dirt showing recent tire tracks from grounds crew.

"We probably shouldn't be doing this," Ty said, voice low despite the empty trail.

"Definitely not."

"Contractual obligations. Professional boundaries. Sticking to the assigned mission. Not getting killed in some third-world shithole." Ty ducked under a low-hanging branch. "Ringing any bells?"

"All the bells."

They moved in silence for another fifty meters. The jungle pressed in from both sides, thick vegetation that could hide anything. Places where visibility dropped to under ten feet.

"She's twenty-two," Lock said finally.

"They're all twenty-two. Or nineteen. Or twenty-five." Ty's voice carried no judgment. "World's full of young women making bad decisions with worse men."

"This is different."

"I know," said Ty. "If it was me I'd have dropped that fat German fuck out of that medevac bird. Let the sharks deal with him."

The trail narrowed ahead, maintenance access giving way to a footpath barely wide enough for single file. Lock checked his watch again. Even if they found Harper immediately, extracted her without incident, and made it back to the resort, they'd be cutting it close.

"What's the play when we find her?" Ty said. "Assuming she's where Nikki thinks. Assuming she hasn't rabbited again. Assuming she doesn't brain us with a rock thinking we're Efron's people."

"We explain Nikki sent us. Get her mobile. Bring her back."

"Just like that?"

"Just like that."

"And when Efron asks how we happened to find a missing woman in the jungle during our routine perimeter assessment?"

Lock paused at a fork in the trail. Left continued along the maintained path. Right disappeared into heavier vegetation. According to Nikki's map, they needed to go right.

"We tell him the truth," Lock said. "Or part of it. We found her during our assessment. She's injured, confused. We rendered aid."

"He won't buy it."

"He doesn't have to buy it. He just has to accept it." Lock pushed into the heavier vegetation. "What's he going to do? Admit they lost a guest then changed the records to say she'd left? Explain why they didn't report her missing? Open that whole can of worms?"

"He could make us disappear too."

Lock stopped, turned to face Ty. "He could try."

They moved deeper into the jungle, the temperature climbing despite the shade. Sweat soaked through Lock's shirt within minutes. The undergrowth grabbed at their clothes, every step requiring effort. This wasn't a nature walk—this was hostile terrain that didn't want visitors.

Lock stopped every hundred meters to listen and check their six. No signs of pursuit yet, but that meant nothing. In vegetation this thick, someone could be twenty feet behind them and remain invisible.

"Movement," Ty whispered.

Lock froze, following Ty's gaze. Thirty meters ahead, a figure in resort security khakis moved perpendicular to their path. Single man, rifle slung casual, cigarette smoke drifting up through the canopy.

They eased behind a cluster of palm fronds, waiting. The guard moved with the lazy confidence of routine patrol—not hunting, just walking his assigned grid. He passed without looking their way, the sound of his movement fading toward the north.

"Expanded patrols," Lock murmured.

They resumed movement, more careful now. The dried creek bed appeared after another ten minutes of hard pushing through undergrowth. Just as Nikki described—a six-foot depression carved by seasonal floods, banks steep enough to require careful climbing.

Lock went first, boot-sliding down the loose earth. The bottom was damp clay, boot prints already marking the surface. Multiple sets, all fresh. Someone else had crossed here recently.

"Company," Ty observed, studying the tracks. "Three, maybe four. Within the last few hours."

"Harper?"

"One set's smaller. Could be." Ty pointed to a scuff mark on the far bank. "Someone slipped climbing out. Grabbed that root for support."

They crossed quickly, hauling themselves up the opposite bank. Lock checked his GPS—half a mile to go. They were losing time with every delay.

The vegetation seemed thicker on this side of the creek. Visibility down to fifteen feet, sometimes less. Every tree could hide an observer. Every sound might be a threat. Lock's shirt clung to him like a second skin, the humidity making each breath feel heavy.

They pushed on, following Nikki's vague directions as best they could. Northeast from the dead palms, she'd said. Two hundred and something meters. In terrain this dense, that covered a lot of ground. A lot of places for someone to hide. A lot of places for someone to die.

CHAPTER
FORTY-FOUR

ETHAN EFRON STOOD before the bank of monitors in the security control room, watching the feed from Camera 47-E go dark. The maintenance trail, eastern sector. Right where Lock and Johnson had been thirty seconds ago.

"They're in the dead zone," the operator said from his station. "Lost visual as soon as they pushed into the heavy vegetation."

"Expected." Efron kept his voice neutral, but his jaw tightened. Two professionals conducting a routine assessment didn't deviate into the jungle. They stayed on marked paths, checked sightlines, documented vulnerabilities. They didn't vanish into the green.

"Should I dispatch a team?"

"No." Efron turned from the monitors. "Get a drone up. Thermal imaging. Let's see if we can find them."

"Yes, sir."

Efron moved to his desk, where a manila folder lay open. Glossy prints spread across the surface, each one timestamped and tagged with camera positions. He picked up the first—Ty Johnson at the pool, 0600 hours, deep in conversation with Nikki Bailey.

The second photo showed Lock at the bar with Astrid, the Norwegian model. Surface reading suggested normal guest interaction, but

Efron knew better. Lock had been mining for information, and Astrid—gossip that she was—had probably delivered.

The third image made him pause. Lock and Johnson talking to Nikki Bailey and Samir Patel.

"Sir?" An aide appeared at the door. "Drone's ready to launch."

"Then launch it." Efron's voice carried an edge that made the aide step back.

Dave Carter had vouched for these two. Called them thorough professionals. Reliable. Discrete.

Efron picked up the photos, studying each one again. Boy scouts, more like. The kind of men who couldn't leave well enough alone.

CHAPTER
FORTY-FIVE

LOCK PUSHED through a curtain of vines, sweat burning his eyes. The jungle fought their progress every step of the way. It had them ducking under branches, untangling from thorny creepers, testing ground that might give way to hidden holes.

The GPS showed them on course, but technology felt inadequate against the raw terrain.

"Hold up," Ty whispered.

Lock froze, following Ty's gaze. Twenty meters ahead, a flash of white against the endless green. They moved forward carefully, and the shapes resolved into three dead palms, their bleached trunks standing like monuments in the living jungle. Triangle formation, exactly as Nikki had described.

"Girl might not know distances," Ty said quietly, "but she got this right."

Lock took a compass bearing. Northeast, into thicker jungle. The canopy overhead was so dense it felt like dusk despite the hour.

They moved in tactical spacing, five meters apart. Close enough to support each other, far enough that one burst wouldn't take them both. Every twenty or so meters they stopped, listened, checked their six. The silence was oppressive—no bird calls, no monkey chatter. Just the buzz of insects and their own controlled breathing.

Lock paused at a massive mahogany tree, buttressed roots giving them natural concealment. He took a knee, catching his breath while scanning their surroundings. The air was thick with humidity, condensing on every surface. His shirt was plastered to his skin, and he could feel the beginnings of heat rash where his belt rubbed.

"You good?" Ty asked, barely winded despite the conditions.

"Never felt better." Lock took a pull from his water bottle, the liquid warm as blood. He capped the bottle, stood. "Let's keep moving."

They pressed on. The terrain began to undulate, hidden ravines and sudden rises that the GPS couldn't predict. Lock's ankle turned on a hidden root, sending a spike of pain up his leg. He caught himself on a tree trunk, hand coming away sticky with sap.

The first signs of human passage appeared ten minutes past the palms. A broken branch at shoulder height, fresh enough that sap still wept from the break. Lock examined it closely—clean break, not the ragged tear of wind damage. Someone had pushed through here, moving fast enough to snap the vegetation.

"Got tracks," Ty called softly.

Lock joined him at a muddy depression where water collected during rains. Boot prints, military tread pattern, size ten or eleven. The edges were sharp, undegraded by time or weather. Recent.

"Security patrol," Ty murmured, examining the tracks. "Maybe six hours old. Two men, moving with purpose."

They adjusted course slightly, paralleling the patrol route rather than crossing it. No point walking into contact they didn't need. Lock's mind worked through the implications. Regular patrols this deep in the jungle meant they were protecting something. Or hunting someone.

The ground began to rise more steeply. They had to use trees to pull themselves up muddy slopes, boots struggling for purchase. At the crest of one rise, Lock paused to check their position. According to the GPS, they should be close. But the jungle revealed nothing, green walls in every direction.

"Hear that?" Ty asked.

Lock stilled his breathing, listened. There—a metallic tick, like cooling metal. Then nothing. They waited, counting seconds. The sound came again, followed by a faint whir.

"Drone," Lock said.

They pressed against the largest tree they could find, using its bulk to break up their heat signatures. The sound grew louder, more distinct.

Through a gap in the canopy, Lock caught a glimpse of it. Matte black against the green, maybe two feet across. The gimbal-mounted camera pod swept back and forth in a search pattern. Thermal imaging, from the look of the lens configuration.

"Grid search," Ty observed.

"Looking for us?"

"Or her."

The drone passed overhead, continuing west. They waited another full minute before moving, knowing it could circle back at any moment.

They pushed forward with new urgency. The jungle began to thin slightly, larger gaps between the trees. Through the vegetation ahead, Lock caught a glimpse of something angular, unnatural. Concrete.

He held up a fist, stopping Ty. They crouched in the undergrowth, studying what lay ahead. The research station squatted in a small clearing like something from a documentary about lost civilizations. Single story, poured concrete construction designed to survive hurricanes. The jungle had been working to reclaim it for decades, vines and creepers turning walls into vertical gardens.

"Water tank," Ty pointed out.

Lock followed his gesture. On the roof, a large metal tank tilted at a dangerous angle, half-collapsed as Nikki had described. Rust had eaten through the supports, and it looked like a strong wind might bring the whole thing down.

They circled wide, staying in the tree line. Standard approach to an unknown structure—observe before committing. The clearing around the station had been maintained, someone had hacked away the worst of the undergrowth recently. Machete marks on cut vegetation, some wilting but not yet brown. Days old, not weeks.

"No movement," Ty reported from his position.

They completed their circuit, identifying exits and potential threats. Main door facing the clearing, a rear service entrance almost hidden by vines. The windows were gone, openings covered by crude barriers—corrugated metal, wooden planks, even what looked like an old tarp. Someone had worked to make this place habitable.

Lock pointed to the main entrance. Ty nodded, understanding the plan without words. Cover and move, standard entry protocol. Even though they expected to find Harper inside, assumptions could be fatal. Better to treat every building as potentially hostile until proven otherwise.

Lock moved first, quick and low across the clearing. The door hung open, rust eating through its hinges. Fresh scratches in the rust showed it had been operated recently. He pressed against the wall beside the opening, listening. No voices, no movement, no breathing. Just the buzz of insects and the distant drone returning on its pattern.

He pivoted into the doorway, checking corners as his eyes adjusted to the darker interior. Concrete floor swept clear of major debris. Makeshift furniture—a table fashioned from an old door laid across concrete blocks, chairs made from broken crates.

"Clear," he called softly.

Ty flowed past him, taking the left side of the room while Lock took right. They moved with practiced efficiency, weapons out now despite the pretense of being consultants. The main room told a story in scattered objects. Water bottles on the table, condensation still beading on the plastic. Food wrappers in a neat pile, organized by type. Medical supplies arranged on a shelf—bandages, antibiotics, antiseptic. A sleeping bag in the corner, unzipped and twisted as if someone had left it in a hurry.

"She was just here," Ty said, examining the medical supplies.

Lock moved to the makeshift medical station. Bloody bandages in a small trash pile, the blood still damp, not the rust-brown of old stains. Packaging from antiseptic wipes torn open with desperate haste. Someone had been treating injuries, and recently. He could smell the antiseptic, sharp against the jungle's organic decay.

A scuff from the back room made them both spin, weapons tracking. Lock moved forward, Ty covering. The doorway led to a smaller space, probably once storage or equipment room. More supplies here—canned food stacked against one wall, bottled water, a first aid kit that had been thoroughly raided. The organization spoke of someone trying to maintain control in chaos.

On the floor, a clear impression in the dust where someone had been sitting. The outline of legs, the scuff marks of repeated movement. Beside it, dark spots on the concrete. Blood, from the color and pattern. Someone had sat here, tending wounds, planning their next move.

"Check this," Ty said from the doorway.

Lock joined him, looking where he pointed. Fresh footprints in the dust leading to the rear exit. Smaller than the patrol boots they'd seen earlier, with an unusual pattern. No tread—these were bare feet. The prints showed detail, individual toes visible in the dust. The left foot dragged slightly, suggesting injury or exhaustion.

"She went out the back," Ty said. "Maybe five, ten minutes ago. Fifteen at most."

They moved to the rear exit. The door had been forced from inside, lock mechanism torn completely free. It hung at an angle, still swinging slightly. Lock caught it, stopped the motion. She'd hit this hard, desperation overcoming caution.

Beyond the door, the jungle pressed in immediately. But the signs were clear—broken branches at hip height, crushed plants, a clear line through the undergrowth where someone had bulled through without care for concealment.

"East," Lock said, reading the signs. "She's heading straight east."

"Running or moving with purpose?"

Lock studied the pattern of disturbance. The broken vegetation showed someone moving fast, crashing through rather than picking a path. A scuff mark where someone had slipped, grabbing a tree for support. Leaves torn from branches at face height.

"Running. Full panic mode." Lock pointed to a smear on a tree trunk. "Blood. Her feet are getting worse."

The drone's sound returned, much closer now. Through the station's missing roof sections, Lock glimpsed it hovering almost directly overhead. The camera pod rotated slowly, methodically. It had found something interesting and was documenting it. How long before that information reached Efron? How long before ground teams arrived?

"We need to move," Ty said.

"If we pursue, we confirm Efron's suspicions."

"If we don't, his ground teams find her first." Ty met his eyes. "Your call, boss."

Lock thought about the bloody bandages, the bare footprints, the desperation implied in that hasty exit. A young woman, injured and terrified, running through hostile terrain. Running because of them, most likely. Their arrival had spooked her into fleeing whatever safety the station provided.

"We go after her," Lock decided. "Quick and quiet. Find her before—"

Voices. Distant but distinct. Multiple speakers, the cadence of military movement. Radio squelch cutting through the jungle sounds. Efron's ground team, vectored in by the drone.

"Three minutes out," Ty estimated. "Maybe less."

"Back door. Now."

They exited fast, plunging into the jungle on Harper's trail. The signs were impossible to miss—she'd abandoned any attempt at concealment in favor of speed. Broken branches marked her passage like blazes on a trail. Deep footprints in soft earth showed where she'd stumbled, fallen, pushed herself back up. Smears of blood on leaves at waist height where she'd used vegetation for support.

Lock pushed the pace, knowing they were racing multiple clocks. The yacht departure, the approaching security team, and Harper's diminishing endurance. She couldn't maintain this pace for long, not with injured feet and days of accumulated exhaustion.

Harper's breath came in ragged gasps as she crashed through the undergrowth. Every step sent lightning through her cut feet, but stopping meant capture. The drone had changed everything. That mechanical whine cutting through the jungle sounds could mean only one thing—they'd found her.

She'd been rationing her last bottle of water when she'd heard it. The sound had grown louder, closer, until it seemed to hover directly overhead. Then voices, muffled by distance but unmistakably human. Coming from the west, the direction of the resort.

Fear had overridden pain. She'd grabbed what she could—water, the knife Nikki had left, a handful of protein bars. No time for anything else. The voices were getting closer, and she could hear the rustle of equipment, the metallic click of weapons.

The back door had resisted at first, rust and humidity sealing it shut. She'd thrown her shoulder against it, feeling something tear in the mechanism. On the third impact it had given way, spilling her into the jungle.

Now she ran without thought or plan. East, always east, because that was away from the resort, away from the men who wanted her silenced. The jungle fought her, demanding payment for passage in cuts and scrapes. Her feet, already raw from two days of barefoot travel, left red prints on leaves and rocks.

Behind her, she could hear pursuit. Heavy bodies moving fast, breaking through the same vegetation she'd just passed. They were following her trail, and she was leaving plenty for them to follow. No energy for evasion, no skill for concealment. All she had was fear and the will to keep moving.

The ground began to rise, then suddenly fell away. She stumbled down a rocky slope, feet skidding on loose stones. Her ankle turned, sending her sprawling. She tasted dirt and blood, pushed herself up. Always up, always forward.

The vegetation was changing, thick jungle giving way to something sparser. Through the remaining trees, she could see open sky. The sound that had been background noise suddenly clarified itself— waves. Ocean waves against rock. She was running toward the coast, toward the same cliffs she'd jumped from nights ago.

But this was different terrain, unknown. The cliffs here could be twenty feet or two hundred. The water below could be deep and safe or shallow and deadly. She didn't know, couldn't know. All she knew was that the sounds of pursuit were getting closer.

Her foot caught on an exposed root, sending her flying. She hit hard, breath exploding from her lungs. For a moment she lay still, body refusing to respond to the desperate commands of her brain. Get up. Move. Run.

She found her knife, the weight of it reassuring. If they caught her, she wouldn't go quietly. Not again. Never again.

She pushed to her feet, weaving like a drunk. The tree line was just ahead, and beyond that, the sound of ocean. Freedom or death, but either was better than letting them take her back.

The jungle ended abruptly. One moment she was pushing through the last of the vegetation, the next she was on open ground. Volcanic rock, black and sharp, stretched toward a horizon that was suddenly, terrifyingly close. The ocean spread before her, endless and blue, but between her and that blue was nothing but air.

Her left foot slipped on the volcanic stone, sending her stumbling toward the edge.

CHAPTER
FORTY-SIX

LOCK BURST from the tree line onto volcanic rock that cut through his boot soles. The terrain angled toward a horizon that ended in empty air. Fifty meters ahead, Harper struggled to regain her footing, her left foot sliding on the treacherous surface.

No more broken girls. Not here. Not now.

That was Lock's promise. A promise he'd sworn to keep, no matter what. If he had to kill, that's exactly what he'd do. No hesitation. No mercy.

But right now, the island's security team wasn't the issue. His issue was Harper Holt standing at the cliff edge, threatening to jump.

Twenty feet away, he watched as she backed up and her left foot slipped on the blood-slicked rock. One wrong step and she'd be gone.

"I'm not bluffing," Harper said. "I'll do it."

A few feet behind her was the cliff face. A sheer drop. Rocks below. Beyond the rocks, ocean. The sound of waves against stone carried up from the darkness, steady and final.

Lock took a step back, palms visible. "I believe you."

"Sure you do."

"We don't work for these people." Lock kept his voice level, non-threatening. Behind him, he sensed Ty adjusting position slightly, ready but not aggressive. Years of partnership had taught them to move as one unit.

"Liar," Harper said, the knife in her right hand catching the afternoon sun.

"On my daughter's life." Lock let the words hang in the salt air. "We're security consultants hired to assess the island. I'm Ryan. This is my business partner, Ty."

Behind him the towering African-American retired Marine offered up a curt nod. Lock caught Harper's eyes flick between them, reading their body language, their positioning. She was scared but not stupid.

"I get you're scared, and you have no reason to trust us, but we came to find you and get you out of here."

Lock read hesitation in Harper's eyes. She was wavering, her weight shifting from foot to foot on the bloodied stone. Should she believe him or not?

"I'd rather die than go back there," she said, almost losing her balance for a second. Her feet left bloody prints on the black rock as she shuffled backward.

"You won't have to," Lock told her. "You have my word. We're going to get you home."

"You have a daughter?"

"Sofia. She just turned four." The words came easier than expected. Lock felt something loosen in his chest, a crack in his professional armor. "She's back home with my wife in Los Angeles. She wants me to bring her back a stuffed tiger. Big Princess Jasmine fan." He paused, watching Harper's face soften slightly.

Her breathing slowed. She was tuned in now, actually listening.

Lock held up his hands, palms open. "One of the other girls told us where we could find you."

"Who?"

That was the question Lock had been hoping for. He passed it off for Ty to answer.

"Nikki Bailey," Ty said. "She told us what happened at Villa Nine. With Drexler."

As Ty started to speak he was cut off by three men emerging from the tree line behind them. Israeli security personnel in tactical gear, weapons at low ready. The three spread out, creating overlapping fields of fire. Professional, silent, lethal. Lock felt a familiar tightness in his shoulders, the automatic calculation of angles and distances.

"Mr. Lock," one of the men, presumably the team leader said. "Step away from the girl, please."

Lock didn't move. Beside him, Ty's hand drifted toward his weapon, the movement casual but deliberate. Lock caught the slight shift in Ty's stance, the almost imperceptible turn that would give him better shooting angles. They'd done this dance before.

"No can do," Lock said.

The team leader's weapon came up, not quite pointing at Lock but close enough to send a message. The barrel tracked with his movements, professional and controlled.

"This doesn't concern you," the team leader said.

"Injured young woman on resort property?" Lock smiled without humor. "I'd say that's exactly our concern."

Lock's hand moved, resting on the grip of his SIG Sauer. Beside him, Ty did the same. The message clear. Make a move and this gets ugly. Fast.

Two more Israeli security personnel emerged from the jungle, boots silent on the damp earth. Five total now, spreading into a half-circle. Lock felt Ty shift position slightly, improving his angles. Harper behind them had gone completely still, sensing the change in the air.

The team leader hesitated, weapon wavering slightly. Lock could see him running calculations, weighing odds. Five against two wasn't terrible numbers, but Lock and Ty weren't typical opposition. Their stance, their calm, their complete lack of concern about being outnumbered all spoke to experience that went beyond weekend warrior training.

"Let's all be cool. Why don't we start over?" the team leader said, first to blink.

"I'm perfectly cool," Lock said. "What about you, Ty?"

"Positively frosty," Ty said.

Back at the edge, Harper made a sound that was half sob, half laugh. "They're going to kill us."

Lock spoke to her. "Want to know something? I don't think they are." He took a beat. "I think they're going to lower their weapons, and then we're all going to walk back in like civilized people."

CHAPTER
FORTY-SEVEN

LOCK CARRIED HARPER through the jungle while the Israeli operatives maintained a loose perimeter around them. The security team knew the efficient routes back to the resort, but their weapons remained visible and their movements stayed tactical. Forty minutes of walking through hostile territory disguised as an escort brought them to the jungle's edge, where manicured resort grounds began and a crowd had gathered.

Guests in designer resort wear mixed with staff trying to maintain professional invisibility, all craning to see what emergency had disrupted their afternoon. The medical team waited with a gurney and trauma kit. Behind them, Lock spotted two figures who weren't quite so happy about this development. Amira Barzani stood rigid in her white linen suit. Patrick stepped forward.

"Everything's fine," Amira announced to the crowd, her smile bright and artificial. "One of our guests went hiking and got lost. Fortunately our security team found her."

"Nothing to see, folks," Patrick added.

Lock reached the medical team but didn't immediately transfer Harper. He wanted witnesses to see her condition—the bloody feet, the dehydration, the clear signs of days of survival.

"What's her status?" the lead medic asked.

"Severe lacerations to both feet," Ty reported. "Probable infection. Dehydration, exhaustion, possible mild hypothermia. She's been running on adrenaline for days."

"Wrist contusions consistent with defensive wounds," Lock added, making sure his voice carried. "She'll need full spectrum antibiotics, wound debridement, possibly surgical repair."

Now he transferred Harper to the gurney. She stirred, eyes focusing briefly.

"The yacht," she mumbled. "I need to get on the yacht."

"We'll handle it," Lock assured her.

The medical team began their work—IV line, vital signs, initial assessment. Professional and efficient, but Lock noticed how they avoided looking at Amira.

"Nikki!" Harper's voice, suddenly clear and desperate. "Where's Nikki?"

Nikki Bailey burst through the crowd, frantic, hair disheveled, mascara streaked. She'd obviously run here the moment she heard.

"Harper! Oh God, Harper!" She tried to reach the gurney but security stepped in.

"Let her through," Lock said quietly.

The security guard looked to Amira, who gave the slightest nod. Nikki rushed to Harper's side, grabbing her hand.

"I'm sorry," Harper whispered. "I'm so sorry. I tried to wait but—"

"Shh, it's okay. You're safe now." Nikki was crying openly. "We're going to get you out of here."

From the crowd's edge, Lock noticed Samir Patel watching. His expression was complex—confusion, anger, betrayal. He stared at Nikki holding Harper's hand, at the obvious connection between them. Lock could see the pieces falling into place in his mind.

Samir turned and walked away without a word.

"We need to move her," the lead medic announced. "She needs immediate treatment."

The gurney began rolling toward the medical facility. Nikki walked alongside, still holding Harper's hand. The crowd dispersed, but Lock knew the real drama was just beginning. Amira remained frozen, Patrick beside her, both watching their world show its first crack.

They reached the medical facility. Harper was whisked inside, Nikki at her side. Through the glass doors, Lock could see Amira on her phone, her gestures sharp. Patrick had disappeared.

"This isn't over," Ty observed.

"Not even close." Lock checked his watch. Nikki and Samir were due to depart for the yacht soon. "But we bought Harper some time. Made her visible."

"Think Efron really believes what you told him?"

Before their escort agreed to walk them back in, Lock had spoken with Efron. He had given the impression that any attempt to obstruct them would lead to the immediate release of an early report detailing everything he and Ty knew so far. It would include the dead body of a young woman washing up on the island and what had happened to Harper Holt. How she'd been offered up, against her will, to a sexual predator in the form of Ulrich Drexler.

"Doesn't matter what he believes. What matters is that he can't take the risk." Lock turned away from the medical facility. "Come on. We've got a security assessment to finish."

CHAPTER
FORTY-EIGHT

"YOU'RE STILL NOT PACKED?"

Nikki looked up from where she sat on the bed, her Louis Vuitton suitcase open but empty beside her. Samir stood in the doorway.

"No, not yet," she said.

"The yacht will be ready in two hours. The helicopter is here." He stepped into the room, closing the door behind him. "I thought you were excited about getting away."

"I am, but..." Nikki picked up a sundress, then set it down again. "Could we ask the captain to delay departure? Just a day or two?"

"Delay?" Samir moved to the minibar, poured himself a scotch. "Why would we want to delay? You've been talking about needing to get away, about how suffocating this place has become."

"Harper's in medical. I can't just leave. She needs me."

"Harper will be fine. The medical staff here are excellent." He sat on the bed's edge, watching her.

"We can't leave her here."

"Why not? She's receiving the care she needs. She'll recover."

"You don't understand—" Nikki stood up, began pacing. "It's not that simple."

"What are you saying, Nikki?"

"I'm not sure Harper's safe here. Not with resort security more concerned about protecting themselves and their guests' reputations."

Samir frowned. "You're being paranoid."

"Am I? Then why haven't the police been called so she can make a report about Drexler attacking her?"

"I don't know. I'm sure they'll get around to it."

"Get around to it?" Her voice came out harsher than she intended. "They've gone into damage control mode. And Harper is the damage."

"So what are you suggesting? That we kidnap Harper from the medical center?"

"I'm suggesting that when she's well enough, we take her with us. Get her somewhere safe, away from all this."

Samir set down his drink. "Nikki, we planned this trip for us. A romantic getaway. You said you needed time away from the resort, from all the drama—"

"I know what I said."

"Then why are you trying to turn it into a rescue mission?"

"Because my best friend was nearly killed!" The panic she'd been suppressing broke through. "Because I can't just sail away and leave her here alone with these people. Because if something happens to her while we're gone, I'll never forgive myself."

"Nothing's going to happen to her. You're catastrophizing."

"You don't know what these men are capable of. You don't know what it's like to be powerless in a place like this."

"And you do?"

The question hung in the air. Nikki realized she'd revealed more than she intended.

"I've seen what happens to girls who cross the wrong people," she said carefully.

"What girls? When?"

"It doesn't matter. What matters is getting Harper safely off this island."

"How?" Samir stood up. "Even if I agreed, how would we get her out of medical without authorization? Without proper discharge procedures?"

"That's why I needed Lock and Ty to find her. That's why I had to make sure you'd help get her off the island. Don't you see? The yacht isn't just for us. It's Harper's only way out."

The words escaped before she could stop them. Samir went very still.

"What did you say?"

Nikki felt the blood drain from her face. "I meant—"

When he spoke his voice was quiet, controlled. "You had to make sure I'd help. The yacht wasn't just for us."

"Samir—"

"Is this why you asked me about borrowing my friend's yacht?" He moved closer, studying her face.

She opened her mouth, then closed it.

"It's not that simple—"

"Isn't it?" His voice was getting louder. "You needed an escape route. I have a friend with a yacht. You needed someone naive enough to arrange it without asking too many questions. And there I was, so eager to impress the beautiful American girl."

"I wanted us to be together too. You know I do care about you."

"Care about me, or care about what I can do for you?" He laughed bitterly.

"That's not fair—"

"Fair?" Samir's composure cracked. "You want to talk about fair? I've been moving mountains for you, and you've been using me like some kind of, I don't know, some kind of travel agent."

"I never meant for you to get hurt—"

"But you knew I would be. Eventually." He grabbed his scotch, drained it. "Tell me something, Nikki. Was any of it real? The dinners, the conversations, the nights we spent together—was I ever anything more than a means to an end? Don't lie to me. Please."

Nikki felt tears threatening. "I don't know. Maybe at first, but then I got to know you—"

"Got to know me?" He slammed the glass down. "Or got to know what I could give you."

"That's not true—"

"Then why didn't you just ask me for help? Why the elaborate seduction?"

"Because I couldn't risk it!" The admission burst out of her. "Harper's life was at stake. I couldn't risk you saying no, or asking too many questions, or deciding it wasn't your problem."

"So instead you manipulated me?"

"I didn't mean to."

"Oh well, that's okay then." Samir moved toward the door. "You calculated exactly what you needed to do to get what you wanted. And it worked perfectly."

"Where are you going?"

"To think." He paused with his hand on the doorknob.

"Samir, please—"

"Please what? Please forgive you for playing me like a fool? Please pretend this was all some misunderstanding?"

"Please understand that I had no choice."

"You had a choice. You chose to lie to me rather than trust me." His voice was cold now. "You chose to manipulate my feelings rather than be honest."

"Would you have helped if I'd been honest?"

Samir stared at her, hurt. "I guess we'll never know now, will we?"

CHAPTER
FORTY-NINE

THE HELICOPTER'S downwash bent palm fronds as Lock and Ty waited at the resort's helipad. Lock's technical assessment team had finally arrived. A Bell 429, civilian markings but flying an approach pattern that suggested former military pilot. Lock checked his watch. His forensic tech team right on schedule.

Fifty meters away, near the departure lounge, Samir Patel stood with a woman who definitely wasn't Nikki Bailey. Natasha, if Lock remembered correctly from the guest manifests. She hung on Samir's arm, laughing at something he said. The body language told the whole story—Nikki was out, Natasha was in, and Samir was pretending he'd planned it that way.

"Trading up already," Lock observed.

"Trading down, definitely down," Ty corrected.

The helicopter touched down. Through the cabin windows, Lock counted four figures moving, gathering equipment. The side door slid open before the rotors stopped spinning.

The tech team lead emerged first—a compact Asian man Lock had worked with on three continents. Former NSA, now private sector where the pay matched the risk. Behind him, three more specialists, all carrying themselves like professionals.

"Ryan," the lead said. They'd worked together enough to skip pleasantries. "Where do you want us?"

"Conference Room B. Full sweep before we plug anything in."

"Copy that."

Lock watched them unload. Pelican cases with tamper seals. Military-spec hardened laptops. A compact antenna array that could do things the FCC didn't approve of. One case in particular drew his attention—thermal lidar system, the kind used to map buildings through walls.

From the upper terrace of the security building, Ethan Efron watched the equipment parade. His expression was neutral, but Lock noticed how his gaze lingered on each case, cataloging capabilities.

Samir and Natasha moved toward the helicopter as the last equipment case came off. The choreography was perfect—new arrivals deplaning, departing guests boarding. Samir paused at the helicopter door, glancing around the helipad. Looking for someone who wasn't there.

Natasha said something, tugging his arm. Samir allowed himself to be pulled into the cabin, but Lock saw his expression in that last moment—confusion mixed with wounded pride.

"Nikki's replacement seems eager," Lock said.

"Replacements usually are."

The helicopter door closed. Within minutes they were airborne, banking north toward wherever Samir's friend kept his yacht moored. Lock wondered if Nikki was watching from somewhere, seeing her ticket out fly away with another woman. Probably for the best. The island was about to become complicated in ways a rich boyfriend couldn't protect against.

The tech team formed up with their equipment, ready to move. Four specialists with enough hardware to peel back whatever digital layers the island might be hiding. Lock had specifically requested this level of capability. Most consultants would pocket the difference, show up with basic gear.

"Interesting times ahead," Ty said, watching Efron disappear from his terrace perch.

"About to get more interesting."

They followed the tech team toward the main building, leaving the helipad empty except for the fading sound of rotors.

CHAPTER
FIFTY

TWO OF EFRON'S men flanked the door to Harper's recovery room, trying to look casual and failing.

"Gentlemen," Lock said, approaching at a steady pace.

"Sir, we have orders not to allow anyone—" the taller one began, stepping in front of him.

Lock stopped. "Terrific. Here's your new order. Ready?"

They both looked at him expectantly.

"Fuck off."

Lock said it conversationally, like commenting on the weather. Both guards straightened, hands moving toward weapons they weren't quite drawing.

"Mr. Efron said—"

"I don't give a shit. I'm conducting a security assessment that includes guest safety protocols. Part of that means interviewing injured guests." Lock smiled thinly. "You want to physically prevent me from doing my job? I'll add it to my report."

The guards exchanged glances. The shorter one reached for his radio.

"Go ahead," Lock said. "Call him. Explain how you're interfering with the assessment his bosses are paying for. I'm sure that'll go well."

The guard's hand stopped. After a moment, both men stepped aside.

"We'll be right here," the taller one said.

"Good. Someone needs to guard this door from all those dangerous medical supplies."

Lock knocked once and entered. The room was more luxury suite than hospital ward—hardwood floors, designer furniture, windows overlooking the garden. Harper lay propped up in bed, an IV line in her left arm.

She looked better than she had at the cliff, which wasn't saying much. Cleaned up, bandaged properly, the wild terror replaced by exhaustion. Her eyes found him as he approached.

"Miss Holt," Lock said, closing the door. "How are you feeling?"

"Like I got hit by a truck. Then the truck backed up and hit me again." Her voice was hoarse but steady. "You're one of the men from the cliff."

"Ryan Lock. My partner and I found you."

"Found me." She shifted, wincing. "That's a nice way of saying hunted me down."

"Not hunting. Looking. There's a difference."

The doctor entered through a side door—a competent-looking woman in her fifties who moved with professional efficiency.

"Mr. Lock," she said, checking Harper's chart. "I was about to update Miss Holt on her condition. Would you prefer privacy?"

"He can stay," Harper said.

The doctor nodded. "The good news is you'll make a full recovery. Seventeen separate lacerations on your feet, all cleaned and sutured. Two are deep enough to concern me, but mobility seems intact. Severe dehydration, which we're addressing. Mild infection in several wounds, but we caught it early. Antibiotics should clear it within forty-eight hours."

"When can I leave?" Harper asked.

"The medical facility? Tomorrow maybe, if you rest tonight. But keep weight off your feet for several days."

"I meant the island."

The doctor's expression didn't change, but Lock noticed the slight pause. "Physically? You could travel in two to three days if needed."

She left them alone. Harper stared at the IV bag, watching drops fall into the tube.

"I want to leave now," she said quietly. "Today."

"Far as I'm concerned, you're free to go whenever you'd like," Lock said. "But I'd prefer if you and Nikki left with us when our assessment is complete."

"Why with you? Am I in danger?"

Lock pulled a chair closer to her bed, sat at her eye level. "I told you before, I have a four-year-old daughter. If something like this happened to her, I'd want someone making sure she got home safe." He paused. "All the way home."

Harper's eyes filled with tears. "She's lucky. Your daughter. Having someone who'd..." She trailed off, swiping at her face. "Sorry. I'm not usually a crier. It's been a really shit week."

"You're here. That's what matters."

She laughed bitterly. "You know what's fucked up? I came here thinking it would be an adventure. Work in paradise for a few months, make some connections, maybe land a job with one of the guests. I speak several languages, have a degree in international relations. I thought I was smart."

"You're alive. That makes you smart in my book."

"Because I got lucky. Because Nikki helped me. Because you found me before..." She stopped, breathing hard. "Can I tell you something? About that night?"

"Only if you want to. You don't owe me or anyone else your story."

"That's just it. I think I do. I think someone needs to know." She twisted the hospital blanket in her hands. "That night with Ulrich—it wasn't random. I'm sure of it."

Lock leaned forward slightly but kept his expression neutral. "What makes you think that?"

"Everything about it was wrong. Usually, there are rules. First dates happen in public spaces. Private villa meetings come later, after trust is established. But with Ulrich, it went straight to Villa Nine."

"Could have been his preference."

"That's what I thought. But then the staff—there were supposed to be servers, a chef. Standard for a private dinner. They were there when I arrived, setting up. Professional, normal. Then Ulrich sent them away. All of them. At once. I tried to leave when things got bad but every exit was shut down. Not just closed. Locked. From both sides."

Lock felt ice in his gut. "You're sure?"

"I know the difference between a stuck door and a locked one. Someone wanted me trapped in there with him." Her voice broke. "The thing is, Ulrich was drunk. Really drunk. And he had... accessories laid out. Handcuffs, masks, things I don't want to describe. But here's what haunts me—I think he thought I might be into it. Like someone had maybe told him that, which is why he'd invited me."

"Who?"

"He wouldn't say. But he was confident. Like he'd been promised something specific." Tears ran down her face now. "I'm not into that. I've never even hinted at being into that. Someone told him lies about me. Set up the whole thing to happen exactly how it did."

Lock handed her the tissue box from the bedside table. "I'm sorry. No one should have to—"

"I'm not done." She wiped her face, anger replacing tears. "After I fought him off, after I ran, I had time to think in the jungle. And I keep coming back to the same question—why me? I'm nobody special. Not rich, not connected, not important. So why set me up?"

"Maybe it wasn't about you specifically."

"What do you mean?"

Lock kept his voice careful. "Maybe you were just the right profile. Young, beautiful, isolated. Someone who could disappear without too many questions."

"A disposable person," Harper said bitterly.

"Their view, not mine."

She was quiet for a moment. "You know what the really sick part is? I think Ulrich was supposed to hurt me. I think that was the whole point. But I don't understand why. What does anyone gain from letting a guest assault a girl?"

Lock didn't answer, but his mind was turning over. He had a good idea of what someone would have to gain.

"I don't know," he said finally. "But I intend to find out."

"Is that why you're really here? Not for some security assessment?"

"The assessment is real. What we find during it... that might be more than anyone expected."

Harper studied his face. "You're not like the others here. Neither is your partner. You actually give a damn."

"Most people do. They just get good at hiding it."

"Not here. Here, nobody gives a damn about anything except money and power and..." She gestured vaguely. "Whatever sick games they're playing."

Lock stood. "Get some rest. Let the antibiotics work. In a few days, we'll get you and Nikki somewhere safe."

"Promise?"

He thought about Sofia, about the world she was inheriting. About young women treated as disposable commodities in games they never agreed to play.

"Promise," he said.

CHAPTER
FIFTY-ONE

THE MATCHMAKER WATCHED Nikki Bailey drag her Louis Vuitton suitcase across the courtyard toward the staff quarters. The wheels caught on the stone path, making her struggle for each foot of progress. From their control room, they could track her on multiple cameras—main pathway, side angle, overhead view. A choreographed humiliation.

She knocked on Astrid's door. A camera mounted over the door gave them the perfect angle—Nikki's face in profile, hope struggling against desperation. The suitcase beside her looked absurd now, designer luggage for a girl with nowhere to go.

Astrid opened the door wearing yoga clothes. The Matchmaker adjusted the audio feed, bringing their voices into focus.

"Nikki?" Astrid's surprise was genuine. "What are you doing here?"

"I need..." Nikki stopped, started again. "Can I stay with you? Just for a few nights?"

The Matchmaker zoomed in on Astrid's face, watching sympathy war with self-preservation. They'd seen this calculation thousands of times.

"I'm sorry about Harper," Astrid said carefully. "Really, I am. But I can't get involved in... whatever this is."

"Please. I don't have anywhere else—"

"I can't." Astrid's voice firmed. "You know how things work here. I'm sorry."

Nikki's shoulders dropped.

"Could I at least use your shower? Just this once? I'm locked out of all the guest villa facilities."

Astrid glanced behind her, then nodded. "Fifteen minutes."

"Thank you."

The Matchmaker switched feeds as Nikki entered Astrid's quarters. The bathroom feed activated as Nikki closed the door behind her.

She moved like someone in a dream, setting down her meager possessions—a designer clutch, phone, the few clothes she'd managed to grab. The Matchmaker noted each item, cataloging what remained of her former life. Amazing how quickly the trappings fell away.

The shower came on. Steam began to fog the mirror. Nikki stepped under the water fully clothed at first, still in the sundress she'd worn to meet Samir. Only after a long moment did she peel it off, letting it drop to the tile floor.

The Matchmaker leaned forward slightly. Such a shame about the market's preferences. The buyers always wanted the pale ones, the blondes, the Astrids of the world. They failed to appreciate the elegance of Nikki's form—the long lines, the fuller proportions.

Nikki stood under the shower spray, and the Matchmaker noticed the moment her composure finally cracked. Her hand moved between her legs, not with desire but desperate need for release, for something she could control. The water pressure, the simple physical sensation—she was using it to escape, if only for a few moments.

The Matchmaker watched clinically, noting how desperation made her movements urgent rather than sensual. Stress relief, nothing more. The body seeking what comfort it could find when everything else had been stripped away.

She finished quickly, efficiently, then stood under the spray as if trying to wash away more than just the day's humiliation. The Matchmaker saved the footage to her file.

A thought occurred. Why waste such a resource? The usual protocol would be removal—an accident, an overdose. Just another girl who couldn't handle island life. But that seemed so... pedestrian.

They thought about their collection, their private archive. They'd never kept one for themselves before. Always the matchmaker, never the match. Of course they had indulged—voyeurism lost its thrill after a time. In a way, guests like Drexler were dilettantes compared to The Matchmaker. Especially when it came to the art of torment.

But they had always been careful to keep their personal and professional lives separate. But now...

Nikki would be perfect. Damaged, friendless, desperate. Truly disposable. No one who counted in their world would miss her.

There would be no need for intermediaries this time. No wealthy fool to fumble what should be savored. They could approach her themselves, offer rescue, salvation. She'd be so grateful. At first.

The Matchmaker pulled up her file, began making notes. Height, weight, measurements—all there. Psychological profile updated to reflect current vulnerability. They added a new classification: "Personal Collection."

On screen, Nikki gathered her possessions. She looked smaller somehow, diminished by the simple act of seeking help and being refused. When she knocked on the bathroom door, Astrid escorted her out without meeting her eyes.

"Thank you," Nikki said quietly.

"Don't come back," Astrid said, avoiding eye contact. "I'm sorry, but don't."

CHAPTER
FIFTY-TWO

THE BUSINESS CENTER conference room buzzed with electronic equipment. Lock counted four laptops, two spectrum analyzers, and enough networking equipment to run a small data center. In next to no time his tech team had transformed the sterile resort meeting space into a proper operations center in less than two hours.

"Initial sweep's running," the team lead announced, eyes fixed on his screen. "We're starting with the main network topology."

Lock positioned himself where he could see the monitors without hovering. Ty leaned against the wall by the door, busying himself with texting the Australian he'd met on their flight out to Dubai. They'd learned years ago that technical specialists worked better without bullet catchers breathing down their necks.

"Getting the baseline?" Lock asked.

"Mapping what should be here versus what is here." The lead worked his keyboard. "Resort this size should have maybe three VLANs—guest services, operations, security. Pretty standard architecture."

"But?"

"But I'm seeing six. Maybe seven." He pulled up a network diagram. "The extra segments aren't documented in their IT brief."

Lock exchanged a glance with Ty. Undocumented networks meant someone was hiding something.

"Could be lazy documentation," Ty suggested. "IT departments aren't always thorough."

"That's what I'm hoping," the team lead said. "Let me dig deeper."

One of the other techs looked up from her packet analyzer. "I've got some weird traffic patterns. Internal streams that don't match standard usage."

"Meaning?" Lock said.

"Heavy data flow where there should be light usage. Consistent streams between buildings that shouldn't need that kind of bandwidth."

"What kind of data?"

"Working on it." She adjusted her equipment. "The packets are evenly sized, evenly timed. Like a heartbeat."

The lead tech pulled up another window. "I'm running vendor lookups on the MAC addresses. Should tell us what kind of devices are talking." He frowned. "That's interesting."

"What?" Lock moved closer.

"Getting hits for equipment that's not on their asset list. Hikvision, Dahua—those are camera manufacturers."

"The resort has security cameras," Ty pointed out. "That's not unusual."

"These aren't on the security VLAN," the tech said. "They're on a separate segment."

Lock felt his instincts sharpen. "Where are these cameras?"

"Give me a second." More typing. "The traffic's originating from multiple guest villas. High-end units."

"Maybe extra security for VIP guests?" Ty suggested, though his tone indicated he didn't believe it.

"Then why hide it on a shadow network?" another tech asked. "And the traffic isn't going to the main security office. It's terminating in Building D."

Lock pulled up the resort map on his phone. "Building D is listed as maintenance and power substation."

"Hell of a lot of data flowing to a maintenance shed," the lead noted. "I'm seeing at least four megabits sustained."

"Which means?"

"HD video streams. Multiple cameras, continuous recording." He looked up at Lock. "Someone's running a parallel surveillance system."

The room fell silent except for the hum of equipment. Lock processed the implications. Cameras in guest villas, feeding to an undocumented location.

"Could be innocent," the lead said, though he didn't sound convinced. "Executive security sometimes runs separate systems."

"But they'd document it," Ty said. "They'd tell us about it in the assessment brief."

Another tech spoke up from his station. "I'm picking up more anomalies. Some of these streams are encrypted—AES-256. That's military-grade."

"Resort security doesn't encrypt camera feeds," Lock said.

"No, they don't. Too much overhead, no real benefit. Unless you're worried about someone intercepting the feeds. Or you're capturing something you really don't want others to see."

Lock considered the implications. Cameras inside guest villas. Military encryption. Secret network infrastructure. Each element alone could be explained away. Together, they painted a more insidious picture.

"Can you tell which villas?" he asked.

"Working on it." The female tech pulled up another tool. "The IP addressing scheme suggests Villas Seven, Nine, Twelve, and Fifteen. All premium units."

"Villa Nine," Ty said quietly.

Lock nodded. The villa where Harper had been attacked.

"How long would it take to set up something like this?" Lock asked.

The lead considered. "To do it right? Integrated into construction, hidden properly? This was planned from day one. You don't retrofit a system like this. Not without going back to the studs and even then it wouldn't be nearly as covert."

"So we're not looking at recent additions."

"Nope. This is built into the bones."

Lock moved to the window. He took a moment.

"Log everything," he ordered. "But don't flag it in any reports yet. I want to understand what we're looking at before we tip our hand."

"Could be nothing," the lead offered without conviction. "Could be a paranoid owner who wants to keep tabs on VIP guests for their own protection."

"Could be," Lock agreed. "But that's not what your gut's telling you, is it?"

The tech shook his head. "No. This feels wrong. The architecture's too sophisticated for simple security. Someone spent serious money to conceal this."

"How much are we talking?"

"Couple of million minimum. Maybe more. Professional grade equipment, custom network design, encrypted channels. This isn't some perverted maintenance guy with a webcam."

Lock returned to the displays. Streams of data flowed across the screens, carrying information the island's owners never intended to share.

"Keep digging," he said. "But carefully. If someone's monitoring this system, they might notice us poking around."

"Already thought of that," the lead said. "We're running passive detection only. Just listening, not interrogating. They won't know we're here."

"Good. What's your next step?"

"Map the full scope. How many cameras, which locations, where the feeds terminate. Then maybe we try to peek inside Building D's network footprint."

"Time frame?"

"Give me four hours for the full picture. Could be less if we get lucky."

Lock nodded. Four hours to confirm what his instincts already knew—this resort was more than it appeared. The hidden cameras suggested blackmail, compromise, control. The encryption suggested professional operations, possibly intelligence related.

Harper's words echoed in his mind: "Someone wanted me trapped in there with him."

CHAPTER
FIFTY-THREE

AMIRA BARZANI'S office suite occupied the top floor of the administrative building, its floor-to-ceiling windows offering commanding views of the resort she'd built into an empire. She stood at those windows now while her two most trusted associates settled into the leather chairs behind her.

"Harper Holt is stable in medical," Efron reported. "Two guards on rotation. She's asking about leaving the island."

"Of course she is." Amira didn't turn from the window. "And our consultants?"

"Ensconced with their technical team in Conference Room B. Running their various scans and assessments. Very thorough."

Patrick shifted in his chair, examining his manicured nails. "How thorough?"

"Thorough's what we're paying them for," Efron said evenly. "Comprehensive security review, remember?"

"Yes, but I don't recall asking them to play detective." Amira finally turned, her white Chanel suit immaculate despite the tropical humidity. "Finding missing girls, carrying them through the resort like some sort of Hollywood heroes."

"They're both ex-military. Force protection is ingrained—" Efron said.

"I don't care about background." Amira's voice was cold. "I care that Dave Carter sold us a boy scout when we needed a businessman."

Efron's expression didn't change. "They were hired because their reputation makes them credible. Discrete, professional, experienced."

"And apparently blessed with inconvenient moral compasses." Amira moved to her desk. "You should have dug deeper, Ethan. Should have found us some leverage before bringing them here."

"I did. Their records are clean. No financial troubles, no compromising relationships, no addictions—"

"Let's all relax, shall we? Everyone has their price." Patrick spoke without looking up from his cuticles. "It's simply a matter of finding the right currency."

Amira studied him with distaste. Men and their need to reduce everything to simple transactions.

"Speaking of prices," she said, "what exactly did Mr. Drexler pay for his evening entertainment?"

Patrick's hands stilled. "The standard rate. Plus discretionary bonus for... special requests."

"Special requests that nearly got him killed and created this entire mess." Amira's voice remained steady. "Remind me again whose idea it was to accommodate his particular tastes?"

"The client requested—"

"The client requested a dinner companion. You provided him with a victim." She let that hang in the air. "And now we have a traumatized girl in our medical facility who knows exactly what kind of special services we facilitate."

"Harper Holt signed the same NDAs as every other girl," Efron interjected. "She knows the consequences of talking."

"NDAs." Amira laughed. "Yes, I'm sure a piece of paper will stop her from describing her attempted rape to whatever journalist or prosecutor Lock puts her in contact with."

"Lock won't—"

"Wouldn't dare? He already has. The moment he carried her through our lobby, he made her visible. Made her real. Made her someone whose disappearance would be noticed." Amira returned to the window. "We've had situations before. Girls who couldn't adapt, who broke under pressure. But they were handled quietly. This... this is public."

"It doesn't have to be," Patrick said. "Harper's medical condition requires extended treatment. Complications from her time in the jungle. Infections, perhaps psychological trauma requiring sedation—"

"No." Efron's interruption was quiet but firm. "Lock's keeping tabs on her."

"Then we need him focused elsewhere," Amira said. "What does he want? What drives him?"

"His wife, his daughter," Efron replied immediately. "Four years old. Wants what's best for her. That costs money in Los Angeles."

Amira considered what he'd just said. "What about the other one?"

"Johnson's simpler. Ex-military, follows Lock's lead. Where Lock goes, Johnson follows."

She moved to the wet bar, poured herself a Perrier. The others knew better than to expect hospitality when Amira was thinking.

"Here's what's going to happen," she said finally. "Ethan, you'll contain this situation. No more surprises, no more missing girls found in jungles. Double the patrols, tighten the surveillance."

"Already in motion," Efron said.

"Patrick, your contact in Dubai. Ensure he's prepared if Miss Holt attempts to file any complaints. We'll need injunctions, gag orders, whatever legal instruments necessary."

Patrick nodded.

"As for Lock and his inconvenient moral center," Amira continued, "I'll handle him personally. Men like him respond better to feminine persuasion. A conversation about the realities of private security work, the importance of discretion, the financial benefits of expanded contracts."

"You think he can be bought?" Efron asked.

"Everyone can be bought. The only question is whether we're willing to meet the price." She took a delicate sip of water. "Offer him a permanent position. Security consultant for all our properties. Seven figures annually. See how his morality holds up against his daughter's college fund and a house in Bel Air."

"And if he refuses?"

"Then we remind him that he's a foreign national on a private island where accidents happen. Boats sink. Helicopters malfunction. The ocean is very deep." She said it without emotion, stating facts rather than making threats.

"What about the Bailey girl?" Patrick asked, his tone too casual. "Harper's friend, Patel's former companion. She knows too much."

"Nikki Bailey is a problem," Amira agreed. "No money, no protection, no reason to keep quiet. We can't have her spreading stories among the other girls."

"I'll handle her," Patrick said.

Amira turned to study him, noting the slight tension in his shoulders, the way his fingers had stilled completely.

"Handle her how?" she asked.

He shrugged. "Leave it to me."

CHAPTER
FIFTY-FOUR

NIKKI EMERGED from the medical facility into afternoon sunlight. Harper was sleeping, finally, after another round of IV antibiotics and pain medication. The infection in her feet was responding to treatment, but Nikki knew that the deeper wounds would take longer to heal.

"Miss Bailey."

She turned to find Patrick Barzani standing near a landscaped palm cluster, hands in the pockets of his white linen pants. Up close, she noticed the telltale signs—dilated pupils despite the bright sun, a slight tremor in his jaw, the way he shifted his weight. Fresh from a bathroom bump, most likely.

"Mr. Barzani," she said carefully.

"Patrick, please. We're not formal here." His smile was warm but calculated. "How is your friend?"

"Recovering."

"Good. That's very good." He stepped closer, and she caught expensive cologne mixed with something chemical. "I wanted to apologize. Personally. What happened to Harper, the way you've been treated since... it's inexcusable."

Nikki said nothing.

"This isn't what we intended," Patrick continued. "We created this place as a sanctuary. When things go wrong, when guests abuse our hospitality..." He shook his head. "We feel responsible."

"Mr. Drexler abused more than your hospitality."

"Yes." Patrick's expression darkened. "He's no longer welcome at any of our properties. What he did to your friend—listen, we want to make things right."

Here it comes, Nikki thought.

"There's an event tomorrow evening," Patrick said. "A small gathering on a yacht. Very exclusive, very refined. We need a few girls to attend—just to add elegance to the party. Conversation, perhaps some light flirting, nothing more."

"Nothing more," Nikki repeated.

"Absolutely nothing. The host is very particular about consent. And boundaries. He simply enjoys beautiful company." Patrick's smile returned. "Each girl who attends will receive nine thousand euros. Cash."

Nikki calculated quickly. Nine thousand euros was close to ten thousand dollars. Enough to get off the island, get Harper proper medical care, start over somewhere safe. It was also far more than the usual rate for a simple party appearance.

"That's very generous," she said carefully.

"It's an important client. Image matters." Patrick shifted again, that cocaine energy needing an outlet. "I thought of you specifically because you deserve something good after what you've endured."

"And what exactly would be expected of me for nine thousand euros?"

"Exactly what I said. Be beautiful, be charming, enjoy champagne and canapés. The yacht will return to port by midnight." He paused. "Think of it as compensation for your difficulties. Our way of apologizing."

Nikki studied his face.

"Just a party?" she said.

"Just a party. I give you my word."

"I appreciate the offer," Nikki said slowly. "Though it feels a bit like buying my silence."

Patrick's eyes widened in apparent surprise. "Buying your silence?

Nikki. May I call you Nikki? I would never ask anyone to compromise their morals. This is simply an opportunity. One that happens to come at a fortuitous time."

The lie came so smoothly she almost admired it.

"When do I need to decide?" she asked.

"By tomorrow morning. The yacht will be here by early evening. You'd need time to prepare, select something appropriate to wear." He produced a business card from his pocket. "Call this number when you've decided. Ask for Claudette—she'll handle the arrangements."

Nikki took the card. Patrick Barzani, Managing Director. No company name, just a phone number with a Monaco prefix.

"I'll think about it," she said.

"Please do. And Nikki?" He touched her arm lightly. "I truly am sorry about your friend. What happened to Harper should never have occurred."

"Right."

She turned to go, but his voice stopped her.

"Oh, one more thing. Given recent events, we're implementing new security protocols. Mr. Lock and his team are helping us ensure everyone's safety. You must feel much better knowing they're here."

There was something in his tone, testing whether she trusted the consultants, whether she'd told them anything.

"They saved Harper's life," she said simply.

"Indeed they did. Real heroes." His smile never wavered. "Though I'm sure they'd be the first to say they were just doing their job. They're both so very... professional."

Another probe. Nikki filed it away.

"I should get back," she said. "Harper might wake up."

"Of course. Do think about tomorrow evening. It would be such a shame for you to miss this opportunity." He stepped back. "After all, you've earned a little luxury after your ordeal."

Nikki walked away without responding, feeling his eyes on her back. Nine thousand euros for a party where nothing would be expected. On an island where a dinner invitation had nearly killed her best friend.

She thought about Lock and Johnson, the way they'd carried

Harper to safety without hesitation. Real men, unlike Patrick Barzani. But they couldn't protect her forever. And nine thousand euros could buy a lot of distance from this place.

At the entrance to the medical facility, she paused and looked back. Patrick was still standing by the palms, phone to his ear now, gesturing animatedly.

Just a party. Nothing expected. His way of making things right.

Nikki fingered the business card. Tomorrow evening, a standard yacht girl party. Easy enough. And nine thousand euros was a lot of money. Money she needed.

CHAPTER
FIFTY-FIVE

THE MORNING SUN cut sharp angles through the windows as Amira Barzani straightened her cream silk suit.

"I owe you an apology," Amira said from her office chair. "The incident with Miss Holt should never have happened."

Ryan Lock kept his expression neutral from the chair across from her. "Things happen. It's how they're handled that matters."

"Precisely." She leaned forward slightly. "Which is why I wanted to speak with you personally. To explain our position and perhaps clear up some misunderstandings."

She rose, moved to a credenza covered with silver-framed photographs.

"Do you know what we really do here, Mr. Lock?"

"Provide luxury experiences for high-net-worth individuals?"

"That's what the brochures say." She selected a photograph, handed it to him. "But our true business is often far more romantic."

The photo showed a couple on a beach—her in a wedding dress, him in a tuxedo. They looked genuinely happy.

"Tori and Mark," Amira said. "She was a waitress from Indiana when she came here. He owns a tech company in Silicon Valley. They met at one of our events three years ago. Now they have a daughter."

She handed him another photo. Different couple, similar joy.

"I'm a matchmaker, Mr. Lock. I take brilliant young women who lack opportunity and introduce them to men with resources. Sometimes it's transactional, yes. But sometimes magic happens."

Lock studied the images. Professional photography, genuine smiles. The kind of success stories that made everything else palatable.

"These women come here knowing exactly what environment they're entering," Amira continued. "They're not victims. They're entrepreneurs, leveraging their assets."

"And Harper Holt?"

Amira's expression darkened. "What happened to Harper was an aberration. A complete breakdown of our protocols. Ulrich Drexler abused our trust."

"But it wasn't the first time, was it?" Lock said quietly.

She paused, Perrier glass halfway to her lips. "I'm sorry?"

"Harper wasn't the first incident. I've documented at least three similar cases in the past eighteen months. Young women who 'left suddenly' after private villa encounters."

Amira set down her glass. "You've been thorough."

"Isn't that what you're paying me for?"

She studied him. "Of course. That was the brief. And you've excelled. Which is why we'd like to offer you a permanent position," she said. "Chief Security Consultant for all our properties. Not just this island, all of it. We have interests in Monaco, Dubai, Singapore."

"I have a company. A partner."

"Of course. We'd contract with your firm. Mr. Johnson would be included." She named a figure that made Lock's expression flicker despite his control. It was three times what he'd make in his best year.

"That's very generous," he managed.

"We believe in paying for quality. There would also be additional benefits. Housing allowance, education fund for your daughter, full medical coverage." She smiled. "I understand Sophie is four. Such a formative age."

Lock noticed she'd gotten the name wrong but didn't correct her. The name drop was subtle but clear.

"The salary would be guaranteed for five years," Amira continued. "With performance bonuses based on discretion. We value partners who understand that not every problem requires a public solution."

"You mean partners who know when to look the other way."

"I mean partners who understand nuance." Her tone sharpened slightly. "The world isn't black and white, Mr. Lock. Sometimes protecting the greater good requires accepting lesser evils."

"Like young women being assaulted by wealthy clients?"

"Like providing financial security for women who would otherwise have none. Do you know what most of our girls would be doing without this place? Waiting tables, cleaning offices, dancing in strip clubs. Here, they have luxury, safety, the chance to change their lives."

"Harper didn't seem to feel very secure."

"No," Amira admitted. "She didn't. Which is why we need someone like you. Someone who can ensure that what happened to Harper never happens again."

Lock weighed his response. The office almost certainly had surveillance.

"It's a significant offer," he said finally. "I'd need to discuss it with Ty. And my wife."

"Of course. Take the time you need." She stood, smoothing her skirt. "But Mr. Lock? Don't take too long. This offer comes with an expiration date."

"Understood."

"Good." She extended her hand. Her handshake was firm, dry, brief.

"One more thing," she said as he turned to leave. "The documentation you mentioned—other incidents. I'd be very interested to review that. If we're going to prevent future problems, we need to understand past failures."

"I'll include it in my final report."

"Excellent. Though perhaps a preliminary copy? So we can begin addressing issues immediately?"

Lock recognized the probe. She wanted to know what he knew, what evidence he'd gathered.

"I'll see what I can do," he said.

In the elevator, Lock forced his expression to remain neutral.

Cameras in the corners, probably audio as well. But inside, his stomach churned.

She believed her own propaganda. That was the worst part. Amira Barzani genuinely saw herself as some benevolent matchmaker, providing opportunities for disadvantaged women. The fact that some of those women ended up traumatized or dead was just a rounding error.

The money was absurd. Enough to secure Sofia's future, expand the company, live without financial worry. All he had to do was become complicit in a system that treated young women as renewable resources.

Outside, the sun felt too bright. Lock walked toward his quarters, knowing he needed to talk to Ty. They'd need to play this carefully, make Amira believe he was considering her offer while the tech team dug deeper.

Three times his maximum annual income. Housing, medical, education funds.

He thought about Harper in the medical facility, feet shredded from running through jungle. About Nikki, adrift without protection. About all the women who'd come before them.

Amira Barzani, the romantic matchmaker.

Lock had met many monsters in his career. The most dangerous were always the ones who truly believed that they were the hero of their own story.

CHAPTER
FIFTY-SIX

"PUT THIS IN YOUR CLUTCH," Ty said, handing Nikki a device no bigger than a car key fob. "Cut a slit in the lining, tuck it deep."

She took the beacon, turning it over in her hands. The plastic casing felt military-grade solid despite its size. "What is it?"

"Personal locator beacon. GPS enabled." He showed her the activation button, covered by a small plastic guard. "If things go bad flip this cover and hold the button until the light flashes red. Then ditch it."

"Ditch it?"

"They'll trace the signal back. You want to be somewhere else when they do." Ty glanced toward the harbor where a sleek yacht bobbed at anchor, maybe three hundred meters out. Its lights were coming on as dusk settled over the water. "That the boat?"

"That's it." Nikki slipped the beacon into her clutch. "There'll be other girls there. Safety in numbers, right?"

Ty didn't answer immediately. He produced a small cylinder that looked like expensive lipstick. "Pepper gel. Better than spray in confined spaces. Won't blow back in your face."

"You're starting to worry me."

"Just being thorough." He demonstrated the activation mechanism. "Point and press. Aim for the eyes, then move. Don't try to fight, don't wait to see if it worked. Create distance and run."

Nikki took the disguised weapon, weighing it in her palm. "Where do I put this?"

"Wherever you can reach it fast. Bra strap, garter, wherever feels natural." He studied her for a moment. "You nervous?"

"Should I be?"

"Fear's not always bad. Keeps you sharp." Ty pulled out a small LED flashlight, showed her the button sequence. "Three clicks activates strobe mode. You get in trouble, hit this and point it at shore. We'll see it."

"We?"

"I'll be watching."

The statement carried more weight than she'd expected. Not a promise to rescue her—that would be fantasy. Just an acknowledgment that someone would witness whatever happened. Someone would know.

"You're different," Nikki said. "From the other men here."

"Lord, I sure hope so."

"No, I mean... You're not trying to impress me or buy me or fuck me. You're just helping."

"Everyone needs help sometimes."

"My mom used to say that." Nikki tested the flashlight's weight, practiced the click sequence. "Before my dad walked out on her. Took her ten years to figure out he just needed to be gone."

Ty's expression shifted slightly. "That's a heavy load for a kid to carry."

"You know about it?"

"Familiar story in my neighborhood. Fathers who can't handle the pressure, take the easy exit." He leaned against the railing, eyes still on the yacht.

"But you didn't repeat the pattern."

"No kids to leave." A ghost of a smile. "I kept things simple that way."

"Lonely, though."

"Sometimes." He turned to her. "Listen, about tonight. Two rules, okay? Non-negotiable."

Nikki nodded, recognizing the shift to business.

"First, know your exits. Soon as you board, map every way off that boat. Stairs, rails, life rafts, everything. Don't trust that there'll be time to figure it out later."

"Okay."

"Second, never go below deck. Never go anywhere alone. You need the bathroom, you take another girl. Someone suggests a private tour, you decline."

"The other girls might not like that."

"Then you be the bitch who ruins the mood. Better rude than trapped." His voice was firm.

Nikki pulled her wrap tighter despite the warm evening.

"You really think something might happen?" Nikki asked him.

"No, but I think it's always better to be prepared."

CHAPTER
FIFTY-SEVEN

THE YACHT'S lower deck hummed with air conditioning and generator noise, but the converted cabin was completely silent. He'd paid extra for the soundproofing—acoustic panels that could muffle screams.

Worth every cent.

He adjusted the overhead surgical light, checking the angle. The table beneath gleamed stainless steel, its drainage channels freshly cleaned. The restraints—medical grade, padded leather—lay open like waiting arms. Everything precisely positioned, everything purposeful.

His hands trembled slightly as he arranged the instruments. Not fear so much as anticipation. The cocaine helped sharpen his focus, made every detail razor-sharp. The IV stand, the monitoring equipment, the careful selection of pharmaceuticals. Propofol for the initial sedation. Ketamine to maintain consciousness while disrupting the pain response. A delicate balance, keeping someone aware but unable to resist.

He'd studied for this. Years of research, careful practice. The human body could endure so much if properly maintained.

The camera mounts took only minutes to install. One directly overhead for the clinical view. Another at eye level for the more intimate moments. The memory cards were fresh, batteries fully charged. Documentation was crucial. Art required proper archiving.

He checked his watch. Twenty minutes until the tender arrived. Time for final preparations.

The medical supplies were already laid out. Saline bags for hydration. Adrenaline if the heart rate dropped too low. Bandages and sutures for anything that might bleed too much. He wasn't a sadist, he was an artist. The goal was duration, not damage. Experience, not extinction.

His arousal was growing intense. He adjusted himself, considering relief, but decided to wait. Anticipation heightened everything. Made the eventual release more profound.

The drugs were hitting perfectly now. That sharp clarity where everything made sense, where his true purpose revealed itself. Not the mundane matchmaking of his public face, but this—the careful curation of human experience pushed to its absolute limit.

He'd done this before, of course. Three times, to be precise. Each experience better than the last, each recording more perfect. The girls who'd "left suddenly" after difficult encounters. Amira thought they'd been simple removal operations. She had no idea about his personal collection.

He moved to the cabin's small mirror, studying his reflection. The pupils blown wide from stimulants. The slight sheen of perspiration despite the air conditioning. The smile that spread across his lips without conscious thought.

Patrick Barzani smiled back at himself, straightening his collar.

Time to prepare for his guest.

CHAPTER
FIFTY-EIGHT

LOCK FOUND Ty in their quarters cross-referencing duty logs with guest departures. He walked past and palmed a folded note against Ty's arm, continuing to the mini-fridge for water.

Ty unfolded it below desk level. Five words in Lock's neat handwriting: *Assume they can hear everything*.

"Thought we could take a walk," Lock said, capping the water bottle. "Check the dock area before dinner."

"Sure." Ty pocketed the note, standing. "Been sitting too long anyway."

They headed out into the cooling evening air, walking like men with nowhere particular to go. The path to the marina wound past the pool area where guests gathered for sunset cocktails.

"Sofia called this morning," Lock said, his tone casual. "Lost another tooth. Carmen says the tooth fairy needs to account for inflation."

"Kids are expensive," Ty agreed. "Getting more expensive every year."

"Tell me about it. Preschool costs more than my first car." Lock paused to admire a yacht coming into harbor. "Makes you think about financial security differently."

"That why you're considering the offer?"

Lock glanced at him. "Five-year guarantee. Medical, housing, education fund. Man would be stupid not to consider it."

"Lot of money."

"More than a lot. Enough to stop worrying, you know? Actually plan beyond the next contract."

They reached the marina proper, evening light reflecting off the boats. A few crew members worked on deck maintenance, but otherwise the docks were quiet.

"Amira made good points," Lock continued. "About understanding the bigger picture. Not everything's black and white."

"She explain the Harper situation?"

"Thoroughly. Drexler was an anomaly. Bad apple who abused their hospitality. They've already implemented new protocols." Lock's voice sounded convincing. "Can't hold the whole operation responsible for one sick individual."

"Makes sense." Ty watched a tender preparing to depart from the main dock. "They run a quality establishment. Few bad incidents don't define the whole."

"Exactly. And with proper security oversight, someone making sure protocols are followed..." Lock shrugged. "Could prevent future problems."

"That someone being you."

"Us. The offer includes you." Lock smiled. "Think about it—steady income, tropical base of operations, working with established infrastructure instead of building from scratch every time."

They'd reached the dock's end, where a small gazebo provided shade during the day. Now it just framed the sunset.

"Amira seemed genuine," Lock said. "About wanting to improve things. She's built something impressive here. Just needs the right security guidance to keep it clean."

"Woman's got vision," Ty agreed. "Takes vision to create a place like this."

"And wisdom to recognize when you need help." Lock turned to watch the tender pulling away from the dock. "I think I'm going to take it. The offer. Pending contract review, of course."

"Of course." Ty's eyes tracked the tender as it headed toward a yacht anchored in deeper water. Single passenger, female, elegant dress visible even at this distance. "Just the one girl on that run."

Lock followed his gaze. "Exclusive party maybe."

"Must be." Ty's voice remained neutral. "Speaking of exclusive, the Red Team still on site?"

"Yeah, other side of the island. Running infiltration drills on the eastern perimeter."

"Good to keep them sharp," Lock said.

CHAPTER
FIFTY-NINE

ETHAN EFRON ENTERED the room carrying a small bouquet of tropical flowers and a leather portfolio. He looked like a thoughtful visitor—pressed khakis, concerned expression, gentle knock on the already open door.

"Miss Holt. How are you feeling?"

Harper pulled the sheet higher despite being fully clothed in a hospital gown. "Better."

"Good, good." He set the flowers on her bedside table, arranging them carefully. "The doctor says you're healing well. No permanent damage to those feet."

She didn't say anything.

"May I?" He gestured to the visitor's chair, already pulling it closer. The leather portfolio rested on his lap. "I wanted to check on you personally. What happened... it shouldn't have occurred."

"No. It shouldn't have."

"Mr. Drexler has been permanently banned from all our properties." Efron's voice carried professional outrage. "His behavior was inexcusable."

Harper watched him perform concern, noting how his eyes never quite matched his expression.

"I've been in security for a long time," he continued. "Seen all kinds of situations. But what bothers me most is when misunderstandings escalate unnecessarily."

"Misunderstandings?"

"Poor communication. Mixed signals. Situations that could be resolved amicably if people just talked." He leaned back, settling in for a story. "Reminds me of a case I handled in Tel Aviv. Years ago, but still instructive."

Harper's skin prickled. She didn't want to hear this story, but interrupting felt more dangerous than listening.

"There was a young woman—bright, ambitious, working for an NGO. She'd become involved with a member of the Knesset. Married man, you understand. These things happen." His tone suggested worldly understanding. "When the relationship ended, she felt used. Angry. Started making threats about going public."

Harper focused on breathing normally.

"The politician was distraught. His career, his family, everything at risk because of what he saw as a consensual relationship that simply ran its course." Efron examined his manicured nails. "He offered her compensation. Generous compensation. Enough to start over anywhere she wanted."

"She refused?"

"She did. Wanted justice, she said. Wanted the world to know what kind of man he was." He sighed. "Young people can be so idealistic."

Harper waited.

"I was brought in to mediate. Spent hours with her, explaining the reality. How these scandals play out. How the woman always suffers more than the man. How much better it would be to accept the offer and move forward."

"But she didn't."

"No. She was determined." Efron's smile was sad, understanding. "She filed complaints. Went to journalists. Made quite a fuss. Very stressful for everyone involved."

The air conditioning hummed. Outside, Harper could hear distant laughter from the pool area. Normal sounds that felt impossibly distant.

"Three months later, she killed herself." Efron said it matter-offactly. "Jumped from her apartment balcony. Tragic. The coroner found she'd been self-medicating for depression. The stress of the situation, the public scrutiny..." He spread his hands. "Sometimes people break under pressure."

"That's terrible," Harper said, not believing for a second that the girl jumped.

"Isn't it? And so unnecessary. If she'd just taken the politician's offer, accepted that relationships end, moved on with her life..." He shook his head. "She'd probably be married now. Children. Happy."

Harper felt her hands trembling and pressed them flat against the bed.

"The saddest part," Efron continued, "was the note she left. Apologizing for causing so much trouble. Saying she should have handled things differently." He met Harper's eyes. "People often gain clarity when it's too late."

He lifted the leather portfolio, extracting a single document. The paper was heavy, expensive, covered in dense legal text.

"Mr. Drexler feels terrible about what happened," Efron said, placing the document on her bedside table. "He wants to make amends."

Harper saw the number before he said it. Five hundred thousand dollars. More money than she'd see in a decade.

"It's a simple agreement. Acknowledging that your dinner was consensual adult interaction that was misinterpreted in the heat of the moment. A mutual understanding that no crimes were committed, just unfortunate miscommunication."

"Consensual," Harper repeated.

"Adult relationships are complex. What seems clear in one moment can feel different in another. Memory is so subjective." He smiled kindly. "Half a million dollars can buy a lot of future. Graduate school. A house. A fresh start anywhere you choose."

The document lay between them.

"Of course, accepting the settlement would include a confidentiality agreement. Standard legal protection for both parties. You couldn't discuss the evening with anyone, ever." His tone remained gentle, helpful. "But why would you want to? Better to put unpleasantness behind us."

Harper stared at the papers. Five hundred thousand dollars to agree that her assault was actually consensual. To legally erase what happened. To become complicit in her own violation.

"I'll need to think about it," she whispered.

"Of course. Take your time. Twenty-four hours should be sufficient." Efron stood, smoothing his pants. "The offer is generous, but not indefinite. Mr. Drexler wants closure so everyone can move forward."

He paused at the door, looking back with paternal concern.

"That woman in Tel Aviv—I think about her sometimes. Such a waste. All that potential, that future, thrown away for what? Pride? Principles?" He smiled sadly. "The dead have no principles, Miss Holt."

CHAPTER
SIXTY

THE YACHT'S salon was understated luxury—cream leather, polished teak, crystal decanters catching the light. Nikki paused at the entrance, taking in the empty space. Soft jazz played from hidden speakers, and champagne waited in a silver bucket, but no other guests mingled with drinks.

"Nikki." Patrick rose from a chair by the windows, setting aside what looked like a financial magazine. "Welcome aboard."

"Mr. Barzani?" She couldn't hide her surprise. "I thought—"

"Please, Patrick." He moved toward her with confidence. "I apologize for the confusion. The other guests canceled last minute. Monaco Grand Prix."

She relaxed slightly. That made sense. The uber-wealthy always had competing invitations.

"I considered canceling entirely," he continued, "but that seemed unfair to you and the other girls who'd already arranged to attend."

"Other girls?"

"Should arrive shortly. Astrid and..." He waved vaguely. "Forgive me, I'm terrible with names. Champagne?"

"Thank you." She accepted the glass, setting her clutch on the nearest surface to free her hands. The yacht's gentle motion made balancing glass and bag awkward.

"Dom Pérignon '96," Patrick said, touching his glass to hers. "From my personal collection."

The champagne was exceptional, though Nikki barely tasted it. Patrick's pupils seemed dilated despite the salon's warm lighting. She'd seen the same look in club bathrooms back home—the aftermath of pharmaceutical confidence.

"Beautiful yacht," she offered.

"Isn't it?" He gestured around the space. "Shall I give you a tour while we wait for the others?"

"Sure."

He led her through the salon, pointing out artwork and amenities with practiced ease. His hand found her elbow once, guiding her around a low table, the touch brief and professional. Still, she noticed how he positioned himself as they moved—always between her and the nearest exit.

"The owner's a Russian. Energy sector," Patrick explained as they admired the bar setup. "Lovely man, though his taste runs a bit excessive for my preferences."

"Seems pretty restrained to me."

"You should see below deck. He had the master suite done in gold leaf." Patrick refilled her glass without asking. "Bit much, even for a yacht this size."

Nikki sipped the fresh champagne, glancing back toward where she'd left her clutch. The beacon Ty had given her sat inside, probably paranoia. Patrick Barzani might be many things—Amira's enforcer, a functioning addict, a man who facilitated questionable relationships—but he wasn't dangerous. Not personally. The girls all said he kept his distance, never made advances.

"How are you finding the island?" he asked, settling into one of the salon's conversation areas. "After recent events, I mean."

"It's been... challenging."

"I imagine so. Your friend Harper—how is she?"

"Recovering." Nikki chose a chair across from him, maintaining distance without seeming rude. "Slowly."

"Good. That's good." He studied his champagne, brow furrowed with apparent concern. "I keep thinking we could have prevented it.

Should have known Drexler's proclivities."

His intensity was unsettling. Those dilated eyes focused on her with an attention that felt heavier than mere sexual interest.

"These things happen," Nikki said carefully.

"Do they? Should they?" He leaned forward, elbows on knees. "I've spent years trying to create something better here. A place where connections could form naturally, safely. And then someone like Drexler—"

He stopped, collecting himself. When he smiled again, it was the polished host returning.

"But that's not your burden to bear. Tonight is about moving forward." He glanced at his watch. "Though I should probably call about the others. Very unlike Astrid to be late."

"I can wait."

"Nonsense. Let me just..." He pulled out his phone, moving toward the windows for better reception. "Make yourself comfortable. There's food in the galley if you're hungry."

Nikki watched him pace by the windows, phone to ear. His free hand gestured as he spoke, that tremor more pronounced now. Whatever he'd taken was hitting its peak. She glanced again at her clutch, sitting forgotten on a side table twenty feet away. Should probably keep it closer, but that seemed paranoid. This was Patrick Barzani, husband to the Ice Queen Amira, not some stranger.

He ended his call with frustration. "Astrid's not answering. Neither is Claudette at the office."

"Maybe they're on their way?"

"Perhaps." He returned to his seat, picking up his champagne. "Though I'm beginning to think we've been stood up."

"I can go if you'd prefer—"

"Absolutely not. You came all this way." His smile seemed genuine, if strained. "Besides, I rarely get to just talk with one of our guests without Amira hovering. She thinks I don't understand the human element of our business."

"Do you?"

"I understand that everyone wants something. Connection, security, excitement." He topped off her glass again. "The trick is matching compatible wants."

"Like a matchmaker."

"Exactly like that." His approval felt oddly intense. "Though matches aren't always romantic. Sometimes they're about finding someone who appreciates what you have to offer."

A door clicked somewhere behind them. Nikki turned to see a crew member in white uniform.

"Sir? The captain asks if we'll be departing on schedule."

Patrick didn't look away from Nikki. "Tell him we're waiting for additional guests. Another thirty minutes."

"Yes, sir."

The crew member disappeared. They were alone again, the yacht rocking gently in its anchorage.

"I should mention," Patrick said, "if we don't hear from the others soon, I'll have to call the evening off. Can't justify the fuel costs for just one guest."

"Of course."

"Though..." He tilted his head, studying her. "We could always do something else. Dinner on shore perhaps? I know a lovely place on the other side of the island."

The offer sounded innocent enough. Dinner instead of a cancelled party. But something in his focus made her skin prickle.

"That's kind, but—"

"Think about it." He stood abruptly, that manic energy needing movement. "I'll check with the captain about weather windows. Sometimes these evening departures get complicated."

He headed toward the bridge, leaving Nikki alone in the salon. She looked at her clutch again, further away now. The beacon inside seemed silly. Patrick was odd, certainly, probably high, definitely intense. But dangerous?

CHAPTER
SIXTY-ONE

LOCK APPROACHED Ty at the outdoor bar, sliding a folded note across when he passed him a beer. They'd agreed to meet here after the tech team briefing—public enough to look casual, noisy enough that surveillance would struggle with audio if they kept their voices low and their mouths partially covered.

Ty glanced down: *Room confirmed compromised.*

"Productive meeting?" Ty asked, pocketing the note.

"The geek squad's making progress." Lock kept his tone light, two consultants discussing work over drinks. "Found some interesting infrastructure issues in Building C. Nothing that can't be fixed with proper investment."

"Infrastructure's always the hidden cost." Ty played along, though Lock could see his mind working behind the casual facade. "Speaking of which, what's our timeline looking like?"

"I'm thinking end of week for the preliminary report. Give them something to chew on while we finish the deep dive."

They moved away from the bar, walking toward the harbor path, late afternoon sun bathing everything in golden light. Other guests wandered past—older men with younger women, same as ever.

"Beautiful evening," Lock said. "Shame to waste it talking shop."

"That's what they pay us for." Ty's attention drifted to the water, where the yacht sat at anchor. "Though I wouldn't mind some downtime. Maybe check out that yacht everyone's been talking about."

Lock followed his gaze to the sleek vessel anchored three hundred meters out. Its lights were coming on as dusk approached. "The Russian's boat? Heard it's something special."

"Heard the parties are better." Ty watched the yacht with an intensity that had nothing to do with its luxury appointments. "Very exclusive gatherings."

Lock checked his watch. "I should head back to the tech team. They wanted me to review some findings. Something about unusual signal patterns they picked up."

"When you see the geek squad," Ty said, his eyes still on the yacht, "ask them to see what they can pick up from that yacht out there."

"Like what?" Lock kept his voice neutral.

"Not sure exactly but it might be worth checking their signals intelligence." Ty's tone was professional, but Lock caught the underlying concern. "Could be interfering with our equipment."

"Roger that." Lock started to leave, then paused. "You coming?"

"In a minute. Want to finish this beer. Enjoy the sunset."

Lock headed off, understanding the real message. Ty needed to work something out, needed to make moves without an audience.

Ty waited until Lock was well out of sight before approaching one of the dock workers securing lines for the night. The man wore the resort's standard whites, his weathered face focused on precise bowline loops.

"Evening," Ty said, keeping his approach casual. "Beautiful night for it."

"Yes, sir." The worker didn't look up from his knots. "Can I help you with something?"

"Just curious—busy night on the water? Saw a tender heading out earlier."

The dock worker finished his knot before straightening. He wiped his hands on his shorts. "Not particularly busy, sir. Pretty quiet actually."

"Any other girls heading out to the yacht tonight?" Ty kept his tone conversational, just idle curiosity from a bored security consultant. "Looked like quite a party setting up."

"Girls?" The worker glanced toward the yacht, then back at Ty. "No sir, not that I know of. Just Mr. Barzani and Ms. Bailey this evening."

Ty felt ice in his stomach, but his expression didn't change. "Just those two?"

"Yes, sir. Mr. Patrick likes his privacy when he entertains."

"I'm sure he does." Ty pulled out his phone, scrolling as if checking messages. "Must be nice, having a yacht like that all to yourself."

"It's a beautiful vessel. Mr. Patrick chartered her special for the season." The dock worker returned to his ropes. "Will there be anything else, sir?"

"No, that's helpful. Thanks." Ty moved away, finding a spot where he could see both the yacht and the dock while appearing to simply enjoy the view. He pulled up the encrypted messaging app.

Need you dockside with the RHIB. Possible extraction scenario.

The response came within seconds: *Copy. Location?*

Main dock. Bring night gear.

Roger that. What's my timeline?

Ty looked out at the yacht again. The jazz music carried clearly across the water now, sophisticated and smooth. Nikki had been out there for at least twenty minutes. Alone with Patrick Barzani. No other guests, no safety in numbers. Just a young woman who'd lost everything and a man who had the power to take what little remained.

How fast can you get here?

Thirty mikes. We're at the north training ground.

Ty's jaw tightened. The north training ground was on the opposite side of the island. Thirty minutes minimum, probably longer with equipment.

Make it twenty if you can.

CHAPTER
SIXTY-TWO

LOCK FOUND the tech team leader waiting for him by the service path near Villa Nine, tablet in hand. Two of Efron's security men lounged against a golf cart fifty meters away, openly watching them.

"Walk with me," Lock said.

They moved along the crushed coral path that wound between the premium villas. Far enough from the guards to speak quietly, close enough to look like a routine inspection.

"You asked me to check Villa Nine," the lead said. "We need to talk about what we found."

"Problems with the assessment?"

"Depends on your definition of problem." He pulled up the tablet, angling the screen away from distant observers. "We ran full spectrum analysis like you requested. NLJD, thermal mapping, RF sweep."

"And?"

"This villa is wired for surveillance. Not security—surveillance. Professional grade, built into the architecture."

Lock maintained his casual pace, aware of their watchers. "Show me."

"Started with RF—looking for wireless signals. Got nothing, which was odd. So we went to non-linear junction detection." The screen showed Villa Nine's floor plan dotted with markers. "Twenty-seven discrete semiconductor signatures. Bedrooms, bathrooms, living areas."

"Cameras?"

"Cameras and audio. The thermal imaging confirmed active components behind walls, following power lines that don't exist on any electrical plan."

Lock studied the data while walking. "Could be for executive protection."

"No." The lead pulled up photographs. "Found this behind an air vent—pinhole lens, four millimeters, IR capable. Another one embedded in what looks like a decorative screw in the headboard. The angles are all wrong for security. They're positioned to capture activity."

"English, please."

"They're bedroom cams, Ryan. Pointed at the bed, the bathroom, the shower. We found MEMS microphones in the crown molding—smaller than rice grains. Eight in the master bedroom alone."

Lock's jaw tightened but he kept walking. The guards had shifted position, maintaining their distance but keeping them in sight.

"Where do the feeds go?"

"Everything's on that shadow network we found—VLAN six. Encrypted data streams, all flowing to the same endpoint. Has to be Building D."

"The maintenance shed."

"Bandwidth analysis shows continuous recording. Someone's capturing everything, twenty-four seven." The lead glanced at the guards. "This isn't a few hidden cameras. It's systematic collection."

They passed Villa Eight, its windows dark behind privacy screens. Lock wondered if it was wired the same way.

"How long has this been running?"

"Based on the integration level? Like we thought, since construction. The TDR shows cable runs behind poured concrete. Fiber splices that predate the finish work. Someone designed this resort with surveillance built into the bones."

"All the villas?"

"Can't confirm without checking, but the network architecture suggests at least all the premium units."

Lock considered the implications. Every powerful person who'd stayed here, every private moment, every indiscretion—all of it captured and stored.

"Previous security reviews should have caught this," he said.

"Only if they were really looking. This level of concealment requires specific equipment and knowledge. Most assessments focus on keeping threats out, not discovering if the resort itself is compromised."

Or they were paid to miss it, Lock thought. Like Amira had tried to pay him.

"Can the resort claim this is legitimate? Security purposes?"

"Not if your USP is complete privacy. Security cameras are visible or disclosed. They don't hide in shower heads. They don't use military-grade encryption." The lead shut down his tablet as they approached Villa Ten. "This is intelligence collection. Kompromat material."

CHAPTER
SIXTY-THREE

"THE OWNER HAS QUITE A COLLECTION," Patrick said, topping off Nikki's glass with more Dom Pérignon '96. "Rothko, Basquiat, even a small Caravaggio. Would you like to see?"

Nikki watched the bubbles rise in her glass.

"I should probably wait for the others," she said.

"Of course." He checked his watch. "Though at this rate, I'm not sure they're coming at all. Astrid can be terribly unreliable."

Through the windows, the island's lights twinkled in the distance. Other boats bobbed nearby, their occupants probably having normal evenings. Normal parties.

The champagne tasted flat, metallic somehow. Nine thousand dollars for a party with no party. Just her and Patrick Barzani, whose pupils were blown so wide she could barely see the brown of his irises. His jaw worked slightly, grinding teeth—the same cocaine tics she'd seen in club bathrooms back home.

"The Caravaggio is extraordinary," he continued, settling into the chair across from her. "Judith Beheading Holofernes. Are you familiar with it?"

"No."

"A biblical scene. A beautiful woman seducing a general, then cutting off his head while he sleeps." His fingers traced patterns on the armrest. "The artist captured the exact moment of death—that transition from life to void. Quite magnificent."

Something in his tone, the way he lingered on 'void,' made her want to pull her wrap tighter despite the warm evening.

"Kind of dark for a party yacht," she managed.

Patrick shrugged. "Great art is about contrasts. Pain and pleasure. Beauty and horror intertwined." He stood. "Come. Just a quick look."

Never go below deck. Ty's voice was clear as a bell in her mind. *Never go anywhere alone.*

But this was Patrick Barzani. The man who owned all of this. Who'd offered her this lifeline when she had nothing. The yacht was staffed; she'd seen crew members. How dangerous could viewing art be? And she's never heard any rumors about Patrick. Sure, he was weird, even a little creepy, but no inappropriate sexual behavior, no assaults. If anything the girls who engaged with him saw him as Amira's little lap dog.

"Five minutes," Patrick said. "Then we'll come back up and wait for the others. Or I'll have the captain take you back if you prefer. The painting, the room, it really is a sight to behold. Something you'll never forget."

What the hell, she thought. She had her distress beacon. Her pepper gel. And it was Patrick.

"Alright," she said, setting down her glass. "But quickly."

"Wonderful." His smile widened. "After you."

He gestured toward a staircase tucked behind the bar. The opening was narrow, brass railings polished to a mirror shine. As she approached, she could smell the lower deck—diesel and cleaning products and something else.

The stairs were steeper than expected. Her heels clicked on each step, the sound sharp in the enclosed space. She gripped the handrail, her clutch bumping against her hip.

"Mind your head," Patrick said behind her. Close behind her. She could smell his cologne mixed with the chemical tang of whatever he'd been taking.

The corridor below felt wrong. After the yacht's expansive upper deck, this was like being inside an expensive coffin.

"The naval architect who built this was a genius," Patrick said. "Maximized every cubic foot. You'd never know from above how much is hidden down here."

They passed closed doors. No sound from behind either one.

The engine noise was louder here, a steady thrum through the soles of her shoes. The air conditioning kept the space cold enough to raise goosebumps on her arms.

A crew member emerged from a side passage—white uniform, eyes that never left the floor. He nodded at Patrick and slipped past Nikki without acknowledgment, as if she didn't exist.

"Climate control is essential," Patrick explained, stopping at an unmarked door at the corridor's end. "Salt air is murder on canvas."

He produced a key card from his jacket. The card reader was hidden behind what looked like a light switch. He waved the card, and something clicked deep in the door's mechanism. Industrial. Serious.

"After you," he said, pushing the door open.

The room beyond was black. Complete absence of light. The air that rushed out was meat locker cold.

"Sorry," Patrick said, his hand finding the small of her back to guide her forward. The touch made her skin crawl. "The automation takes a moment."

She stepped inside because stepping back would mean pushing into him. The floor felt different—smooth and hard. Like a hospital.

The door swung shut behind them with a soft pneumatic hiss. Sealed. The silence was complete.

"Patrick?" Her voice sounded small.

"One moment."

She heard him moving but couldn't place where. Her eyes strained for any light, but the darkness was total. Professional.

The air smelled wrong. Under the antiseptic surface were other scents. Metal. Leather. Something organic.

"Almost there," Patrick said from a different place than expected. He was circling.

Soft clicks. Not light switches. Something else.

Dim red light bloomed from the corners. As her eyes adjusted, the truth hit her.

Stainless steel dominated the room. A table in the center with drainage channels. Above it, surgical lights hung like mechanical spiders. IV stands flanked the table, bags already hanging, tubes coiled and waiting.

The walls held restraints—medical-grade leather straps with metal buckles. Monitoring equipment. Cameras mounted at precise angles. On a side table, instruments laid out with surgical precision.

This wasn't a gallery.

CHAPTER
SIXTY-FOUR

"PATRICK," she said, her voice steady despite her hammering heart. "I'd like to go back up now."

"Would you?" His voice came from behind her, between her and the door. "But you haven't seen the collection yet."

She turned slowly. He stood with his back against the door, and in the red light, he looked like someone else entirely.

"There's no Caravaggio," she said.

"Isn't there? I'm sure it was kept here. Ah well, never mind." His smile was terrible. "We can create our own art. Something much more intimate than oil on canvas. Something more contemporary."

Nikki's hand moved toward her clutch. Casual, like adjusting the strap.

"Don't," Patrick said sharply. "I know Ty probably gave you some self defense party favors. Did you really think we don't monitor our employees, even the contractors?"

Her fingers kept working anyway. The beacon was there, deep in the lining where she'd cut the slit. Just flip the cover, hold the button.

"Here's what's going to happen," Patrick continued, reaching into his pocket. "You're going to undress. Slowly. Then you're going to lie on that table. If you cooperate, this will be transformative. If you fight—"

The taser appeared in his hand. Blue electricity arced between the prongs.

"Please," Nikki said, her fingers finding the beacon inside her clutch. "The money. I'll give it back. I won't tell anyone—"

"Tell anyone what?" He took a step forward. "That you came to a party that doesn't exist? On a yacht that was never here? That you disappeared like your friend Harper is about to?"

Another step.

"No one knows you're here, Nikki. No one's coming."

Her thumb found the plastic guard over the activation button. Flip and press.

"You're wrong," she said.

"Am I?" Another step. "Your protector Samir is with Natasha right now. Your friend Harper is a dead girl walking. And your new friend Tyrone? He thinks you're at a party with other girls, having champagne and making small talk."

The plastic guard flipped up with a tiny click.

"What was that?" Patrick's head tilted.

"Nothing." Her thumb found the button. "Just my bracelet. The clasp is loose."

He studied her. Then: "Show me your hands."

"Patrick—"

"Show me your hands!"

He lunged forward with the taser. Nikki pressed the button, feeling it depress as she tried to dodge. But he was faster.

The prongs caught her shoulder. Electricity shot through her body like liquid fire. Every muscle seized at once, her jaw clamping shut so hard she tasted blood. Her legs went out from under her.

She hit the floor hard. The clutch flew from nerveless fingers, skittering across the smooth surface. Through the haze of pain, she saw Patrick standing over her. The taser clicked off.

"Now then," he said, not even breathing hard. He walked to where her clutch had fallen, picked it up. "Let's see what toys you brought to my party."

The door was locked. The room was soundproofed.

And somewhere in her fallen bag, invisible in the red light, a small

LED blinked steadily. Calling for help that might never come.

CHAPTER
SIXTY-FIVE

TY'S PHONE vibrated against his ribs—three pulses, then steady buzzing. Not a call. Not a text. The emergency frequency.

He pulled it from his pocket, the screen showing a red dot pulsing on a maritime chart. Nikki's beacon. The GPS coordinates placed way offshore. Right where the yacht sat at anchor.

"Shit."

He thumbed open the encrypted channel. The Red Team leader answered on the first ring.

"Go ahead."

"Beacon's active. Need immediate extract from the yacht. Where are you?"

"Roger that. Fifteen mikes out." The leader's tone was professional but urgent. "We had an engine failure. Just got it running again."

"Fifteen minutes?" Ty felt his jaw clench. In fifteen minutes, Nikki Bailey could be dead. "How bad was the failure?"

"Catastrophic. Fuel line split clean through." A pause. "Looked almost surgical, if I'm being honest. Like someone scored it to fail under pressure."

Of course they did, Ty thought. There were no coincidences here. No consequences either.

"Can you make it faster?"

"Negative. We're already pushing it. Engine's running rough. Any harder and we'll be swimming."

Ty looked out at the yacht. Its lights glowed peacefully in the distance. Somewhere inside, Nikki was in trouble bad enough to activate an emergency beacon. Fifteen minutes was way too long.

"I'm going in," Ty said.

"That's not advisable."

"Noted. Get here when you can."

He killed the connection and turned toward the dock. Two resort tenders bobbed at their moorings, engines off, their operators lounging nearby. One was playing cards with a security guard. The other—younger, maybe twenty-five—was cleaning equipment.

Ty approached the younger one. "I need a boat to take me out. Now."

The kid looked up, taking in Ty's expression. "Sir, I need authorization from—"

"Emergency." Ty kept his voice level. Professional. "Medical situation on the yacht. We gotta go."

"I need to call it in." The kid reached for his radio. "Protocol says—"

Ty's hand closed over the radio, gently but firmly pushing it down. "What's your name?"

The kid swallowed. "I... need to verify—"

"Listen to me." Ty stepped closer. "There's a woman on that yacht who's going to die if we don't move right now. Every second we waste discussing protocol is a second she doesn't have. Are you going to help me save her life, or are you going to explain to the authorities why you let her die?"

The operator's eyes flicked to the security guard, still absorbed in his card game fifty feet away. Ty could see him weighing options—job security against human life.

"I could lose my job."

"I'll make sure you don't." Ty's voice was certain. "But we need to go. Now."

The kid looked at the yacht, then back at Ty. Something in Ty's expression convinced him because he nodded once.

"Tender Two's the fastest. Come on."

They jogged to the second boat. The operator fired up the engine while Ty cast off the lines. The motors rumbled to life—not the sharp bark of military RHIBs but adequate.

"Cast off," the kid said, working the controls.

Ty threw the lines aboard and jumped in as they reversed away from the dock. The security guard looked up from his cards, frowning. Ty gave him a casual wave—nothing to see here.

As soon as they cleared the dock, Ty pulled out his phone again. Lock answered immediately.

"Go."

"Nikki activated her beacon. She's on the yacht with Barzani. I'm en route on a resort tender."

"Backup?"

"Red Team's fifteen mikes out. Engine trouble."

Lock's paused, "How convenient. You armed?"

"Always."

"Barzani won't be alone. The yacht crew—"

"Don't worry." Ty glanced at the kid steering, who was focused on navigation. "I'll handle it."

"Ty?"

"I'm not letting another girl die on this island." The words came out harder than he'd intended. "Not happening."

"Copy that. I'll see what I can shake loose from this end. Watch your six."

Ty ended the call and moved forward to where the operator was steering. The yacht grew larger ahead, its sleek lines hiding whatever was happening inside.

"Can't we go faster?" Ty asked.

"This is full throttle." The kid had to shout over the engine noise. "Any more and we'll blow the motor."

The tender bounced over a swell, spray soaking them both. Ty wiped salt water from his eyes, never taking his gaze off the yacht.

"What's on the yacht?" the operator asked. "Really?"

"Someone who trusted me to keep her safe."

The kid nodded, understanding more than Ty had said. "There's a boarding ladder on the starboard side. Away from the main deck. Less visible."

"You know the boat?"

"I ferry supplies sometimes. The crew..." He hesitated. "They're not regular yacht crew. They don't talk much."

Of course they weren't. Nothing on this island was regular. The whole place was like some kind of billionaire freakshow.

The yacht loomed larger now. Ty could make out details—the gleaming hull, portholes glowing with warm light, the radar array turning lazily on the bridge.

"Two minutes," the operator said.

Ty checked his weapon. SIG Sauer P229, thirteen rounds. Against an unknown number of irregular crew. The odds sucked, but odds didn't matter anymore. He was done playing nice.

"Soon as I'm aboard, you get clear," Ty said. "This isn't your rodeo. Anyone asks, tell them I threatened you, that you had no choice in the matter. Understand?"

The yacht filled their vision now. Ty could hear music drifting across the water. Jazz. Sophisticated. The soundtrack to nightmares dressed up as dreams.

One minute.

His phone buzzed. Red Team leader: "Engine's gone again. We're working on it but no guarantees when we can get there."

CHAPTER
SIXTY-SIX

EFRON CAUGHT up with Amira as she walked past Villa Twelve, her heels clicking on the path.

"We need to talk," he said, falling into step beside her.

"I have a conference call in ten minutes." She didn't slow her pace. "Whatever it is can wait."

"No, it can't."

His tone made her glance at him. Efron's face remained professionally composed, but she'd known him long enough to read the tension in his jaw, the way his hand kept touching his phone.

"Walk with me," she said.

They continued along the path that wound between the premium villas. Lights glowed behind privacy screens, the murmur of conversation and soft music drifting from terraces. The kingdom of pleasure they'd built, running like clockwork.

"Lock's technical team swept Villa Nine today," Efron said.

"So? That's what we're paying them to do."

"They found everything."

Amira's stride broke for just a moment. "Impossible. We've had dozens of assessments."

"They brought military-grade detection equipment. NLJD units, thermal mapping, spectrum analyzers." Efron kept his voice low. "They didn't just find cameras. They have the entire infrastructure. The shadow network, the encrypted feeds, even traced the data flow."

She stopped walking, turning to face him. In the landscape lighting, her face was cold marble.

"How thorough was their search?"

"Thorough. All the devices in Villa Nine. They mapped the power draws, identified the recording equipment, even dated the installation to original construction." His hand touched his phone again. "This isn't some security guard with a bug detector. The people he brought in know exactly what they're looking at."

"And Lock?"

"Knows everything. Or enough." Efron glanced around, confirming they were alone. "He had them document it all. Off-network storage, encrypted files. He's building a case."

Amira's lips thinned. "This is your failure, Ethan. Your security protocols—"

"My protocols?" His voice rose slightly before he caught himself. "I wanted to contain them after they found the body. You're the one who insisted on playing nice. 'Buy him off,' you said. 'Everyone has a price.'"

"Because that's how civilized people handle problems. Not with your Israeli tendency toward—"

"Toward what? Efficiency?" Efron stepped closer. "We had them isolated, controlled. I could have had an accident arranged within hours. Clean, professional. But no, you wanted to try to sweet talk them, make offers, play your games."

"Games?" Her voice turned dangerous. "Everything we've built here is built on games. Connections I nurtured. My ability to read people, give them what they want."

"Your ability to whore them out, you mean."

The slap came fast, her palm cracking against his cheek. A couple walking past quickly looked away, hurrying off toward their villa.

Efron touched his face, a smile playing at his lips. "Truth stings, does it?"

"How dare you—"

"How dare I what? State facts?" He moved closer, his voice dropping. "You think I don't know about Harper? Your husband didn't just randomly assign her to Ulrich. Patrick knew exactly what would happen. Violent client, isolated girl, hidden cameras. Perfect blackmail material."

"You're talking about my husband—"

"I'm talking about a sick fuck who gets off on this." Efron's composure cracked. "And you know it. You've always known it. You just choose to look the other way because it suited you, helped you land the whales who like the really sick stuff."

Amira's hand moved to strike him again, but he caught her wrist.

"Did you really think I didn't know?" he continued. "Every time a girl goes missing, every time there's an 'accident,' every time Patrick takes special interest in the matching process? You knew, and you let it happen because the recordings were so valuable."

"Let go of me."

He released her wrist but didn't step back. "We're past the point of pretending, Amira. Lock knows about the surveillance. His team is documenting everything. And your husband—"

"Is a necessary evil." The words came out flat, empty of emotion. "Do you think I enjoy being married to him? Watching him pretend to be charming while his mind works through his sick fantasies? But he serves a purpose. The clients trust him. The girls think he's harmless."

"Harmless? He's practically a serial killer. At least a proxy one," Efron laughed bitterly.

"Patrick's activities have never compromised operations before—"

"Because I clean up after him!" The words burst out. "Every mess, every body, every hysterical girl who sees too much. Who do you think handles that? Who makes the problems disappear?"

They stood facing each other in the tropical darkness. In the distance, music drifted from the main resort—a string quartet playing for guests who had no idea their paradise was built on surveillance and suffering.

"We need to contain Lock," Amira said finally. "Whatever it takes."

"Too late for that now. They have our secrets."

"Then we need better leverage. Something that makes him understand the consequences of talking."

"What leverage? They found our entire operation. They know—"

"They know about equipment in walls. They don't know how deep this goes."

"Yet."

Amira smoothed her dress, composing herself. "Your friends in Tel Aviv—"

"Are not going to be happy about any of this." Efron's tone turned icy. "They won't let this operation be compromised." He stepped back, the power dynamic suddenly clear. "You've been playing hotelier, Amira. Thinking you run this place. You're middle management, at best. A useful asset who's become a liability."

"You wouldn't dare—"

"Wouldn't I?" His smile was cold. "Who do you think suggested this location? Who arranged the permits, the protection, the immunity from local law? You and Patrick were selected because you fit a profile. Persian exile desperate to matter, perfect for fronting an operation. Never forget who you really answer to."

His phone buzzed. Then again, insistent. He pulled it from his pocket, frowning at the screen.

"What is it?" Amira asked.

He answered, listening. His expression moved from annoyance to alarm to panic.

"When?" he barked into the phone. "How many?" A pause. "And Patrick's where?"

He lowered the phone slowly, his face draining of color.

"What?" Amira demanded.

"Ty Johnson just commandeered a resort tender. The Red Team's mobilizing with full tactical gear." His voice was hollow. "They're heading for the yacht."

"Which yacht?"

"Which yacht?" he scoffed. "The one where your husband is alone with Nikki Bailey."

CHAPTER
SIXTY-SEVEN

THE IV DRIP marked time in Nikki's peripheral vision. One drop. Two. Three. She tried counting them, needing something for her mind to hold on to, but the numbers kept sliding away.

"Propofol and ketamine," Patrick said, adjusting the flow rate with practiced fingers. "A delicate balance. Too much propofol and you'll sleep through everything. Too much ketamine and you'll dissociate completely. I want you present."

His voice had changed. Gone was the manic energy. The cocaine-fueled chatter had begun to subside. This Patrick moved precisely, each gesture deliberate. He'd removed his jacket and rolled his sleeves with the same precision someone might use to wash for an operation.

Nikki tried to turn her head, to track his movement, but the padded restraints held her immobile. Leather against her wrists and ankles, another strap across her forehead. She could feel them without being able to see them, phantom pressure points mapping her helplessness.

"Ketamine truly is a fascinating drug," Patrick continued, checking her pupils with a penlight. "Dissociative anesthetic. You'll feel everything but be unable to process it properly. Pain becomes... almost abstract. Like watching a film of someone else suffering."

The light hurt. Everything hurt. But distant, muffled, like hearing music through walls. She tried to speak and managed only a low moan. Her tongue felt thick, foreign.

"Shh." He placed a finger against her lips. His skin smelled of antiseptic soap. "Vocalization is limited. The propofol affects the laryngeal muscles. But don't worry—I don't need you to speak. Your body will tell me everything."

The red emergency lighting made shadows dance on the ceiling. Or maybe that was the drugs. Nikki couldn't tell anymore. She'd lost track of time, moments stretching and compressing without pattern. How long had she been here? Minutes? Hours?

Patrick moved to the side table, fingers dancing over instruments laid out on surgical cloth. Each piece precisely aligned, organized by function. He selected something that caught the light—thin, silver.

"I need you to understand something," he said, not looking at her. "This isn't about anger. It's not about power. Those are pedestrian motivations, the kind they talk about in dull textbooks."

He held the instrument up, examining it. A probe of some kind, medical grade, designed for purposes she didn't want to fathom.

"This is about transformation. About finding the exact moment when someone becomes something else. When the social construct of identity dissolves and only the essential remains."

Nikki's fingers twitched, trying to form fists. The small movement sent waves of pins and needles up her arms. The restraints weren't tight enough to cut circulation, she realized. He wanted her to feel everything.

"Harper was meant for Ulrich," Patrick continued, setting the probe aside and selecting something else. "A crude man with crude appetites. No artistry, no finesse. Just animal brutality." He turned to study her with those dilated pupils that seemed to eat light. "But you... you're mine."

A sound escaped her throat. Not quite a word, not quite a scream. The drugs had turned it into something pitiful.

"That's it," he encouraged. "Don't fight the medication, Nikki. Let it carry you. Fighting only exhausts you, and we have so much ahead of us."

He moved closer, and she could smell him now—cologne mixed

with a cocaine flop sweat. Excitement, she realized. He was sweating from excitement.

"Do you know what the most fascinating part of the human body is?" His hand hovered over her stomach, not touching, just close enough for her to feel the heat. "The nervous system. A hundred billion neurons, all firing, all processing, all capable of such exquisite sensation."

His hand moved to her arm, fingers finding the median nerve at her wrist. He pressed, gently at first, then with increasing pressure. Pain bloomed—sharp despite the drugs, traveling up her arm in electric waves.

"See? Even sedated, even dissociated, the body knows. The body remembers." He released the pressure, and the absence of pain was almost worse. "We're going to explore every pathway, map every response. By the end, I'll know you better than you know yourself."

Nikki tried to focus on the ceiling, on the IV drip, on anything but his voice. But the ketamine made concentration impossible. Her thoughts scattered, reforming in patterns that made no sense. She was in the yacht. She was back home in Atlantic City. She was drowning in champagne while Ty's voice told her to know her exits.

The exits. Where were the exits?

"You're trying to orient yourself," Patrick observed. "Admirable, but futile. The drugs won't allow it. You're here, Nikki. With me. Nothing else exists for us."

He moved to the camera mounted above the table, adjusting its angle with an artist's care. The lens stared down at her, a mechanical eye recording her helplessness.

Another camera, positioned at the foot of the table. He checked its focus, made minor adjustments. His movements were loving, reverent. This was ritual for him, she realized through the chemical haze. Sacred.

Nikki's eyes tracked to her clutch, abandoned on a counter near the door. So close. So impossibly far. The beacon inside, still blinking probably. Calling for help that wouldn't come in time, if it came at all.

"I never asked you. Are you religious, Nikki?" Patrick asked, selecting a new instrument. This one she recognized—a scalpel, its blade catching the red light like a tiny flame. " I never thought I was. But I find myself thinking about God during moments like these."

He set the scalpel within easy reach but didn't pick it up. Not yet. The anticipation was part of it, she understood. The waiting. The dread.

"The Catholics had it wrong with their mortification of the flesh. They thought suffering brought you closer to God through denial, through punishment." He adjusted her IV again, and warmth flooded her arm. "But suffering is revelation. It strips away pretense, showing us what we truly are."

Nikki felt tears sliding down her temples, pooling in her ears. The drugs made even this sensation distant. She was watching someone else cry. Someone else strapped to a table while a madman prepared to dissect her.

"Oh, look at you crying Nikki. It's so beautiful," Patrick whispered.

He pulled on surgical gloves with practiced movements. The latex snapped against his wrists, a sound that would haunt her if she survived. When she survived. She had to survive. Ty was coming. Someone was coming. They had to be. Her story couldn't end like this.

"We'll start slowly, shall we?" Patrick said, his gloved hand trailing along her arm. "Establish some baselines. The body has limits, even with medical support."

His fingers found pressure points—here at her elbow, there at her shoulder. Each touch precise, calculated.

"I've studied for years," he continued conversationally. "Medical texts, anatomy courses, even worked with a mortician for a while. But corpses teach you nothing about suffering. They're just architecture. You need someone to still be alive to understand pain."

The yacht rocked gently, and Nikki's drugged mind latched onto the movement. They were on water. Water meant shore. Shore meant people. Help. But the soundproofing ate her moans, turned them into whispers that died inches from her lips.

"Shall we begin?" Patrick asked, though he didn't expect an answer. He reached for the scalpel, then paused. "No. Too crude for an opening. Let's start with pressure. See how your nervous system responds to focused stimulus."

He produced something she couldn't identify—a device with a rounded tip that looked medical but wrong somehow. When he pressed it against the inside of her elbow, she understood. Pain bloomed—not sharp but deep, traveling along nerve pathways like electricity through wires.

"Ulnar nerve," he noted, watching her face. "Minimal surface damage but maximum neural response. See how your pupils dilate despite the propofol? Fascinating."

Nikki's back arched involuntarily, muscles fighting restraints. The movement was small—the drugs saw to that—but Patrick noticed everything.

"Yes," he breathed. "That's what I was looking for. The body is always honest. No matter what the mind wants, the body tells truth."

He moved the device to her knee, finding another nerve cluster. The pain was different here—shooting down her leg, making her foot cramp despite her inability to move. Patrick watched with the intensity of a scientist observing crucial data.

"You're lasting so much better than I expected," he said. "Most are screaming by now. But the drugs help, don't they? Keep you right at the edge without letting you fall over. We can continue like this for hours this way."

Hours. The word echoed in Nikki's fractured consciousness. She tried to hold onto Ty's face, Lock's voice, Harper's smile—anything that wasn't this room, this man, this careful deconstruction of her humanity.

"I'm going to tell you a secret," Patrick said, setting the pressure device aside. "We have surveillance in the villas. Cameras that capture the vital moments. My idea. But not for blackmail, not for leverage—that would be Efron and Amira's pedestrian thinking. I wanted to study. To observe how people behave when they think they're unseen. The intimate moments. The truth revealed in privacy."

He selected another instrument, this one with multiple thin prongs.

He held the instrument up, letting her see it. "This stimulates multiple nerve endings simultaneously. The sensation is... unique. Some describe it as burning. Others say it's like insects under the skin. We'll see which camp you fall into."

Nikki's fingers twitched again. She focused all her will on moving, on breaking free, on doing something. But the drugs held her in chemical chains stronger than any restraint.

"Oh," Patrick said, noticing her efforts. "Still fighting. How wonderful. He touched her cheek with disturbing tenderness. "You're special. You're going to last long enough for me to show you everything."

Somewhere above, through tons of steel and soundproofing, jazz still played. The yacht still rocked. The world still turned.

But in the red-lit room, time had stopped. There was only Patrick's voice, the drip of the IV, and the patience of a monster who'd waited their whole life for this.

"Shall we continue?" he asked.

And then he began for real.

CHAPTER
SIXTY-EIGHT

THE BOARDING LADDER rose from black water into darkness. Ty hauled himself up. Somewhere above, jazz still played—Duke Ellington maybe, sophisticated and smooth. The music pissed him off. Nikki was in trouble bad enough to activate an emergency beacon, and these fuckers were playing dinner music.

He climbed fast, weapon tucked at the small of his back. The yacht's hull was slick with salt spray. Ten feet. Twenty. His shoulders ached from the angle, but he'd climbed worse in Iraq, usually with people shooting at him.

"Stop right there!"

The voice came from above. Vaguely French accent, commanding tone. Ty looked up to see a uniformed figure leaning over the rail—captain's stripes on his shoulders, gray beard trimmed.

"This is a private vessel," the captain continued. "You're committing an act of piracy under international maritime law. I'm authorized to use force—"

Ty reached the rail and vaulted over. The captain stepped back, hand moving toward his hip. Radio or weapon, didn't matter. Ty closed the distance before he could complete the motion.

"Where are they?" Ty grabbed the man's wrist. "Patrick Barzani and the girl. Where?"

"I don't know what you're—"

Ty spun him, arm across his throat in a blood choke. Not enough to put him out, just enough to focus his attention. "Try again."

"You can't... this is piracy... I'll have you arrested..."

The threats died as Ty increased pressure. The captain's face went red, then purple. Ty eased off just enough to let him breathe.

"Final chance. Where?"

Movement to his left. Another crew member emerging from a doorway—built like a nightclub bouncer, moving like he knew how to fight. He saw Ty, saw his captain in a chokehold, and charged without hesitation.

Brave but stupid.

Ty released the captain with a shove, pivoting to meet the charge. The crew member threw a wild haymaker. Ty slipped inside the arc, driving an elbow into the man's solar plexus. Air rushed from his lungs. As he doubled over, Ty brought his knee up hard, catching him in the face. Something cracked. Blood sprayed across the teak decking.

The man went down and didn't move.

Ty turned back to the captain, who was pressed against the rail, eyes wide. "Your boy's not getting up. Next one won't either. Where's Barzani?"

"Below," the captain stammered. "Mr. Barzani's in one of the private areas below."

"Show me."

"I can't—he doesn't like to be disturbed when—"

Ty drew his weapon, letting the captain see it clearly. "You're going to take me there. Now. Or I'm going to paint this deck with your brains and find it myself."

The captain's hands shook as he raised them. "Okay. Okay. This way."

He led Ty through a salon that reeked of money—crystal decanters, leather furniture, art that probably cost more than most people's houses. The music was louder here, masking their footsteps. No other crew visible, but Ty kept the captain close, gun pressed against his kidney.

They descended narrow stairs to the lower deck. The change was immediate—gone was the luxury, replaced by functional corridors that felt cramped. The music faded, replaced by engine noise and the hum of generators.

"Which way?"

The captain hesitated at a junction. "It's... I should warn you. The cabin is special. Soundproofed. Reinforced. Mr. Barzani values his privacy. Even I'm not allowed inside."

"Move."

They passed doors marked as crew quarters, storage, mechanical spaces. The captain tried to slow at one intersection, maybe hoping to mislead. Ty jabbed the gun harder into his back.

"Don't get creative. Straight to Barzani."

At the corridor's end, an unmarked door stood apart from the others. Heavier. No visible handle, just a card reader glowing red. As they approached, Ty heard it—muffled but unmistakable. A woman's scream, distorted by soundproofing but carrying pure terror.

"Open it."

"I can't." The captain's voice cracked. "Only Mr. Barzani has access. It's biometric and keycard. I swear, I can't—"

Ty slammed him face-first into the bulkhead. The captain dropped, blood streaming from his nose. Ty tried the card reader—dead. He kicked the door where the lock mechanism should be. Solid steel. Didn't budge.

Another sound from inside. Nikki's voice, he was sure of it now.

He shot the card reader. Sparks flew, plastic melted, but the door remained sealed. He shot the lock area—two, three times. The bullets barely dented the metal.

"Nikki!" He pounded on the door with his fist. "Nikki, I'm here! Hold on!"

The sounds from inside stopped. Worse somehow than hearing them continue.

Ty stepped back, evaluating. The door was serious business—military-grade reinforcement, probably with deadbolts that went deep into the frame. He'd need explosives or cutting tools, neither of which he had.

Multiple footsteps on the deck above. The captain must have triggered an alarm, or someone had heard the shots. Didn't matter. More crew meant more obstacles between him and Nikki.

He grabbed the semi-conscious captain by the collar, dragging him up. "Override. Emergency code. Something."

"There's... nothing..." Blood bubbled from the captain's broken nose. "He designed it... that way. Total privacy. Can't be overridden."

Ty dropped him and turned back to the door. Somewhere behind that steel, Patrick Barzani was doing things to the girl. And Ty, for all his training and violence and determination, couldn't reach her.

He heard footsteps on the stairs now. Coming fast.

CHAPTER
SIXTY-NINE

THE POUNDING on the door broke through her haze. Metal on metal. A voice, muffled but urgent. Her name—someone was calling her name.

"Nikki! Nikki, I'm here!"

Ty. The recognition hit her immediately. Ty had found her.

Her body tried to respond. Vocal cords strained against the propofol's paralysis, managing only a low, animal sound. But it was enough. Patrick heard it too, his hands stilling on her arm where he'd been mapping nerve clusters.

"Interesting," he said.

The pounding continued. Then gunshots—three sharp cracks that made the door ring. Patrick didn't flinch. Instead, he tilted his head, studying the door with satisfaction.

"Military-grade steel composite," he said, loud enough for his voice to carry. "Your friend could shoot at it all day."

He moved to the door, pressing his palm against it. "Can you hear me out there? Ty, was it? I'm Patrick Barzani. I believe you've been looking for Nikki."

The pounding stopped. Silence stretched, filled only by the hum of equipment and Nikki's labored breathing.

"She's here with me," Patrick continued, his voice becoming theatrical. "Very much alive. Very much aware. Would you like to know what we're discussing?"

"Open this fucking door!" Ty's voice.

"I'm afraid that's not possible." Patrick turned back to Nikki, his dilated eyes bright with excitement. "Isn't this delicious? He's so close."

Nikki fought to make sound, any sound. The drugs made her throat feel thick, but desperation drove her. A moan escaped, louder this time. Proof of life.

"That's it," Patrick encouraged. "Let him hear you. Let him know you're still capable of response."

He returned to the table, selecting a new instrument. His movements became theatrical, playing to his unseen audience.

Nikki's eyes tracked to the door. If she could just make enough noise, give Ty something to focus on. She pulled against the restraints, muscles fighting chemical paralysis. The leather creaked—small sound, but in the soundproofed room it seemed loud.

He touched the rod to her inner arm, finding the radial nerve. Electricity shot through her arm, making her fingers spasm. This time she managed a scream—weak, distorted, but unmistakably a scream.

The pounding resumed with renewed fury. "Nikki! Hold on!"

"She can hear you," Patrick said, adjusting the device's intensity. "Every word."

He moved the device to her leg, finding the sciatic nerve. The pain was different here—deeper, radiating from hip to ankle. Nikki's back arched as much as the restraints allowed. Another scream, stronger this time. Her body was fighting now, survival instinct burning through the drugs.

"That's it," Patrick breathed. "Show him you're alive. Show him exactly what he can't stop."

The IV bag swayed with her movements, the drip rate increasing. Patrick noticed, adjusting the flow with practiced fingers. "Can't have you going into shock. Not yet. We have an audience now. That changes everything."

Through tears she didn't remember shedding, Nikki could see his transformation. The controlled clinician was becoming something more primal. His breathing had quickened, sweat beading on his forehead despite the cool air. The audience—Ty's presence—had excited him in ways she couldn't have anticipated.

"You know what's remarkable?" Patrick continued, speaking to both of them now. "The human body's capacity for sensation. We think of pain as simple—damage equals response. But it's so much more complex."

He demonstrated, touching the device to points along her torso. Each contact brought different sensations—burning, freezing, electric, crushing. Her nervous system couldn't process them all. She screamed again, the sound raw and desperate.

"Stop!" Ty's voice cracked. "Just stop!"

Nikki's vision was starting to fracture. The red emergency lighting blurred, each pulse of pain adding new colors. She could feel her heart racing, too fast, too hard. The monitors beside the table showed numbers that meant nothing to her but made Patrick frown.

"Tachycardia," he noted. "Heart rate approaching dangerous levels. The emotional stimulus of rescue proximity is affecting her more than anticipated."

He set aside the neural stimulator, moving to adjust her medications. The clinical care was somehow worse than the torture—the pretense that this was medicine, that he was helping.

"Ty," she managed to croak. The word cost her everything, but she needed him to know she was still here, still fighting.

"I hear you!" His response was immediate. "I'm not leaving! I'm right here!"

Patrick selected a new instrument—Nikki couldn't focus enough to identify it. Her vision was tunneling, darkness creeping in from the edges. But she could still hear. Ty's voice, Patrick's breathing, the steady drip of the IV.

"She has perhaps ten minutes," Patrick announced. "Fifteen if I intervene medically. Her system is approaching cascade failure. The combination of trauma, drugs, and emotional stress is proving too much."

The new instrument touched her skin. Fresh pain, but distant now. Her nervous system was overloading, unable to process new input.

She heard herself scream but it sounded like someone else. Someone far away.

"Nikki!" Ty's voice, desperate. "Stay with me! Don't you quit on me, girl!"

She tried to respond but her throat wouldn't work anymore. The drugs or the damage or simple exhaustion—she couldn't tell. Patrick's face swam above her, those dilated pupils pulling her down.

"This is the moment," he whispered, but his words seemed to echo from a great distance. "The transition."

Nikki's eyes found the IV drip one last time. Still counting drops, though the numbers meant nothing now. One. Two. Three.

Darkness crept in from all sides. Ty's voice fading, Patrick's breathing receding. Even the pain, that constant companion, slipping away.

Her last coherent thought was absurd in its simplicity: She'd never make it back to Atlantic City and her family. Never use that nine thousand dollars. Never get to see her friend Harper again.

Then thought itself dissolved.

CHAPTER
SEVENTY

THE RHIB'S engines cut to idle as it bumped against the yacht's swim platform. The Red Team leader—the same operator who'd found the body days ago—was first up, gear bag slung over his shoulder. Two more operators followed, weapons at low ready, scanning for threats.

"Sitrep," the leader said, taking in Ty's blood-spattered appearance and the barely conscious captain.

"Girl's locked below with Patrick Barzani. Torture scenario. Door's reinforced military-grade." Ty's words came fast, clipped. "Been quiet in there for two minutes."

The leader's expression didn't change, but his hand signals sent one operator toward the upper deck. Clear and secure. No surprises.

They descended quickly, Ty leading. The team leader examined the door—noting the bullet strikes, the damaged card reader, the solid construction.

"Good grouping," he said, running fingers over the impact points. "But this is serious hardware."

"Can you breach it?"

The leader was already gesturing to his second operator, who unslung his pack. "Rig it."

The second operator pulled out blocks of C4, working efficiently.

His hands shaped the plastic explosive around the lock mechanism while the team leader unspooled detonation cord.

"How long?" Ty asked.

"Ninety seconds to rig, five to clear." The leader glanced at him. "Your girl?"

"Asset. Civilian."

"Copy."

The silence from beyond the door pressed against them. No screaming. No taunting. No sounds of movement. Just the hum of the yacht's systems.

"Upper deck's clear," the first operator reported over comms. "Crew's gone. Looks like they rabbited."

"Roger that. Take overwatch position."

The explosives operator finished molding the C4, inserting the blasting cap with delicate precision. The team leader ran det cord along the door's hinges—a backup in case the lock charge wasn't enough. Everything by the book, even with time burning away.

"Stack up," the leader ordered.

They formed against the wall—the second operator with a ballistic shield, Ty behind him, the leader bringing up rear security. Standard breach formation.

"I go in first," Ty said.

"Negative. Shield leads, you're second." The leader's tone brooked no argument. "We do this clean."

The explosives operator held up five fingers. Silent countdown.

Five. Four. Three. Two. One.

The blast shook the yacht. The blast wave hit them, ears popping despite their protective stance. The door buckled inward, lock mechanism vaporized, hinges sheared. Smoke and debris filled the air.

"Go, go, go!"

The second operator moved through the breach, shield leading. Ty followed, weapon up, searching for threats through the smoke.

The red emergency lighting bathed everything in crimson. The torture table dominated the center, Nikki's still form strapped to it. IV lines running, monitors showing weak vitals. Patrick Barzani lay crumpled against the far wall, hands pressed to his ears, blood running between his fingers.

"Clear!" the second operator announced.

"Medic up," the leader called, moving to secure Patrick.

Ty went straight to Nikki. Her skin was gray, lips blue-tinged. The restraints had left deep marks on her wrists. He started unbuckling them, trying not to see the instruments laid out with surgical precision, trying not to think about what they'd been used for.

"Don't touch the IVs," the leader said, working over her efficiently. "Need to know what's in her system."

He checked her pulse—thready but present. Pupils—unequal, sluggish. Breathing—shallow and irregular.

"She's dying," he announced. "We need medevac."

Patrick stirred against the wall, eyes unfocused. The blast had blown out his eardrums, blood trickling down his neck. He tried to speak but only managed a wet cough.

Ty crossed the space in two strides and kicked him in the ribs. Hard. Patrick doubled over, gasping.

The leader grabbed Ty's arm. "Easy there."

"Fuck him," Ty said, but stepped back.

"Call it in," the leader ordered. "Medical emergency, civilian critical, need immediate dustoff." He turned back to Nikki. "We move her topside. Carefully. Get a litter."

They worked efficiently. The operator produced a collapsible stretcher from his pack. Together they transferred Nikki, careful of the IV lines, the evidence of systematic torture written on her body.

"What about him?" the second operator nodded at Patrick.

"Secure him," the team leader said.

They zip-tied Patrick's hands behind his back, ignoring his moans. The leader did a quick assessment—concussion, blown eardrums, possible internal injuries from overpressure. He'd live.

"Moving," the leader announced.

They carried Nikki through the yacht's corridors, up into the main salon where jazz still played softly. The contrast was jarring—torture room below, luxury above. Through the windows, dawn was breaking over the water.

On deck, they laid the stretcher on the helicopter pad. The leader worked to establish a better IV line while the others scanned for threats. Ty knelt beside Nikki, checking her pulse again. Still there. Still fighting.

"Dustoff's fifteen mikes out," the operator reported from his overwatch position. "But we got ourselves some company."

Ty looked up. Three boats moving fast in formation. Even at distance, he could make out the armed men on deck.

"Efron's people," he said.

"How many?" the leader asked, not looking up from Nikki.

"Three boats, maybe four men each. Coming in hot."

The leader finished securing the IV and stood to issue new orders. "Roach, southwest corner. Tierney, northwest. Watch the stairs."

They moved into position efficiently. Weapons weren't raised—not yet—but fingers rested on trigger guards.

The lead boat was two hundred meters out and closing. Through binoculars, Ty could see Efron himself at the helm, face set in hard lines. The boats spread into an attack formation, preparing to come alongside from multiple angles.

"Medical emergency on board," the leader called across the water. "We have a critical patient waiting for dustoff."

Efron's boat didn't slow.

One hundred meters.

"Think they're here to help?" one of the Red Team asked.

Ty checked his weapon's chamber. "Not a chance."

CHAPTER
SEVENTY-ONE

THE YACHT SAT in a pool of light from its own deck lamps, surrounded by circling boats. Ryan Lock stood at the helm of another of the Red Team's RHIBs, hands visible but ready. No sudden movements. No aggressive postures. Ice cold as it played out.

Efron's voice crackled through a megaphone from the lead boat, his Israeli accent thickening with stress. "This ends now, Lock. Surrender for medical evacuation."

On the yacht's deck, two forms lay under the harsh lighting. Nikki on a stretcher, unconscious, skin gray. An oxygen mask covered her face, IV lines running to bags held high by one of the Red Team operators. Beside her, Patrick Barzani sat slumped against the rail, wrists zip-tied behind him, blood crusting around his ears from the breaching blast.

"Both patients go," Lock called back, his voice carrying across the water without electronic aid. "No negotiations."

Three of Efron's boats maintained a loose perimeter, each with four armed men visible. The Red Team had defensive positions on the yacht —one at the bow, one at the stern, the team leader crouched beside Nikki monitoring her vitals. Ty stood near Patrick, ostensibly providing security but looking like he wanted to finish what the blast had started.

"The girl is dying," Efron said through the megaphone. "Every minute we waste—"

A high-pitched scream cut across the water. Another tender was racing from shore, engine whining with the strain. Amira Barzani stood in the bow despite the chop, one hand gripping the windscreen, the other pointing at the yacht.

"We need to get Patrick medical attention. Now!"

They hit the wake from one of the circling boats and Amira nearly went overboard, catching herself at the last second.

The tender pulled alongside Efron's boat, Amira already trying to climb across before they'd properly tied up. Her designer dress was torn, hair wild, makeup streaked down her face. She looked nothing like the composed woman who'd tried to buy Lock's silence days ago.

"Why are you just sitting there?" She grabbed Efron's tactical vest, shaking him. "Storm the yacht! Save Patrick!"

Efron carefully removed her hands. "Mrs. Barzani, we have a tactical situation—"

"I don't care about your tactics." She wheeled on his men. "I need you to save him."

On the yacht, the medic looked up from Nikki's still form. "BP's dropping. Sixty over forty. Heart rate's all over the place." He glanced at Lock. "She's dying. Five minutes, maybe less."

"You heard him," Lock said into his radio, knowing Efron was monitoring the frequency. "Clock's ticking."

Patrick stirred at the sound of his wife's voice, managing to lift his head. Through his concussion and perforated eardrums, he could barely process what was happening, but he knew Amira was near.

"Amira," he croaked, trying to stand. He made it to his knees before swaying dangerously. "Help... please..."

"That whore can die for all I care." Amira's scream was raw. "I need you to save Patrick."

Patrick managed to get his feet under him, using the rail for support. Blood had dried in trails from both ears, giving him a grotesque appearance in the harsh lighting. His pupils were different sizes—clear concussion signs—and his expensive clothes were soiled with vomit and other bodily functions from the blast trauma.

"Please," he said again, louder this time. "Amira... I'm hurt..."

Ty stepped behind him, casual as a man moving to get a better view. "Here," Ty said. "Let me help."

He planted both hands on Patrick's back and shoved. Hard.

Patrick went over the rail with a surprised yelp, hitting the water with a graceless splash. For a moment, he surfaced, sputtering. Then the zip-ties registered. His hands bound behind him, he had no way to swim. No way to even tread water properly.

"Amira!" He managed one clear word before going under.

"Oops," Ty said flatly. "Slipped."

Amira's scream was piercing. "No! Save him! Efron, save him!"

Patrick surfaced again, fifteen feet from Efron's boat, eyes wide with panic. He tried to kick, to stay afloat, but the concussion made coordination impossible. He went under again, came up gasping.

"Do something!" Amira turned on Efron, fists beating against his chest. "He's drowning! Save him, you coward!"

Efron didn't move. Neither did his men. They stood and watched Patrick struggle.

"Jump in yourself if he's that important to you," one of them muttered.

Amira heard him. She spun, slapping the man hard enough to rock his head back. Then she was on Efron, clawing at his face, screaming incoherently. He caught her wrists, trying to restrain her without hurting her, but she was beyond reason.

Patrick surfaced one more time, further away now, carried by the current. His movements were weaker, uncoordinated. More reflex than conscious effort.

"He's drowning" Amira broke free from Efron's grip and lunged for his sidearm. "If you won't save him, I swear, I'll kill every one of—"

"Please be quiet, Amira." Efron's voice was tired. "I need to think."

"I don't care who you think you are, Ethan. You're going to pay for this—" Amira started.

The Glock appeared in Efron's hand. The shot was flat, undramatic in the open air. A small hole appeared in Amira's forehead, just above her left eyebrow. Her expression shifted from rage to surprise to nothing at all.

"I said I needed to think," Efron repeated to no one in particular.

He grabbed her body before it could fall, lifting it with surprising ease for his size. Two steps to the rail and he heaved her over. She hit the water near where Patrick had gone under for the last time, her designer dress spreading like ink in the dark water.

The silence that followed was complete. Even the boat engines seemed to idle quieter, as if the machinery itself was shocked by the sudden violence. On the yacht, the Red Team operators exchanged glances. Lock remained still, processing what they'd just witnessed.

Efron holstered his weapon with the same precision he'd drawn it. When he looked up at the yacht, his expression was blank.

"The girl needs medical evacuation," he said, as if the last two minutes hadn't happened. "Shall we discuss terms?"

Before Lock could respond, someone pointed toward shore. Another boat was approaching—a resort tender. The driver was clearly visible in the deck lights: a heavy-set man in cargo shorts and a polo shirt stretched over an ample belly.

Dave Carter, former SAS, current deputy head of security, completely oblivious to the fact he was motoring into a massacre.

"Oi! Lock!" His Essex accent carried clearly across the water. "What's all this then? Your boys made a right mess of that control room!"

He puttered closer, finally noticing the tactical positions, the weapons, the bodies floating in the water between the boats.

"Bloody hell," he said, killing his engine. "Did I miss something?"

On the yacht, Nikki's monitor alarmed. The medic worked frantically, adjusting IV flows, checking vitals. "We're losing her!"

Ty looked at the water where Patrick had disappeared, then at Efron's hollow expression, then at Dave Carter sitting in his inflatable like a lost English tourist on the Costa Brava who'd fallen asleep on a rented Paddle Boat only to wake up in a shipping lane.

"Yeah, Dave," Ty said quietly. "You missed something."

The bodies of Patrick and Amira Barzani drifted further apart, carried by different currents toward the same dark horizon. On the yacht's deck, Nikki Bailey fought for each breath.

And Dave Carter, sweating in the tropical night, tried to make sense of a world gone mad.

CHAPTER
SEVENTY-TWO

THE BODIES DRIFTED in the black water, Amira's designer dress spreading wide, Patrick facedown. Efron wiped a speck of bloody gristle from his cheek. Around the yacht, boat engines idled, crews frozen in the aftermath of sudden violence.

"Now that you've simplified the command structure," Lock said, his voice carrying across the water with practiced calm, "let's talk about what happens next."

No judgment in his tone. No shock at the executions. Just business, one professional to another. The bodies were facts now, nothing more.

Efron spoke first. "The girl needs medical attention. We're wasting time."

"We are," Lock agreed. "But you need to understand something first. We have your archive."

The words carried across the water. Efron's expression didn't change, but Lock caught how he tensed, the way his hand drifted toward his radio.

"Every video," Lock continued. "Every client. Every crime. Years of material, catalogued by date, name, and act. Quite the collection."

"You're bluffing." Efron's voice remained steady, but there was calculation behind it now.

"Am I?" Lock pulled out his phone, the screen bright in the darkness. "Should I describe what Ulrich did to Harper Holt in Villa Nine? Or the other sick shit you're using for kompromat?"

Efron's men shifted on their boats, uncomfortable with the specifics. They'd known about the surveillance in abstract terms. Hearing it described made it real.

"Maybe we should discuss Mrs. Baka," Lock scrolled through his phone as if checking notes. "The Hungarian security minister with the expensive tastes? You remember—May of last year, Villa Twelve. The Albanian girl who wouldn't stop crying. Baka beat her with a champagne bottle until her orbital bone cracked."

One of Efron's men muttered something in Hebrew. A prayer or a curse, Lock wasn't sure.

"Then there's your American friend," Lock's voice sharpened. "The one with the big ego and the tiny penis. Arrived on his private 757, brought his own security. Except they weren't there to protect him—they were there to procure for him. Two girls who had barely hit puberty. Children. Your cameras caught everything, didn't they? I believe he paid extra for the one you'd found who looked like his daughter."

Dave Carter's boat bounced through the chop, the man himself visible in cargo shorts and a sweat-stained polo that had seen better decades. But Lock noticed how Dave's hand rested on the gun at his hip, his eyes taking in every shooter's position.

"Ethan," Dave said as he pulled alongside, killing his engine as he came alongside.

"Dave." Efron's tone was neutral. "This is a security matter."

"So I gathered." Dave's gaze took in the floating bodies without comment. Twenty years of special operations had shown him worse. "He's not bluffing, sunshine. Your control room's stripped bare back there, mate. Ryan here has everything. Even found your backup servers in Building D."

The confirmation was worse than Lock's claims. Dave Carter didn't bluff, didn't exaggerate. If he said the control room was compromised, it was compromised.

Efron pulled out his radio, eyes never leaving Lock. "Control, this is Efron. Status check on Building D."

Static. Then: "Sir, which... which control room are you asking about?"

The question was telling. Efron's jaw tightened as his temper shortened. "The secondary facility."

More static. Lock could hear panic in the voice when it came back. "Sir, we have a breach. The secondary control room has been accessed. The archive is... they're in everything. The upload started twenty minutes ago. We can't stop it remotely."

On the yacht's deck, Nikki's monitor began alarming. The medic bent over her, checking leads. "V-tach!" he announced. "She's going into cardiac arrest!"

Ty dropped beside the stretcher, positioning himself for compressions. His large hands found the proper position on her chest, beginning the rhythm of chest compressions that every soldier learned.

"Come on," Ty muttered between counts. "Don't you quit on me, girl."

The medic prepared a syringe of epinephrine while the other operator continued bagging oxygen. Nikki's face had gone from gray to death-pale.

"How much?" Efron asked, his voice cutting through the medical emergency.

"Of the archive?" Lock kept his tone conversational. "Forty-seven terabytes so far. Financial records, correspondence, and of course, the video collection. Your greatest hits, all backed up to servers you'll never find."

"Impossible. The encryption—"

"Was excellent. Your cyber security team should be proud. Took our specialists a while to crack." Lock pocketed his phone. "Though the facial recognition index made sorting easier. Searching by name, date, specific acts. Very impressive."

"Fifteen seconds," the medic announced. On the yacht, they'd managed to get Nikki's heart rhythm back, but it was irregular.

"The intelligence services who sanctioned this operation..." Efron began.

"Will cut you loose the moment this goes public," Lock finished. "You know how this works. Plausible deniability. You were a rogue asset, operating without authorization. They'll probably help prosecute you to prove their innocence. Then while you're waiting for your day in court, the guards will disappear and you'll kill yourself. Just like Epstein."

Efron's men were looking at each other now, doubt showing. They'd signed on for close protection and maritime security, not international blackmail operations, especially not ones that ended up with one or more of them in a jail cell on suicide watch. The bodies floating nearby were a clear reminder of how quickly loyalties could shift in this kind of world.

"But the good news is," Lock said, pausing. "We're not interested in destroying intelligence networks or starting international incidents. I mean, we're interested, but we know we wouldn't make it out alive either. We just want the girl to live and certain guarantees for our safety."

"What kind of guarantees?"

"The kind backed by mutually assured destruction. The archive stays private as long as we stay healthy. Anything happens to us, to the women, to anyone connected to this—everything releases. Every video, every client, every transaction."

On the yacht, Ty's compressions had settled into a steady rhythm. Push, push, push. The medic administered another round of drugs. Nikki's color hadn't improved, but she was still fighting.

"You're assuming I care about exposure," Efron said.

"I'm assuming you care about living." Dave Carter's voice was mild, but his hand had shifted to a better grip on his weapon. "Because if those videos release, you won't just have the coppers after you, mate. You'll have forty-seven terabytes worth of very rich, very powerful people who'll want their revenge."

The math was clear. Efron just might survive legal prosecution, assuming he didn't have an accident or suicide himself—his government connections ran deep. But he wouldn't survive the victims of his blackmail operation coming for revenge.

"She needs a hospital," the medic called out. "Now. Or we lose her."

Efron stood motionless for ten seconds that felt like ten minutes. Around him, boats circled, weapons ready, everyone waiting for his decision. The bodies of Patrick and Amira had drifted further apart, pulled by different currents toward the same oblivion.

Finally, he raised his radio. "Medical flight, this is control. You're cleared for departure. Repeat, cleared for immediate departure."

The yacht's engines started up. On deck, the Red Team moved with practiced efficiency, preparing to transfer Nikki to the helicopter that was already approaching, its navigation lights blinking against the stars.

"We're not done," Efron said.

"Roger that, asshole" Lock agreed. "We're not."

Ty never broke rhythm with the compressions, even as they prepared to move Nikki. His shirt was soaked with sweat and blood—hers and Patrick's—but his face showed the focused determination of a man who refused to let death win.

The helicopter touched down on the yacht's helipad, rotors spinning loudly. Medical crew poured out with proper equipment—a real stretcher, portable monitors, a full trauma kit. They took over from the Red Team with professional efficiency, loading Nikki quickly.

"I'm going with her," Ty announced. It wasn't a question.

Lock nodded. There was no discussion, no debate. Ty climbed aboard as they secured Nikki, taking a position where he could see her face, willing her to keep fighting.

As the helicopter lifted off, its rotor wash blew away the evidence of violence—blood diluted by spray, spent shell casings rolling into scuppers. The downdraft churned the water into whitecaps that lapped against the yacht's hull.

The bodies of Amira and Patrick rode the swells. The churn nudged them closer until their bodies nearly touched, spinning the bodies in a slow waltz.

CHAPTER
SEVENTY-THREE

THE HELICOPTER'S interior was cramped with purpose—medical equipment, two flight medics, Ty, and Nikki's failing body at the center of it all. The rotor noise made normal conversation impossible, everything shouted over the mechanical roar and rush of wind through the open door.

Ty gripped Nikki's hand, careful of the IV line taped to her wrist. Her fingers were cold, too cold, but he felt the slightest pressure when he squeezed. Still there. Still fighting.

"Hey," he said, leaning close enough that she might hear him over the noise. "You stay with me, understand? We're almost there."

Her eyelids fluttered—not quite opening, but movement. Response. The medics worked around him, adjusting drips, checking monitors, speaking in medical shorthand that meant nothing good.

"BP's still dropping," one shouted to his partner. "Seventy over forty."

"Push another unit of plasma. Get me that epi ready."

Ty ignored them, focused on Nikki's face. Someone had wiped away the worst of the blood, but bruises were already forming—dark flowers blooming under her brown skin. Evidence of what that monster had done.

"You know what I was thinking about?" Ty said, his mouth close to her ear. "That morning at the pool. Remember? You were swimming laps, perfect form. Like you'd been on a team or something."

Her hand twitched in his. Acknowledgment.

"Remember the pool that morning, Nikki? I knew right then you were a fighter. Way you cut through that water. Strong." He used his free hand to smooth a damp cloth across her forehead. The helicopter's medical kit included everything, even small comfort items. "That's what you need to do now. Just keep swimming, okay? One stroke at a time."

One of the medics reached across him to inject something into her IV port. "We need to intubate," he said to his partner. "She's not maintaining O2 sats."

"Not yet," the other replied. "Let's see if the bronchodilators work."

Ty didn't know what that meant, but he heard the uncertainty in their voices. These were good medics—he could tell by their efficiency—but they were fighting a losing battle with limited tools.

"How much longer?" he asked.

"Fifteen minutes to landing."

"Can't this thing go any faster?"

"We're at max speed, sir. Pilot's pushing it as hard as—"

"Push harder!" The words came out as a snarl. Ty caught himself, saw the medic's expression. "Sorry. I'm sorry. Just..."

"I get it." The medic squeezed his shoulder. "We're doing everything we can."

Ty turned back to Nikki. Her eyes had opened to slits, unfocused but aware. Looking for something. Someone.

"I'm right here," he said. "Not going anywhere."

Her lips moved. No sound, but he could read the shape: Harper?

"She's safe," Ty said quickly. "Harper's safe. You saved her, Nikki. You got her out."

Relief flickered across her features. Then her lips moved again. He leaned closer, trying to catch words that wouldn't come.

"My..." The word was barely a whisper. "Family..."

"Your family?" Ty's throat tightened. "You want me to call them?"

A tiny nod. More lip movement. He made out: "Tell them... I'm sorry... I love them..."

"No." The word came out harder than he intended. "You're going to tell them yourself. You hear me? You're going to call them yourself."

Tears leaked from the corners of her eyes, trailing down toward her ears. She squeezed his hand—once, deliberately. Then her lips formed two words he couldn't mistake: "Thank you."

Something broke inside Ty's chest. This girl—woman—who'd been tortured within an inch of her life, was using what might be her last words to thank him. To worry about others. To apologize to family she might never see again.

"Listen to me," he said, his voice rough with emotion he couldn't contain. "You don't thank me. You don't apologize to anyone. You survived. You fought. You protected your friend when everyone else would have run. You're the bravest person I've ever met, and believe me, I've met some brave fucking people in my life."

The helicopter banked, changing course slightly. Through the open door, Ty could see lights below—the island's medical district coming into view. So close now.

"Five minutes," one of the medics announced.

Nikki's breathing had gone shallow, rapid. The monitors showed numbers that made the medics exchange worried glances. Her hand in his felt smaller somehow, as if she was already beginning to fade.

Ty suddenly realized he was crying. When had that started? Salt tears mixing with the sweat on his face. He turned his face away so she couldn't see it and swiped the tears away with the back of his hand.

"Heart rate's dropping," a medic said. "Forty-two BPM."

"Starting atropine."

The helicopter descended sharply. Through the door, Ty could see the hospital's helipad rushing up to meet them—a concrete circle painted with a red cross, ground crew already waiting with a trauma gurney.

"Almost there," Ty told Nikki. "Thirty seconds and you'll have real doctors, real equipment. You just hold on thirty more seconds."

Her eyes had closed again, but her hand still gripped his. Weak but present. Still fighting.

The skids touched down with a bump that jolted through the cabin. Before the rotors had even begun to slow, the ground crew was moving. Trauma doctors, nurses, equipment that looked like it belonged in a spacecraft.

One of the flight medics was already shouting. "Twenty-three-year-old female, multiple trauma, post-arrest times two."

They were pulling the stretcher out, Ty moving with them, refusing to let go of her hand. The transfer to the hospital gurney was smooth, professional. Someone tried to separate him from her.

"Sir, you need to let go. We've got her."

"I'm not—"

"Sir." A doctor, older woman with kind eyes behind surgical glasses. "The best thing you can do for her now is let us work. I promise you, we'll do everything possible."

Ty looked down at Nikki one last time. Her face was peaceful now, unconscious but still beautiful despite the bruises. He leaned down, whispered in her ear: "You swim, you hear me? You swim like that morning in the pool. I'll be right here when you wake up."

He let go.

They rushed her through the emergency doors, a controlled chaos of medical professionals doing what they did best. Ty stood on the helipad, watching until the doors swung shut behind them. The helicopter's rotors were still spinning down, washing him with warm air that did nothing for the cold in his chest.

Blood on his hands. Hers. Patrick's. His shirt was soaked with it, sticking to his skin. He looked at his palms, seeing the half-moon marks where Nikki's nails had dug in during the worst of the pain.

CHAPTER
SEVENTY-FOUR

PATRICK'S BODY bobbed face-down twenty meters from the yacht, hands still zip-tied. Amira floated closer to him now, her designer dress spread across the surface like spilled ink, one shoe missing.

"Left side," Lock called to the Red Team leader. "Get the woman."

Efron's men worked from their RHIB, boat hooks extended. No one spoke beyond operational necessities. The sound of metal against flesh carried across the water as they snagged clothing, hauled dead weight toward boat rails.

Patrick came up heavy, waterlogged, the zip-ties still binding his wrists. Two of Efron's men struggled to lift him over the gunwale. His body hit the deck with a wet thud.

"Your boss next," Lock said, watching Efron direct the recovery.

Amira's retrieval was easier—less body mass, but the dress complicated things. It wrapped around the boat hook, requiring careful maneuvering. When they finally got her aboard, blood from the head wound had mixed with seawater, creating pink rivulets across the deck.

Efron stood between the two bodies, hands clasped behind his back like he was reviewing an honor guard. "They'll need to be presentable for the families."

"Families," Lock repeated. "Right. Speaking of which—how exactly do you explain putting a bullet in your boss's head to your handlers?"

Efron looked up from the corpses. "Amira wasn't my boss."

"She paid you."

"She signed checks. Different thing entirely." Efron gestured at the boats, the men, the floating crime scene. "You think a woman who married into money and played resort hostess was running this operation?"

Lock studied him. "Who was?"

"People who matter. People who'll understand that sometimes assets become liabilities." Efron's smile was cold. "Amira and Patrick served their purpose. Now they're a problem solved."

"And your handlers are fine with you solving problems by execution?"

"My handlers like results." Efron stepped over Patrick's body to face Lock directly. "Which brings us to our situation. You have forty-seven terabytes of their work. They'll want it back."

"They can want all they like." Lock pulled out his phone, showed the upload progress bar. "Sixty-three percent complete. Takes sixteen hours total."

"I could stop the transmission."

"You could try. But the tech team's already gone dark. Even I can't reach them now." Lock pocketed the phone. "System's automated. Miss two consecutive check-ins, everything releases to seventeen different news outlets."

Dave Carter's inflatable puttered closer. "Bloody hell, this is getting morbid. Can we discuss terms somewhere that doesn't smell like a morgue?"

Efron nodded. "I agree. I'm sure we can come to an arrangement."

Lock stared at him. "Oh, I'm certain we can."

CHAPTER
SEVENTY-FIVE

FIFTEEN MINUTES. Ty had counted every one of them on the industrial clock mounted above the nurses' station. Fifteen minutes of pacing the same twenty feet of corridor, his shoes leaving faint bloody prints on the polished floor that maintenance would have to clean later.

The mainland trauma center's corridors stretched longer than the island's compact medical suite, institutional and impersonal.

People passed—visitors, staff, other walking wounded—and their eyes would catch on him, then slide away. A large Black man covered in blood, wearing the thousand-yard stare of someone who'd seen too much. They gave him space, hurrying past like he might be contagious.

His shirt had dried stiff against his skin. Nikki's blood. Patrick's blood. His own sweat. The smell of copper and fear and helicopter fuel clung to him. He should clean up. Should at least wash his hands. But that would mean leaving this corridor, and he couldn't do that. Not until he knew.

A door opened down the hall. Trauma Suite 3. A young doctor emerged, surgical cap still on, scrubs fresh but his face wearing the exhaustion of a failed fight. He looked at his tablet, then up at Ty.

"Are you with the patient from the helicopter? Nikki Bailey?"

Ty stopped pacing. "Yes."

The doctor approached, and Ty could read it in his walk. The careful steps of someone about to deliver the worst news possible.

"Are you family?"

"Friend." The word felt inadequate. They'd known each other for days, really. But she'd trusted him, taken his equipment, held his hand while dying. What did that make them?

"Do you have next of kin information? Parents? Siblings?"

Ice spread through Ty's chest. "Why?"

The doctor met his eyes directly. No soft lead-in, no gentle preparation. The clinical approach of someone who'd learned that clarity was kinder than false hope.

"Ms. Bailey passed away three minutes ago. We tried everything—massive transfusion protocol, full resuscitation efforts. But the damage was too extensive. Her heart gave out just as we got her into surgery."

The news landed like a punch. Three minutes ago. While he'd been pacing this hallway, counting minutes, she'd been dying in the next room.

"She was twenty-three," Ty said. He didn't know why that mattered, but it did.

"I'm very sorry." The doctor's voice had softened now that the information had been delivered. "If it's any comfort, she wasn't alone. The surgical team was with her. She wasn't in pain at the end."

Wasn't alone. But Ty hadn't been there. He'd promised to be there when she woke up, and instead she'd died surrounded by strangers trying to save her life.

"She mentioned a sister," Ty said, the memory surfacing through his shock. "In Atlantic City. Said she was sick."

The doctor made a note. "We'll need to make notifications. Is there anyone we can call for you?"

For him? Ty almost laughed. He was covered in blood in a hospital corridor, and a doctor was asking if he needed someone to call. What he needed was for time to reverse. For different choices. For a world where twenty-three-year-old women didn't die because they tried to help their friends.

"No," he said.

The doctor hesitated, clearly wanting to offer more comfort but not knowing how. "There are grief counselors available if—"

"Thank you."

It was a dismissal, and the doctor recognized it. He nodded once and retreated back through the trauma suite doors, leaving Ty alone in the corridor with his bloody footprints and the weight of failure.

Three minutes ago. While he'd been watching that clock, counting off seconds like they mattered, Nikki Bailey's heart had stopped beating. All that fight, all that strength he'd seen in her—gone.

Twenty-three years old.

If Patrick Barzani wasn't already dead, Ty would have hunted him down and killed him with his bare hands. Slowly. Making it last. The way Patrick had made Nikki's suffering last.

But Patrick was fish food now, and Nikki was dead, and the math didn't balance. Would never balance.

Ty stood frozen in the hospital corridor, blood on his clothes and grief in his chest, fury coiling behind his ribs.

Somewhere, Lock was negotiating with killers. Somewhere, Harper Holt was recovering from her ordeal. And somewhere back home, a family was about to get the worst phone call of their life.

CHAPTER
SEVENTY-SIX

THE BEACH BAR stood empty under string lights that swayed in the offshore breeze, casting moving shadows across abandoned tables and chairs. Someone had left the music on—Bob Marley singing about three little birds. Armed men stood at the perimeter, watching each other across the sand.

Lock stood at the bar itself, not drinking, just needing something solid to lean against. Efron sat across from him on a barstool, the picture of casual control except for the blood still staining his shirt. Dave Carter had positioned himself at the end, where he could see both groups and the approaches from the resort.

"Before we begin," Lock said, his voice cutting through the reggae, "Ty called. Nikki Bailey died at the hospital. They couldn't save her."

One of the Red Team operators muttered a curse. Dave's face went grim. Even Efron's men shifted uncomfortably, studying their feet.

"She was twenty-three. Her whole life ahead of her," Lock added, because someone needed to mark that fact.

Efron broke the silence. "If you hadn't interfered—"

"She'd be dead or in a psychiatric ward." Lock's voice stayed level, but anger ran beneath it. "Don't pretend you gave a damn about any of these girls."

"Enough." Dave stood, hands flat on the bar. "A young woman's dead. We can't change that. But we can stop more from dying. So let's do what we came here to do."

Lock nodded, pulling himself back to business. Outside, waves broke against the shore in steady rhythm.

"Terms," Lock said. "Safe passage for my people. Tonight. We leave, no interference, no tracking, no future contact."

"Agreed," Efron said.

"Compensation for Harper Holt. Two million US dollars. Clean transfer to accounts I'll designate."

Efron's eyebrow rose. "That's four times what was originally agreed."

"That was then, this is now."

"And if I refuse?"

"Then in sixteen hours, every major news outlet gets a teaser reel. The whole sick catalog. With feature length footage to follow."

Efron considered, then nodded. "Okay, two million. What else?"

"Every woman who was targeted, assaulted, or trafficked through this operation gets compensation. Half a million minimum. You have the records—you know who they are."

"That could be dozens of women."

Lock leaned forward. "This isn't negotiable. These women, hell some of them were children, were victims of systematic abuse. They deserve something."

"Some won't want money. They'll want justice."

Lock took a breath. "We both know how this works. Too many powerful people with too much to lose. They'll be silenced one way or another. At least with money, they can rebuild their lives."

Dave spoke up. "He's right, Efron. You know he's right. Pay up, close the books, everyone walks away."

"And the archive?"

"Destroyed," Lock said. "You can watch me do it. Every file, every backup. Complete erasure."

"How do I know you won't keep copies?"

"Because I'm tired." The admission surprised Lock even as he said it. "I'm tired of this world, these games, these compromises. I want to go home to my daughter and pretend places like this don't exist. Pretend people like you don't exist either."

Efron studied him. "That's either the truth or an excellent lie."

"It's the truth. But I need guarantees too. My team signs NDAs, yes. But if anything happens to any of us—accidents, suicides, sudden illnesses—I'll hold back one or two of the more explosive items as insurance."

"My handlers won't like that."

"Your handlers?" Lock laughed, short and bitter. "Your handlers will deny you exist the moment this becomes inconvenient. We both know that."

Efron's jaw tightened, but he didn't argue.

"Speaking of handlers," Lock continued, "this whole operation shuts down. The resort closes. Permanently."

"That's not my decision."

"Make it yours. Structural problems, environmental concerns, fucking termites—I don't care what excuse you use. But this place dies."

"And if they just restart it somewhere else?"

"Then that's someone else's problem." Lock hated the pragmatism in his own voice. "I can't save the world. I can only clean up this corner of it."

Bob Marley finished his song. Another started—"No Woman, No Cry."

"The report," Efron said. "Barzani Hospitality hired you for a security assessment."

"No report needed if there's no resort." Lock managed a grim smile. "Congratulations. You had a good run. Made a lot of money, destroyed a lot of lives. Now it's over."

"You think it's that simple? The people involved—governments, intelligence services, men with unlimited resources—they won't just let this disappear."

"I know." Lock thought of the archive, terabytes of evidence that would never see a courtroom. "Look at Panama Papers. Eleven million documents, massive revelations. A few resignations, one or two arrests, then business as usual. Look at Epstein. Everyone knew, no one cared enough to stop it."

"So why bother?"

"Because I can save a few. Get Harper home. Get the other women some money. Shut down this specific hell." Lock met his eyes. "It's not enough. It's never enough. But it's what I can do."

Efron stood, walked to the bar's small window, looking out at his resort. "My handlers have technology you can't imagine. Phones that explode. Cars that drive off cliffs. Heart attacks that leave no trace."

"I know that too."

"Yet you think your insurance policy will protect you?"

"I think mutually assured destruction worked for the Cold War." Lock joined him at the window. "You could kill us all, yes. But the scandal would destroy operations across the globe. Is removing a few security consultants worth burning decades of intelligence assets?"

Efron weighed this, then turned from the window. "My people will need verification that the archive is destroyed."

"Tonight. In your security office. You can watch every file deleted, every drive destroyed."

"And Amira Barzani? Her husband?"

"What about them?"

"The bodies need explanations. Stories for families, authorities."

"Boating accident," Efron said without hesitation. "Tragic. Patrick fell overboard, Amira dove in to save him. Very romantic. Very stupid."

"Anyone going to question that?"

"Patrick was known for his drug use. Amira for her temper. A late night boat ride, too much champagne, an accident..." Efron shrugged. "Things happen."

They stood facing each other in the empty beach bar, two professionals concluding the ugliest of business. Outside, the resort sprawled in artificial paradise, hiding surveillance equipment and suffering behind manicured gardens.

"Your fees," Efron said. "The original contract plus?"

"Triple rate for my team. Hazard pay. They signed on for security assessment, not this."

"Done."

"Plus medical coverage for Harper Holt. Lifetime. Whatever she needs."

"Agreed."

Lock extended his hand. The gesture felt wrong, sealing this devil's bargain with civilized ritual. But Efron took it, his grip firm and dry.

"By dawn," Efron said. "Be gone by dawn."

"We will be."

They held the handshake a moment too long, each man taking the other's measure one last time. Then Efron turned and walked away, his men falling in behind him. They disappeared into the darkness beyond the string lights, heading back to manage their collapse.

Dave Carter waited until they were gone, then poured himself a rum from behind the bar. "Anything else you need?"

"A shower." Lock watched the lights of the resort. "Maybe ten showers."

"That girl Nikki deserved better."

"They all did. Harper, Nikki, every woman who walked into this trap thinking they'd found opportunity." Lock turned away from the window. "But this is what we can do. Save who we can, get paid, go home."

"And live with it."

"And live with it."

Dave raised his glass in a mock toast. "To compromise. To pragmatism. To pretending we didn't just shake hands with the devil."

Lock didn't have a glass. Even if he had, he doubted his capacity to swallow, so he nodded. In a few hours, they'd be gone. The resort would close. The women would get their money. The archive would disappear. And somewhere in Atlantic City, a family would be planning a funeral for a girl who'd died trying to save a friend.

It wasn't justice. Not even close.

But it was what they had.

CHAPTER
SEVENTY-SEVEN

A FEW HOURS LATER, the old security office felt like a crime scene being sanitized. Outside, demolition crews worked with industrial efficiency, their excavators and bulldozers shaking dust from the ceiling tiles. Inside, men stood around a bank of monitors, watching terabytes of evidence prepare to disappear forever.

"Biometric confirmation required in three minutes," the tech team leader announced, his voice carefully neutral.

Lock stood at the primary terminal, watching countdown timers tick down. Forty-seven terabytes of surveillance footage, meticulously organized, tagged, and indexed. In three minutes, it would begin its path to deletion.

Efron leaned against the wall, arms crossed, watching with the satisfaction of a man seeing loose ends tied up. His own technical specialist—a nervous Israeli who kept checking his phone—monitored from a secondary terminal.

"The system's elegant," the tech lead said, filling the silence. "Every forty-eight hours, we had to confirm or it auto-uploads to seventeen different destinations. Journalists, law enforcement, NGOs. All using quantum-resistant encryption."

"Overkill," Efron commented.

"Insurance," Lock corrected. "Your people would have found ways around anything less."

Through the window, an excavator's claw tore into Villa Nine's roof. Pink insulation scattered across the ground in the morning sun. By evening, the entire structure would be rubble. By week's end, the whole resort would exist only in carefully edited memories.

"Two minutes," the tech lead announced.

On the monitors, the archive's interface displayed its grim inventory. Folders within folders, organized human misery. The root directory showed the scale:

VIDEO_ARCHIVE > CLIENT_SESSIONS > 2,847 FOLDERS

Lock did the math. Over thirteen years of operation. That averaged to one new victim every two days. The numbers felt clean, abstract. The reality they represented was anything but.

"Beginning pre-deletion verification," the Israeli tech said. His screen showed deeper layers:

VID_001_2011-03-15 > VILLA_FOUR VID_002_2011-03-22 > VILLA_NINE

VID_003_2011-03-27 > YACHT

File names scrolled past—timestamps and camera angles, reducing human suffering to efficient data points. Occasionally, a thumbnail would flash before being marked for deletion. A room. A bed. A figure too distant to identify.

"It's a shame Amira isn't here to see this," Efron said, watching another villa get demolished outside. "She had opinions about the renovation. Wanted to go ultra-modern. Glass and steel."

Even though Lock had no time for Amira Barzani it took everything he could not to walk over and punch Efron in the face.

"One minute."

Lock placed his hand on the biometric scanner. The tech lead did the same at his station. Two keys to turn simultaneously, preventing any single person from destroying the evidence alone. Or in this case, preventing them from preserving it.

"Thirty seconds."

More files scrolled past. Lock caught names he recognized:
BAILEY_Nikki_2024-06-14 HOLT_Harper_2024-06-11

Each name a person. Each person a story that would never be told. The system showed their final footprints—camera angles, timestamps, duration of recordings. Nikki's files were marked with a red flag: "INCIDENT - ARCHIVED TO SPECIAL COLLECTION."

Patrick's special collection. Now Patrick was feeding fish, and his collection was about to follow him into oblivion.

"Confirmation required," the tech lead said. "On my mark. Three... two... one... mark."

Lock pressed his palm to the scanner. A green light swept across his hand, reading the whorls and ridges that made him unique. Beside him, the tech lead did the same. For a moment, nothing happened.

Then the monitors came alive.

"AUTHORIZATION ACCEPTED - BIOMETRIC 1/2 VERIFIED"
"AUTHORIZATION ACCEPTED - BIOMETRIC 2/2 VERIFIED"
"SECURE DELETION INITIATING... PASS 1 OF 3"

The file structure began collapsing in on itself. Folders vanished in rapid succession, each deletion triggering the next. Progress bars appeared for each drive segment:

"Purging 2011_LAUNCH_YEAR/VID001-VID244/" "Deleting 5,826 files (341.2GB)... Estimated Time: 00:23:17"

"It'll take about four hours for complete secure deletion," the tech lead explained. "Three-pass overwrite with random data between each pass. DoD standard."

"No recovery possible?" Efron asked.

"Not unless you've got a quantum computer and a time machine."

Outside, Villa Nine's remains were being loaded into dump trucks. Where Harper had fought for her life, where cameras had captured her terror, there would soon be only empty land. Ready for whatever came next.

"I notice Villa Two is being preserved," Lock said.

"Structural considerations," Efron replied smoothly. "The architects need an intact reference point for the rebuild."

Bullshit. Villa Two housed the secondary control room. Even with the archive deleted, the infrastructure remained. Ready for the next operation, the next set of victims, the next carefully organized folders.

The deletion continued its methodical progress. Years compressed into progress bars:

"Purging 2015_PEAK_YEAR/VID1001-VID1744/" "Purging 2019_-EXPANSION/VID2301-VID2890/"

"Look at that," the Israeli tech said. "2019 was busy. Almost eight hundred sessions."

Sessions. As if they were therapist appointments or yoga classes. Not systematic violations of helpless young women captured in high definition and organized for maximum leverage.

Lock watched names scroll past in the deletion queue. Some he recognized from the sample he'd shown Efron—politicians, celebrities, titans of industry. Others were just identification numbers, their real names protected even in documentation of their crimes.

A subfolder caught his eye before vanishing: "SPECIAL_PROJECTS/RECRUITMENT"

Inside, for the brief second before deletion, he glimpsed file names that turned his stomach. Not clients being serviced, but staff being trained. Young women learning their roles in this machine. How to smile. How to survive. How to become complicit in their own exploitation.

"Your partner," Efron said quietly. "Johnson. How's he doing?"

"How do you think?"

"The girl—Bailey—she wasn't supposed to be there. Patrick went... off script."

"She's still dead."

"Yes." Efron watched another villa collapse outside. "If it helps, Patrick's replacement will be more... controlled. We've learned from this experience."

Lock turned from the monitors. "You're starting up again?"

"Not me. Not here. But somewhere, yes. The demand doesn't disappear just because one supply point closes." Efron's smile was thin. "Don't look so surprised. You knew this was bigger than one island."

The demolition crew had moved to Villa Twelve. Lock remembered the intelligence briefing—a German politician had beaten a girl there, Frau Meintz losing control after too much champagne and cocaine. Now it was just timber and drywall, waiting for the excavator's claw.

The system showed its work with clinical precision:

"SECTOR 94,012 of 11,230,441 - Purging VID3847_2023-11-15_VILLA_NINE" "CONFIRMED - Sector Wiped" "FINAL PASS - Removing shadow volume copies..."

Each confirmation another crime erased, another victim forgotten, another perpetrator protected. Lock watched his insurance policy evaporate one file at a time. Soon, all that would remain were memories and money transfers. The stories the survivors told themselves in the dark.

"I'm curious," Efron said. "What will you tell your wife about this job?"

"Nothing."

"Come now. She must ask about your work. Where her husband goes, what he does."

"I tell her I help keep people safe."

"And do you? In the grand scheme?" Efron gestured at the demolition. "The resort is closed. The immediate threat removed. Some women have money for their silence. You've kept people safe, in a fashion."

Lock didn't answer. Outside, Villa Fifteen joined its siblings in ruin. How many horror stories had those walls contained? How many cameras hidden in crown molding and smoke detectors? How many lives destroyed for the entertainment of those who could afford anything except consequences?

The monitors showed the archive's final moments:

"Purging FINAL_YEAR/VID4400-VID4761/" "SYSTEM NOTICE: Archive 91% destroyed" "Preparing final verification sequence..."

"Almost done," the tech lead said unnecessarily.

When the last file vanished, when the progress bars all showed 100%, when the system confirmed complete destruction, Lock felt nothing. No satisfaction, no relief. Just the weight of necessary compromise.

"DELETION COMPLETE - ZEROED FILE SYSTEM - SYSTEM SHUTDOWN IN 60s"

The monitors began going dark one by one. Outside, the demolition continued, erasing physical evidence as thoroughly as they'd erased the digital. In a month, no one would know what had happened here. In a year, it would be mythology. In a decade, perhaps even the survivors would wonder if it had all been real.

"Excellent work," Efron said, pushing off from the wall. "Clean, professional. I'll inform my superiors that all obligations have been met."

He extended his hand. Lock looked at it—the same hand that had executed Amira, that had overseen years of systematic abuse, that would build another operation somewhere else—and shook it. Because that was the deal. That was the compromise.

The tech lead was already packing equipment. The Israeli specialist had vanished the moment confirmation came through. In sixty seconds, the system would shut down forever, taking its secrets to digital graves.

Lock walked out of the security office into morning sun that felt too bright, too clean for what they'd just done.

CHAPTER
SEVENTY-EIGHT

"WHERE'S NIKKI?" Harper asked, fumbling with the ties on her hospital gown. "They said she was hurt, but no one will tell me... Is she already on the plane?"

Ty stood in the doorway, unconsciously placing himself between Harper and the corridor. Behind him, Lock waited with professional patience, giving them space for what had to be said. Ty had done this before—delivered news that would shatter someone's world—but it never got easier. Each time carved away another piece of him.

"Almost ready," Harper said, still focused on the gown. Her fingers trembled against the generic fabric. "The doctor says I'm cleared to travel. Just need to finish..." She fumbled with a button, cursed softly.

"Take your time," Ty said, gentling his voice the way he would for a spooked animal.

Something in his tone made her hands stop. She looked up, really seeing him for the first time. The blood was gone—he'd changed clothes—but exhaustion lined his face like scars. In his eyes, she saw something that made her chest tighten with recognition she wasn't ready to accept.

"She's okay, right?" The words tumbled out faster now, denial building momentum. "I mean, I know she was hurt. I saw... But she's tough. You don't know her like I do."

Harper pushed to her feet, swaying slightly, one hand gripping the bed rail. Ty stepped closer without thinking, ready to catch her if she fell. The movement was automatic, protective, the kind of response beaten into him by years of watching over people who couldn't watch over themselves.

"This one time back in Atlantic City, she got food poisoning and still worked a double shift. Said the show must go on." Harper's laugh cracked in the middle. "That's Nikki. She doesn't quit."

Ty watched her construct the wall of words, each story another brick against the truth. He'd seen it before—the way people talked faster when they knew silence would let reality creep in.

"Harper." His voice carried the weight of bad news delivered in hospital corridors, funeral homes, family kitchens. "I need you to listen."

Her hands clenched the shirt fabric. "No."

"Nikki tried to get help. She was brave. Braver than anyone should have to be." Ty kept his eyes on hers, willing her to hear what he couldn't quite say directly. "But she was hurt too badly. The doctors did everything they could."

"No." Stronger this time, but her voice was breaking around the edges. "You're wrong. Where is she? I want to see her."

Ty stepped closer, close enough to catch her if she fell, far enough to let her process. The balance of proximity and space, learned through too many conversations like this one.

"She died."

The words hung between them, brutal in their simplicity. Harper stared at him, waiting for the punchline, the correction, the 'just kidding' that would make this another nightmare instead of reality. When it didn't come, something fundamental shifted in her face.

"She can't be dead." The break in her voice was audible now. "We had plans. We were going to travel. See the pyramids. She always wanted to..." Her legs gave out. She sank back onto the bed, and Ty moved with her, settling beside her but not touching, reading her body language for permission he didn't have yet.

"Oh god. This is my fault."

"No." The word came out harder than he intended. "This is not your fault."

"If I hadn't been so stupid—"

"Stop." Ty's command voice, usually reserved for operations, but softer at the edges. Harper's eyes snapped to his, swimming with tears that hadn't fallen yet.

"The people who hurt you, who hurt Nikki—they're responsible. Not you. Never you." He let his voice gentle, the way he'd learned to modulate for the aftermath. "Nikki chose to try to help. That was her choice, her courage. Don't dishonor that by blaming yourself."

"But if I hadn't—"

"If you hadn't wanted a better life? That's nothing anyone can blame you for."

The tears came then, silent at first, then building to sobs that shook her whole body. Ty felt the familiar tug of wanting to reach out, to offer the comfort of human contact, but held back. Sometimes grief needed space to breathe, and Harper had already had too many boundaries violated. Instead, he stayed present, a steady presence in her peripheral vision.

Harper's crying gradually subsided. She pressed her palms against her eyes, trying to stop the flow, to regain some control.

"What happened to her?" she asked.

Ty weighed his words. She didn't need the details of the torture, the machinery, the calculated cruelty. That knowledge would only add to her burden.

"Something that shouldn't have," he said simply. "But because of her, you're here. Safe. Going home."

"Home." The word sounded foreign in Harper's mouth, like she was testing a language she'd forgotten. "How do I go home without her?"

"I've been here. Want to know how you deal with stuff like this? One day at a time. One hour if that's too much." Ty had given this speech before, to soldiers who'd lost brothers in arms, to families shattered by violence. It never got easier, but the words had worn smooth with use. "You honor her by living. By healing."

Lock appeared in the doorway, a folder in his hand. He read the scene in a glance—Harper's tear-streaked face, Ty's careful positioning, the weight of grief filling the small room. His eyes met Ty's in silent question: *How bad?* Ty's barely perceptible nod answered: *Bad, but manageable.*

"Harper," Lock said gently, his voice carrying the professional compassion of someone who'd delivered difficult news before. "I'm sorry to interrupt, but we need to discuss some logistics."

She wiped her face with her sleeve, muscle memory of composure taking over. "The NDA. They mentioned I have to sign something."

Lock set the folder on the bedside table within her reach but not forcing it on her. "This is your copy. Read it on the plane. The compensation will be transferred once it's signed. Two million U.S. dollars."

Harper's laugh was bitter and broken. "Blood money."

"Maybe," Lock said simply, no sugar-coating. "But it's also a future. Therapy. Education. Whatever you need to rebuild."

Harper looked between them—Lock with his folder and careful pragmatism, Ty with his exhausted compassion. Two men who'd seen too much, carrying their own burdens while trying to shoulder hers. Outside the window, the sky was darkening, the island's paradise facade dissolving into something more honest.

"When do we leave?" she asked finally.

"Twenty minutes. There's a car waiting."

She nodded, went back to buttoning her shirt. Her hands were steadier now, grief hardening into something she could carry. Ty watched her armor herself for what came next, recognizing the process from his own mirror.

"Will the men who did this face justice?" she asked without looking up.

Lock and Ty exchanged another look, years of partnership compressed into a single glance. Ty's slight head shake said *Be honest*, and Lock's nod acknowledged the advice.

"What do you think of when you say justice," Lock said.

"Prison. Trial. Something."

"The resort is closing. Some people are dead. Others have lost their power." Lock chose his words carefully, honestly. "It's not what they deserve, not by a long shot, but it's what we could manage."

Harper absorbed this, another blow on top of too many. Her shoulders sagged slightly, and Ty felt the urge to close the remaining distance between them, to offer the steadying touch she might need. But she was still too fragile, still too raw for that kind of contact from a man she barely knew.

"And if I don't sign? If I want to tell everyone what happened?"

"Then you become a target. The NDA protects you as much as them."

"Some protection." She stood, testing her balance, finding it better now. Grief was settling into something she could work with, at least temporarily. "Nikki's dead and I'm being paid to pretend it didn't happen."

Both Ty and Lock didn't say anything. There was nothing to say. No real counter-argument. None they wanted to make anyway.

Harper looked up at Ty, really looked, and saw her own grief reflected and magnified. He'd been there when Nikki died. Held her hand. Carried that weight. The recognition passed between them wordlessly—two people bound by shared trauma, by the weight of what they'd witnessed.

"Was she in pain?" The question came out whispered, the most important thing she needed to know. "At the end?"

Ty thought of the helicopter, the blood, the desperate fight to keep her conscious. The promises he'd made that she'd be okay, lies told with the best intentions.

"No," he lied again, the kindness automatic. "She wasn't alone, I was with her."

Harper nodded, accepting the deception because she needed it. She picked up the folder, held it like it might explode. Two million dollars and a lifetime of silence. The price of survival in an unfair world.

"I'm ready," she said.

They left the medical suite together, a small procession bound by circumstance and shared purpose. Lock led, professional and alert. Harper walked in the middle, clutching her folder like a lifeline. Ty brought up the rear, close enough to catch her if she stumbled, far enough to give her space to breathe.

The hallways were empty, cleared for their departure. Through windows, they could see the demolition continuing—paradise being unmade one building at a time, the resort's careful facade crumbling to reveal the rot beneath.

"She wanted to see the pyramids," Harper said suddenly, her voice carrying the hollow quality of someone speaking to themselves as much as to others. "Maybe I'll go. Take her ashes."

"That sounds right," Ty said, meaning it.

They reached the exit where a nondescript SUV waited, engine running. The driver didn't look at them, professionally invisible in the way that suggested Lock's careful arrangements. Harper climbed in, and after a moment's hesitation, chose the seat directly behind Ty rather than isolating herself in the back corner.

As they pulled away from the medical building, Harper pressed her face to the window, watching the island recede. The confined space of the car created an unexpected intimacy—three people who'd shared something terrible, now sharing the silence that followed. Ty could see her reflection in his side mirror, ghostly and lost, and found himself adjusting his position so she could see his face if she needed the reassurance of human connection.

The island disappeared into darkness behind them, taking its secrets and its dead. Harper pressed her face to the window until there was nothing left to see, then settled back into her seat, closer to the others than she'd been to anyone in days. Sometimes survival meant accepting the comfort of strangers who'd become something more through shared witness to the worst of human nature.

In the driver's mirror, Lock watched them all, reading the dynamics, understanding that some bonds were forged in fire and couldn't be easily broken. Tomorrow, Harper would fly home to rebuild her life. But tonight, they were three people who'd seen hell together, and that created a kind of family, however fleeting.

CHAPTER
SEVENTY-NINE

LOCK CLOSED Harper's door and stood in the hallway, listening to the silence. The Jumeirah's thick carpet absorbed his footsteps as he moved to the adjoining suite. Through the door, he heard ice against glass—a sound that told him everything he needed to know about Ty's current state.

Ty sat by the floor-to-ceiling window, Dubai sprawled below like a circuit board of lights. A bottle of whiskey stood on the side table—Macallan 18. Three fingers already gone. Lock had seen him drink maybe five times in fifteen years. Never on a job. Never when they had a principal to protect. Not even when grief was eating him alive from the inside.

"She okay?" Ty said without turning. His voice carried the careful steadiness of someone working hard to sound normal.

"Sleeping. Finally." Lock moved to the minibar, selected a water, buying time to read his partner's emotional temperature. "Doc gave her enough to knock out a horse. She'll be out until morning."

Ty lifted his glass, studied the whiskey like it held answers he couldn't find anywhere else. Lock settled into the opposite chair, close enough to intervene if needed, far enough to give Ty space to process. They'd done this dance before—Ty internalizing everything until it threatened to implode, Lock providing steady presence without pushing.

"We're really just going to let him walk?" Ty's words came out flat, but Lock heard the rage underneath. "Efron."

Lock watched his partner's profile against the city lights, reading the tension in his jaw, the way his free hand had formed a fist against his thigh. Seventeen years of working together had created a language of silent communication.

"I wouldn't say no consequences," Lock said carefully.

Ty's head snapped around, and Lock saw the dangerous glitter in his eyes that meant violence was being considered. Time to redirect that energy into something more productive.

Lock pulled out his phone, swiped to a video file. "Tech team pulled this before we left the yacht."

He turned the screen toward Ty. Grainy security footage, but clear enough. The boat's deck. Amira Barzani lunging for Efron's weapon, screaming. Efron drawing his Glock. The muzzle flash. The small hole appearing in her forehead.

Ty's entire body went still, the glass frozen halfway to his lips. Lock knew that stillness—it was Ty processing information, recalibrating, his tactical mind spinning up scenarios.

"Yacht had comprehensive security. Cameras everywhere." Lock let the implications hang in the air. "Tech team pulled the hard drives while we were having our chat with him on deck."

Ty set down his glass with deliberate care, his movements suddenly precise in the way that meant he was transitioning from grief to operational thinking. Lock felt some of the tension in his own shoulders ease. This was territory they both understood.

"Murder," Ty said simply.

"Gets better." Lock swiped to an audio file. "Remember when he and I had our heart-to-heart?"

Efron's voice filled the room, metallic through the phone speaker but unmistakably his: "The kompromat operation was never about money. It was about leverage. Strategic assets in key positions. Senators. Judges. CEOs. Even a few generals."

Ty straightened, and Lock watched him cataloging every word, every implication. This was why they worked so well together—Lock's strategic thinking paired with Ty's tactical precision, both minds processing the same information from different angles.

The recording continued. Efron's clinical explanation of the operation. The hidden cameras. The careful cataloging.

"We had files on over three hundred individuals. Americans. British. Germans. Even a few Israelis who got careless."

Lock stopped the playback and watched Ty's face transform. The grief was still there, but now it had direction, purpose. Something they could work with.

"Your iPhone?" Ty said, and there was almost admiration in his voice. "You recorded this on your fucking iPhone?"

"Sometimes simple is best." Lock felt a flicker of satisfaction at Ty's reaction. After everything they'd been through, his partner could still appreciate elegant tradecraft. "He was so focused on the big picture, he missed the basics."

Ty reached for his glass again, hesitated, then pushed it away entirely. Lock noted the gesture—Ty choosing clarity over numbness, grief giving way to operational focus. Good. They'd need that focus for what came next.

"So we have him cold. What's the play?"

"Seventy-two hours." Lock pulled up a contact list, angling the phone so Ty could see. Partnership meant transparency, especially when planning someone's destruction. "Once we're stateside and Harper's safe."

Lock scrolled through names, watching Ty read over his shoulder.

"The Guardian has a journalist who's been investigating intelligence services. Sarah Kellerman." Lock paused, letting Ty process. "But media's only part of it."

He shifted to another list, felt Ty lean closer to read the names. "Senator Harrison. His operation had video of him with a nineteen-year-old in Monaco. Cost him the Intelligence Committee chair."

Lock could feel Ty's understanding building, the way his partner's mind was racing ahead to see the full picture.

"Margaret Thorne. British MP. Career ended overnight when photos surfaced." Lock scrolled down. "David Krasner. Federal judge whose wife got an envelope of photos. She killed herself. He resigned from the bench."

"Christ." Ty stood abruptly, moved to the window. Lock watched him in the glass reflection—the way grief and rage were being channeled into something colder, more focused. More dangerous.

"Three hundred files," Lock continued quietly. "Three hundred people whose lives got destroyed. Most of them probably suspected they were set up but could never prove it."

"And now they'll know exactly who to blame," Ty said to the window.

Lock nodded, though Ty couldn't see it. "He spent fifteen years making enemies. Powerful ones. They've been waiting for someone to pay."

Ty turned from the window, and Lock saw his partner had found his center again. The drinking was done. The self-recrimination over Nikki's death was being transformed into something they could both work with.

"His handlers won't protect him. Not once this goes public."

"Can't protect him," Lock agreed. "He becomes radioactive. Every intelligence service will distance themselves."

"Man like that doesn't retire." Ty moved back to his chair, settled in with the fluid grace of someone whose body had stopped fighting itself. "He disappears."

"One way or another."

Ty studied Lock's face, reading him the way Lock had been reading him all evening. "You sure about this? He's got reach. Resources."

"In seventy-two hours, he'll be too busy staying alive to worry about revenge."

"And Harper?"

Lock felt the weight of that question, the shared responsibility they carried for the young woman sleeping in the next room. "She goes home thinking justice will come through official channels. Doesn't need to know about this."

Ty was quiet for a long moment, processing not just the plan but its implications, its risks, its necessity. Lock waited, understanding that his partner needed to arrive at the same conclusion independently.

That was how they worked—presenting options, allowing for individual assessment, trusting in their shared judgment.

"Nikki deserved better," Ty said finally.

"Yeah, she did."

"She was twenty-three. Thought she was going on an adventure." Ty's voice roughened, and Lock heard the guilt that would probably never fully leave his partner. "Ended up on a slab in the mortuary because she tried to do the right thing."

Lock said nothing. Sometimes silence was all you had to offer, and after fifteen years, Ty knew that Lock's quiet presence was its own form of support.

"This won't bring her back," Ty said.

"No."

"But he pays."

"Everyone pays eventually."

Ty lifted his glass—still three-quarters full, Lock noted—in a gesture that was part toast, part promise. "To consequences."

Lock raised his water bottle, understanding the ritual, the way they were sealing something between them. They drank, and Lock felt the familiar satisfaction of perfect operational alignment. This was what partnership meant—two minds, two skill sets, two different ways of processing trauma, coming together in shared purpose.

Through the adjoining door, Harper slept, sedated and safe. In three days, she'd be home. In four, the story would break. By the end of the week, Efron would be the most hunted man on three continents.

Lock opened his phone's calendar, set a reminder. Seventy-two hours. He showed the screen to Ty, who nodded once, committing the timeline to memory.

"Get some sleep," Lock said, rising. "Long flight tomorrow."

Ty nodded, but his eyes went back to the window, to the lights below, to a world where men like Efron built empires on others' misery. Lock paused at the door, reading his partner's posture, the set of his shoulders. Still processing, but no longer drowning. Good enough.

"Lock." Ty's voice stopped him at the threshold. "The beach. When you shook his hand. You already knew you were going to do this?"

Lock smiled, feeling the cold satisfaction of a plan coming together. Justice delayed but not denied. "Sure did. Fuck that guy. And all the others like him."

Ty's answering smile was sharp as a blade, dangerous in all the right ways. The grief was still there, would always be there, but now it had company. Now it had purpose.

"Chess, not checkers."

"Fuckin'-A," Lock said.

CHAPTER
EIGHTY

MUNICH, GERMANY

MONTHS LATER

SNOW FELL on Grünwald's empty streets, muffling sound and softening edges. The neighborhood slept behind walls and gates, secure in its wealth. At 3:00 AM, even the ambitious were dreaming.

Two figures moved through the falling snow, shadows against shadows. One black, one white, both dressed for winter work—dark clothing, thin gloves, equipment distributed to avoid telltale bulges. They'd left their vehicle three blocks away, approaching on foot through the small park that bordered Ulrich's property.

The mansion squatted behind its perimeter wall, a modernist box of glass and concrete that somehow managed to look both expensive and cold. Security lights created pools of yellow against the snow, but there were patterns to avoid, blind spots to exploit. They'd been watching for three days. They knew.

The black man raised a thermal scope, scanning. The security guard's heat signature bloomed near the gatehouse, right on schedule. Every ninety minutes, the man took a smoke break. Seven minutes of nicotine and boredom. More than enough.

Hand signals. Move.

They crossed the lawn in synchronized steps, footprints filling with snow almost immediately. The white man extended a telescoping pole, mirror attached, angling it to catch the IR beam from the nearest camera. Redirect the beam, create a blind corridor. Old trick, still effective.

At the study window, the black man produced a reed switch magnet, placing it against the frame. The sensor would think the window remained closed even as they lifted the pane. No wires cut, no alarms tripped. Just physics and preparation.

Inside. Warmth and the smell of leather and old books. An oil painting on the wall—Ulrich shaking hands with a former Chancellor. Another photo showed him at a charity gala, arm around a young actress who'd later claimed assault. The accusations had disappeared, of course. Money had that power.

The white man checked his tablet, house plans glowing dimly. Master bedroom, second floor, east wing. The Telenot alarm panel would be in the utility closet under the stairs. Thirty seconds once they moved past the entry sensors.

They moved. The black man found the panel, already pulling out a preprogrammed card. The maintenance override was a gift from a technician who'd worked on the system six months ago. He'd been expensive but thorough. The system accepted the override, switching to test mode. No signals to the monitoring company. No backup alerts.

Up the marble stairs, testing each step before committing weight. The house was a museum of wealth—sculptures that belonged in galleries, paintings worth more than most people's homes.

The master suite door presented a final obstacle. Biometric lock, fingerprint and retinal scan. But every system had maintenance protocols. The Black man worked at the access panel with practiced efficiency. Not hacking—just convincing the system that routine service was required.

Click.

They entered together, taking positions on either side of the California king bed. Ulrich slept on silk sheets, unconscious in every sense.

The white man pulled out a medical kit, removing two syringes. Propofol in one, ketamine in the other.

Poetic justice had its appeal.

The black man's hand covered Ulrich's mouth as his eyes snapped open. For a moment, confusion. Then the recognition hit of why they were likely here and what they were going to do. His struggles were brief, pointless. A soft man's panic against hard men's purpose.

"This is for Harper Holt, asshole." The man's voice was conversational, matter-of-fact.

Ulrich's eyes widened. Harper's name hit him like a physical blow.

"And Nikki Bailey," the white guy added. "And all the others."

The needle went in clean, finding the vein on the first try. Propofol first, the world's edges going soft for Ulrich. Then the ketamine, sending him on the same journey Nikki had taken. But she'd had someone holding her hand, telling her to fight. Ulrich had only the impassive faces of his executioners.

His body began its betrayal. Convulsions, labored breathing, the heart struggling against the chemical assault. The white man monitored his vitals on a small device, watching the numbers fall with clinical detachment.

Four minutes. Five. Ulrich's body made one final effort, back arching, hands clawing at nothing. Then stillness. The monitors confirmed what their eyes already knew.

They worked efficiently. Body positioned to suggest accidental overdose—a rich man's recreational habits gone wrong. The syringes went back in the kit

Exit protocols were mirror images of their entry—reset the door, down the stairs, alarm system returned to normal status. Out through the study window, reed switch magnet removed. The guard was still smoking.

They crossed the snowy lawn, footprints already vanishing. The park swallowed them, two shadows returning to shadow. At the tree line, they paused, looking back at the mansion. In a few hours, someone would find Ulrich. Police would be called. An investigation would find evidence of drug use, high-risk behavior, a man who'd lived dangerously and died predictably.

Case closed.

But for tonight, in the falling snow of a Munich winter, Harper Holt had her justice. Nikki Bailey had her vengeance.

The snow continued to fall, covering tracks, muffling sound, making everything clean and white and new. By morning, it would be as if they'd never been there at all.

Just another rich man dead in his bed, and two ghosts vanishing into the winter night.

EPILOGUE

LOS ANGELES, CALIFORNIA

DECEMBER 23RD

THE ARRIVALS LEVEL at LAX was deep into holiday madness—families clutching oversized teddy bears, college kids home for break, business travelers looking defeated by delays. Christmas music competed with flight announcements. Lock emerged from Terminal B looking like any other weary traveler, rolling carry-on in one hand, duty-free bag in the other.

He'd changed clothes in Munich, trading tactical black for business casual. Just another road warrior business guy heading home for the holidays. The duty-free bag held wooden ornaments, a hand-carved nativity set, a nutcracker that cost more than it should have. Normal souvenirs from a normal trip. Each one carefully chosen to erase the memory of what his hands had done forty-eight hours ago.

The Rivian pulled up to the curb right on time, Carmen behind the wheel. Through the tinted back window, he could see Sofia bouncing against her car seat restraints, small hands already waving frantically. An airport security officer was approaching, ready to wave them along—no stopping, no waiting, keep it moving.

Lock tossed his bag in the back and slid into the passenger seat in one smooth motion. The car smelled like peppermint—Sofia's candy cane remnants—and Carmen's vanilla lotion. Home distilled into scent.

"Daddy!" Sofia's voice filled the car before he'd even closed the door. "Did you bring me something?"

He turned, taking in his daughter—red velvet dress with white trim, tiny reindeer antlers headband already askew, chocolate smudge on one cheek. Perfect and completely unaware that monsters existed in the world.

"Maybe I did," he said, leaning back to kiss her forehead. His hand lingered on her small shoulder, grounding himself in her warmth.

Carmen leaned over for her kiss, and he caught her wrist gently, holding her there a moment longer than usual. Her eyes searched his face, reading the micro-tells that said *I missed you* without words.

"How was Germany?" she asked as she pulled away from the curb.

"Quiet."

"Quiet's good." She navigated the departure lanes with practiced ease, one hand finding his briefly before returning to the wheel. "Ty make his connection?"

"Different flight. He had someone to see." Lock watched her process this, connecting dots the way she always did.

"The girl from the news?"

Lock nodded. Carmen had watched enough coverage to know Harper Holt had been hurt, even if she didn't know why or how Lock was connected.

He pulled out the duty-free bag, angling it so Sofia could see. "Want to see what I found at the Christmas market?"

Her squeal could have shattered glass. He pulled out the ornaments one by one—a wooden angel with real feathers for wings, a tiny carved sleigh, painted stars that caught the light. Each one was met with gasps of delight, her small hands reaching eagerly before remembering to ask permission.

"And this," he said, producing the nutcracker, "is to protect your room from mice."

"We don't have mice!"

"Exactly. He's very good at his job."

Carmen glanced over, her smile carrying warmth and gentle accusation. Lock shrugged—guilty as charged. Sofia was already arranging the treasures in her lap, creating some elaborate hierarchy known only to four-year-olds.

"Next year, I was thinking we could all go," he said quietly. "Spend Christmas over there. They have markets everywhere, lights, music. Snow if we're lucky."

"Snow!" Sofia bounced. "Real snow! Can we, Mama?"

Carmen's eyes met his in the rearview mirror. A whole conversation passed between them—*are you sure, can you promise, will you be here?*

"We'll see," she said, but her smile said yes.

They merged onto the 405, traffic thick but moving. Los Angeles glittered with its own version of holiday cheer—palm trees wrapped in lights, inflatable Santas in shorts, menorahs in windows. Home in a way that made his chest tight with relief he hadn't known he'd been carrying.

Sofia was creating elaborate stories for her ornaments, something about the angel protecting the sleigh from bad weather. Her voice rose and fell with dramatic emphasis, the nutcracker apparently now involved as backup security. Lock found himself smiling at her tactical thinking.

"She had three candy canes at a party," Carmen murmured. "Fair warning."

"Sugar crash incoming?"

"Twenty minutes, tops."

The familiar rhythm of family communication settled over them. Code words, shorthand, the kind of partnership built over years of shared responsibility. Lock let it wash over him, each mile putting distance between who he'd been back there and who he was now he was back with his family.

By the time they reached the South Bay, he could almost believe they were different people entirely.

"You were quiet when you got back from that island job," Carmen said suddenly. Her tone was casual, but he knew that tone. It was the one that meant she'd been thinking, connecting pieces he'd thought he'd kept separate.

Lock glanced in the rearview. Sofia had stopped mid-story, the angel ornament clutched to her chest, eyes already heavy. The sugar crash arriving on schedule.

"She asleep?"

"Getting there. But that's not an answer."

He watched his daughter fight sleep, determination losing to exhaustion. Her head tilted, found the side of her car seat. The angel stayed clutched in her small hand like a talisman.

"Rich people stuff," he said finally.

Carmen's fingers drummed once against the steering wheel—a tell that meant she was deciding how hard to push. "What kind of rich people stuff?"

He thought of Nikki Bailey dying in a helicopter. Of Patrick Barzani disappearing beneath dark water. Of Ulrich's eyes in the Munich darkness. Of compromises that tasted like ash and decisions that he would never wash from him.

"They're not like us."

Carmen reached over, took his hand. Her fingers were warm, callused from her daily gym sessions, real in a way that grounded him to this life, this moment. "Thank heavens."

"Thank heavens," he repeated.

She squeezed once, understanding the weight he carried without needing the details. They both knew there were things he couldn't tell her, burdens he had to bear alone. But she also knew he'd come home to them. That was what mattered.

"Ty okay?" she asked after a moment.

"He feels responsible for what happened."

"But he's not."

"No, he's not."

They turned onto their street, houses glowing with Christmas lights. The Berry family had gone all out again—synchronized LED show that probably violated several city ordinances. Sofia stirred at the familiar sights, blinking awake with the confusion of children waking in cars.

"We're home?"

"Almost, baby," Carmen said, her voice carrying the gentle patience that made Lock fall in love with her all over again.

Their house sat at the end of the cul-de-sac, tastefully lit compared to the neighbors. Carmen had put up white lights along the roofline, a Christmas wreath on the door. Normal. Safe. Everything he'd fought to protect without them ever knowing they'd needed protecting.

In the driveway, Lock grabbed the bags while Carmen extracted a drowsy Sofia. The nutcracker had joined the angel in her grip, apparently now best friends in whatever story she'd been spinning.

"Can we put them on the tree?" Sofia asked, words slurring with exhaustion.

"First thing tomorrow. After breakfast."

"Pancakes?"

"If you're good."

"I'm always good." The indignation in her sleepy voice made Carmen snort softly.

"Tell that to the Christmas cookies that mysteriously disappeared," Carmen said.

Sofia's eyes widened with four-year-old cunning. "That was Daddy."

Lock followed his girls inside, breathing in the scent of home—pine from their tree, cinnamon from whatever Carmen had been baking, the lingering sweetness of Sofia's bedtime routine. His go-bag would need attention—clothes to wash, equipment to clean and store. But not tonight. Tonight was for being Ryan Lock the father, not the man who made hard choices in dark places.

Sofia was asleep again before they reached her room, head on Carmen's shoulder, trust absolute. They tucked her in together, moving with the synchronized efficiency of parents who'd done this dance a thousand times. Lock placed the nutcracker and angel carefully on her nightstand while Carmen adjusted the covers. Standing guard, just as he'd promised.

In the hallway, Carmen turned and pulled him close, her arms sliding around his waist. The move was practiced but never routine, her body fitting against his like they were designed for each other.

"I'm glad you're home."

"Me too." He buried his face in her hair, breathing her in.

"Whatever happened out there..."

"Is done."

She pulled back enough to study his face, her thumb brushing across the tension line between his eyebrows. Something in his expression made her decision for her.

"Okay," she said simply, and pulled him closer.

His phone vibrated against his chest where it pressed between them. He almost ignored it, but Carmen was checking Sofia's door, making sure it was cracked just right for the nightlight.

Lock glanced at the screen. News alert from a monitoring service he'd forgotten to disable.

Former Israeli Intelligence Officer Eitan Efron Killed in Car Bombing. No Suspects.

His face showed nothing.

"What is it?" Carmen asked, reading his stillness the way she read everything about him.

"Old business." He deleted the alert without another glance. "It's finished now."

She studied him, her hand finding his chest, feeling his heartbeat steady beneath her palm. Whatever she saw there satisfied her.

"Okay," she said again, and he pulled her back to him.

Later, they stood in the hallway of their home, holding each other while their daughter slept surrounded by Christmas ornaments. Carmen's warmth seeped through his shirt, real and present and everything worth protecting. Outside, the neighbor's light show cycled through "Silent Night" in electric blues and greens. Somewhere, Ty was sitting with Harper Holt, making sure she was healing. Somewhere in Munich, snow was falling on a mansion where inside a monster would never hurt anyone again.

But here, in this hallway, Ryan Lock was just a father home for

Christmas. A husband holding his wife. A man who'd done necessary things in dark places so that his daughter could sleep safely surrounded by wooden angels.

"Merry Christmas," he whispered to Carmen.

NEW TITLES FROM SEAN BLACK

THE REMOVAL (RYAN LOCK #14)

From the author of *Lockdown* and *The Yacht Girl* comes the fourteenth Ryan Lock thriller.

A black van. Men in tactical gear. A violent arrest that doesn't look quite right.

When ex-military bodyguard Ryan Lock witnesses a raid in Manhattan Beach, his trained eye catches details others would miss. The boots are wrong. The procedures are wrong. And the man being dragged away is screaming something in Spanish that makes Lock's blood run cold.

One question too many makes Lock a target.

Now someone wants him to stop digging. They've frozen his accounts. They've threatened his family. They've made it clear: walk away or disappear like all the others.

But Lock has never been good at walking away.

In a city where immigration raids happen every day, Lock discovers something far more sinister—a conspiracy where badges become weapons, where law enforcement becomes lawless, and where the disappeared don't just vanish. They're erased.

Some lines, once crossed, can't be uncrossed. Some witnesses never get to testify. And some patriots aren't who they claim to be.

PRE-ORDER HERE

THE BURN PIT (BYRON TIBOR #4)

No backup. No rules. No forgiveness.

Military veteran Byron Tibor has spent years on the run—from the government that turned him into a weapon, and from the wreckage of a life he can never reclaim. But when he finds himself among a band of fellow veterans—hardened, discarded, and living by their own code—he's drawn into a new kind of war.

They don't look like heroes. They're wounded, hunted, and haunted. But together, they've seen too much to keep their heads down. And when a buried injustice threatens to destroy what little they have left, the fight comes to them. Outgunned and outnumbered, they'll take on the system that burned them—all they need is a spark.

Byron Tibor is back in the explosive next chapter of the award-nominated series that blends pulse-pounding action with raw emotional power.

PRE-ORDER HERE

DON'T MISS YOUR FREE COPY OF THE FIRST RYAN LOCK THRILLER

Meet Ryan Lock in the explosive bestseller that started it all — *Lockdown*.

When a peaceful protest in the heart of New York City erupts into a deadly bloodbath, ex-military bodyguard Ryan Lock is thrown into a high-stakes game of survival. Caught between corporate secrets, animal rights extremists, and professional killers, Lock must protect his client at all costs — even as a child's life hangs in the balance.

Join my readers' club today and I'll send you the complete ebook of *Lockdown* — absolutely free.

Your email will never be shared and you can unsubscribe at any time.

Claim your free copy now by clicking **HERE**.

ALSO BY SEAN BLACK

The Ryan Lock Series

Lockdown

Deadlock

Gridlock

The Devil's Bounty

The Innocent

Fire Point

The Edge of Alone

Second Chance

The Red Tiger

The Deep Abiding

Avenue of Thieves

The Last Bodyguard

The Yacht Girl

The Removal

The Byron Tibor Series

Post

Blood Country

Winter's Rage

The Burn Pit

ABOUT THE AUTHOR

To research his books, Sean Black has trained as a bodyguard in the UK and Eastern Europe, spent time inside America's most dangerous Supermax prison, Pelican Bay in California, undergone desert survival training in Arizona, and ventured into the tunnels under Las Vegas.

A graduate of Oxford University, England and Columbia University in New York, Sean lives in Dublin, Ireland.

His Ryan Lock and Byron Tibor thrillers have been translated into Dutch, French, German, Italian, Portugese, Russian, Spanish, and Turkish.

When he's not writing, Sean trains in Brazilian Jiu Jitsu. In Paris in 2023 he became the only amputee to ever become a European champion in Brazilian Jiu Jitsu competing against able-bodied athletes. He is also the only amputee Pan-American champion in the sport.

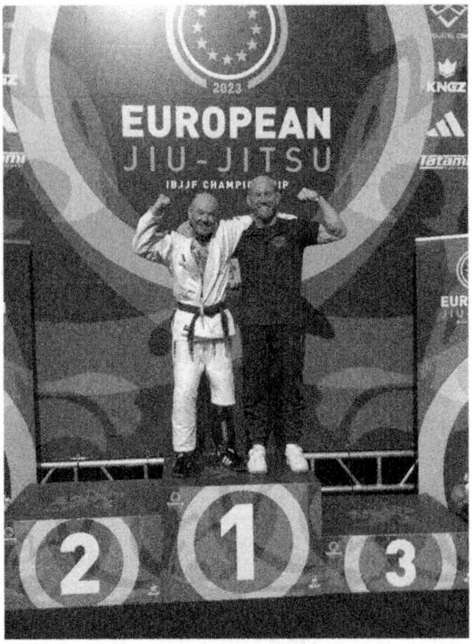
2023
EUROPEAN
JIU-JITSU
KNGZ
2
1
3

Printed in Dunstable, United Kingdom